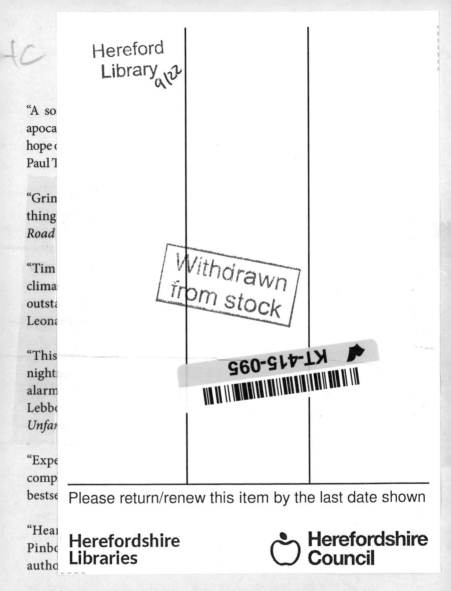

"A so
apoca
hope
Paul T

"Grin
thing
Road

"Tim
clima
outsta
Leona

"This
night
alarm
Lebbo
Unfa

"Expe
comp
bests

"Hea
Pinbo
auth

"Lebbon's near-future fable has a power and urgency all its own."—
M. R. Carey, bestselling author of *The Girl With All the Gifts*

"A wildly ambitious look at family ties, survival, and the magic of
hope."—Sarah Langan, a

"Tim Lebbon's *The Last Storm* is apocalyptic horror at its very best. A scorched-earth nightmare that is all too believable, *The Last Storm* is Lebbon's finest creation, and that's saying something."—Richard Chizmar, *New York Times* bestselling author of *Chasing The Boogeyman*

"Lebbon is a master of the cross-genre thriller, and *The Last Storm* is one of his absolute best!"—Tim Waggoner, author of *We Will Rise*

"I've loved Tim Lebbon's writing since *The Silence* but this is next level stuff. A hyper-surreal look into a post-climate change future with rich characters, heart, action, terror, and a relentless voice that drags you out and won't let you go. Tremendous."—Adrian J. Walker, bestselling author of *The End of the World Running Club*

"Beautifully written, *The Last Storm* depicts a near future beset with the terrifying consequences of climate change. But out in the desert, one family has a peculiar talent that may begin to quell the fires… or unleash a new Armageddon. Another must-read from Tim Lebbon, this book grabs you by the throat with the first paragraph and doesn't let up."—A.J. Elwood, author of *The Cottingley Cuckoo*

"Lebbon is the undisputed master of the post-apocalyptic thriller."— Michael Marshall Smith, bestselling author of *The Straw Men*

"With *The Last Storm*, Tim Lebbon brings unflinching apocalyptic terrors but infuses the storm with heart and relatable characters. A thinking person's apocalyptic novel. Bravo!"—Jonathan Maberry, *New York Times* bestselling author of *Kagen the Damned*

"Tim Lebbon has long been Britain's finest horror writer, but he has outdone himself with *The Last Storm*, a novel that paints its apocalyptic world so clearly you can feel the heat from the page. Like all the best horror fiction, it is the novel's humanity, not its monstrosity, that will cling to the reader."—Stuart Neville, author of *The House of Ashes*

THE
LAST
STORM

ALSO BY TIM LEBBON
AND AVAILABLE FROM TITAN BOOKS

Eden
Coldbrook
The Silence

THE RELICS TRILOGY
Relics
The Folded Land
The Edge

The Cabin in the Woods: The Official Movie Novelization
Alien: Out of the Shadows

THE RAGE WAR
Predator: Incursion
Alien: Invasion
Alien vs. Predator: Armageddon

Kong: Skull Island – The Official Movie Novelization
Firefly: Generations

THE
LAST
STORM

TIM LEBBON

TITAN BOOKS

This novel was written during the first Covid lockdown, so it is dedicated with love to my wonderful family, who kept me safe and sane. My wife, Tracey, my daughter Ellie, and my son Dan. The three best people I know.

The Last Storm
Print edition ISBN: 9781803360423
E-book edition ISBN: 9781803360508

Published by Titan Books
A division of Titan Publishing Group Ltd
144 Southwark Street, London SE1 0UP

First edition: July 2022
1 3 5 7 9 10 8 6 4 2

A CIP catalogue record for this title is available from the British Library.

Printed and bound in Great Britain by CPI Group Ltd.

TWENTY YEARS AGO

THE STORM BEFORE THE CALM

JESSE

The room was full of bad things. Three wooden crates stacked in one corner contained zip-locked bags of drugs. The lid had slipped from the top crate, and no one seemed concerned. There was nothing hidden here. The table pushed against the opposite wall was strewn with empty liquor bottles, overflowing ashtrays, a cracked mirror dusted with what looked like heroin, a fat roll of dollar bills stained with something that wasn't water, and a handgun. Propped against the table was an AR15 with a bump stock. Jesse wondered if it was there to intimidate him. It was probably just there.

"So you're sure you can do this?" the man asked. He was one of the bad things in the room. He sat on a plastic chair, right ankle resting on his left knee. He was heavily bearded, hair expensively cut, and a delicate ring glimmered in his left nostril. He'd said his name was Wolf. It was ridiculous, but Jesse didn't feel like laughing. A man and a woman stood just behind Wolf. Neither of them had spoken, but they both watched Jesse with calm weariness. He did not know their names, and didn't want to know. He thought of them as Snake—the tall white guy with a bald head and tattoo of a python eating his left ear—and Harley, the short, muscled black woman in a Harley Quinn T-shirt.

"Yes," Jesse said.

"Only, we've let you in now," Wolf said, glancing around the place as if it was anything other than a wretched fucking pit. But he didn't mean the room. "Let you see. Let you know. And you can't unsee and unknow."

"I don't see anything," Jesse said. "And like I told you, it works best outside."

"I don't want you doing it outside," Wolf said. "People might see."

"Who?" Jesse asked. Perhaps there was too much challenge in his voice. Snake crossed his arms. Harley shifted from her left foot to her right and back again. *Stay calm*, Jesse thought, even though calm was the last thing he felt.

"People," Wolf said, drawing the word out. "Eyes in the sky."

The man's alleged concern made no sense. It was absurd. The small blockwork building stood within acres of poppy plants, and if anyone saw Jesse out there doing his thing, they'd also see them. Maybe the guy's own product was making him paranoid.

Jesse felt sweat running down his back. *I'm such an idiot.* He should have turned the other way when this opportunity arose, but when contact was first made he and Karina were too broke for him to accept what he was getting into—the secrecy, the guns, and the murdering thugs. And when he realised, he was already in too deep. When he tried to go back on his agreement, they threatened his family with violence. In the end, he had no choice.

The only positive was that he was doing this a thousand miles from home. Karina and his sweet little Ash didn't even know where he was, and until this was over and he returned home with a wad of much-needed cash, that was how it would remain.

"Don't worry, nobody knows me," Jesse lied.

Wolf looked him up and down. Jesse let him, glancing instead at Snake and Harley. He wondered how many people they'd killed between them—and how—and cursed his vibrant imagination. They returned his gaze, expressionless.

He had to stay calm, level, unruffled. It wouldn't work otherwise.

But he looked at the AR15, and the dusting of heroin, and the roll of stained cash that was probably meant for him, and realised again what a total idiot he'd been.

"Outside, then," Wolf said, standing from his chair. He clapped his hands together and grinned. "But not for long."

"It'll be quick," Jesse said. Another potential lie. He never really knew how long it would take, and that piled on more pressure. Once, in Omaha, he sat on his own in a dry riverbed for almost five hours before the first patter of light rain speckled the dusty ground.

Snake picked up the AR15 and handgun and left the hut. Harley inclined her head at the door to indicate Jesse should go next, and she and Wolf followed him out. Over his shoulder, Jesse carried a small wooden case on a leather strap. The strap was worn and darkened from years of use. The case was inlaid with an intricate design of a large tree, canopy and roots mirroring each other. Different types of wood had been used to create the design, and over the years some of it had shrunk and fallen out, leaving only a shadowy memory. He had no idea who had made the case or where it came from. It had called to him from an old antique store. It had been empty, and he had filled it with his apparatus.

Wolf had not told his minions to search inside the case. He knew what it contained.

Outside, the heat struck Jesse a physical blow. He squinted, dropping the sunglasses from his forehead back down over his eyes. He plucked the cap from his back pocket and pulled it tight onto his head.

Everything was dust. It coated his damp skin, scratched its way into his eyes and ears, his nostrils, and the cracked creases of his lips. He felt it inside his clothing, settling into the contours of his body and chafing when he walked. It was the dust of dead things. Jesse looked down as he walked and kicked up dry, sterile grit, the ground begging for water to bring it back to life. The sun beat at the back of his neck, seeking to dry him out, leach from him the waters of life. Everything he did was to prevent that from happening, and to stop it from happening to others. He told himself that, time and again. He told Karina and thought she believed him, hoped she did. He *needed* her to believe. Jesse needed the firm understanding that everything he did was from a position of control. That was the only way it would work. Confusion, stress, tension, fear: all were the enemy of his gift.

Stretching in every direction were row upon row of sickening poppy plants. Suspended above them on a grid of bamboo struts and wires, just above head height, were other creeping plants. He didn't know their species, only that they too were almost dead. There were irrigation channels and a network of flexible hoses trailing beneath the loose planting structures, but many of the hoses were old and desiccated in the intense, unrelenting sunlight. Wolf had told him that for many years they'd been tapping into the nearby river: then, when that dried up, the reservoir six miles away in the hills. Last year, that had also gone dry. The shrubs used to camouflage the crop had dried and died first, leaving the poppy fields exposed to aerial surveillance. It was only a matter of time before they were found out.

That was why Jesse was here, with his apparatus in the wooden case slung over his shoulder. He had come to make rain to save the crop and fill their water storage facilities. For that, Wolf had promised him sixty thousand dollars.

The art of his gift was what drove him, but there was also the money. And there was also his unspoken certainty that, whether his attempt worked or not, this crop was doomed. If he could not bring rain, the plants would not last another month. If he could usher in a downpour, it would not only be a mere shower. That was not how it worked. His level of control was not quite as refined as he had claimed to Wolf. If and when his rains fell, they would do so in a storm that might wash away the loose, dried soil, flood the fields, strip away and drown many of these illicit crops.

Jesse knew he was an idiot. He only hoped he could take the money and run before the full deluge arrived and Wolf realised what he had done.

"Where?" Wolf asked.

"Here is fine," Jesse said.

"You're sure?" The drug farmer was eager and excited to see what Jesse could do. It was a normal reaction, but Jesse didn't regard Wolf as a normal man.

Snake and Harley moved away, giving him distance and space as he stood looking around. The suspended camouflage crop was mostly pale, a sandy colour with occasional wan green patches where some plants clung to life. It was a familiar scene. The drought was deep and long; the world continued to change and, however much Jesse tried to help, he was little more than a speck of sand on a vast beach.

"So, what happens now?" Wolf asked.

"I set up," Jesse said. He paused, looking directly at Wolf. "I need peace. And quiet. And solitude."

Wolf gazed at the wooden box hanging from Jesse's shoulder.

"Is it true you have to stick needles in your arms?" Wolf asked.

"It's nothing like *that*," Jesse said, trying to keep the disgust from his voice. But as Wolf shrugged, turned, and walked away, he had to wonder whether it was more similar than he'd care to admit.

Jesse breathed deeply a few times and turned his face to the sky. It was clear and pale blue, scorched almost cloudless by the unrelenting sun. He remembered his mother doing the same, and he had a rich, living memory of the first time he'd asked what she was doing. He'd been maybe five years old then, and she had been five years away from the flames that would consume her.

I'm wishing upon a cloud, she'd said, laughing as Jesse assumed the same position. *See that one, son? It looks like an elephant.*

He saw no elephants now. There were a few scattered cirrus clouds so high up that they were barely smudges against deep blue infinity. Other than that, the sky offered no signs of rain.

Jesse shrugged the box from his shoulder and opened the metal fastenings. Placing it carefully on the dusty ground, he knelt before it and opened the lid. The lid's underside was still vibrant with the inlaid tree design, as if only the outside had been weathered and worn away by time. He sometimes wondered whether he was also like that. He was approaching forty, but sometimes it felt as though he'd already lived two lifetimes.

Continuing his deep breathing, he took out the apparatus. It was light and small, the length of his forearm, comprised of a series of tubes and bulbs, electrical components and brass casings, and other pieces gathered and gleaned from many sources. He'd built it as a teenager, hearing his mother's whispered encouragement in his mind with each element he added, the turn of every screw. At one end was the focus, and he turned the dial that extruded the small, pointed horn that would aim at the sky.

Closing the lid of the box, he placed the locator pins in their corresponding holes, and then he was almost ready.

Almost.

He took two long wires and unspooled them, ensuring that both ends were connected correctly to the apparatus. Then he extracted two sterile needles from their lined container on one edge of the device and fitted them to the ends of the wires.

He glanced up to see Wolf watching from twenty metres away.

"I need to be on my own," Jesse said.

"Right. On your own." Wolf scuffed the dried soil with one of his boots, kicked at a plant stem. It crumbled beneath his foot, showering crumpled stem and leaves to the ground. "Just fix my place," he said, and he turned away.

It was a strange turn of phrase. It almost left Jesse feeling sorry for him.

He pumped his fist, pushed one needle into his right forearm and stuck it there with surgical tape, then did the same with the other. A tingle of anticipation made him shiver, even in the heat. Twin droplets of blood ran around his arms and dripped to the dusty ground, and were sucked down into the parched land. He wondered how much blood had been spilled into this arid soil, then he closed his eyes and shut away the idea. That was not his business. He dealt not in drugs, but in rain, and his rush was not balanced with pain.

Feeling the sun stretching the skin on his face, sweat running down his neck and torso, and the dusty, gritty reality of this dying land, Jesse closed his eyes and brought himself inward.

Soon, he heard the inner tides of his own personal storms as the thrilling flow began to build. He drifted with those tides. He let them carry him, knowing that he would always remain afloat, comfortable. Sometimes, he believed it was the only safe place. Even when he was with Karina he felt exposed and in danger. Everywhere he looked he saw the world stealing back control from humanity, punishment for so many years of abuse.

Jesse opened his inner eye to view the vague, dark pebbly beach he could not feel beneath his feet, the sea he would never smell, and the distant shadow of tall cliffs to his right. He felt himself balanced perfectly between them all. This was his place. He called it The Shore.

At some distance he heard the soft whirl of his apparatus starting to spin, turn and cycle, and smelled the faintly familiar tang of ozone on the air.

Eyes still closed, he waited for the first drops of rain to fall.

When Jesse opened his eyes, Harley was crouched before him, pointing a pistol at his face.

"I call bullshit," she said. "I don't know how you were ever taken in by this."

"Have faith, Lucy-Anne," Wolf said from somewhere behind Jesse.

The name didn't suit her. It was too nice. She didn't look nice.

Harley tilted her head slightly. "He's awake."

"I don't sleep," Jesse said.

"We've been calling your name," Harley said.

"And like I told your boss—"

"His name's Wolf."

"Like I told Wolf, I need peace and silence, otherwise it might not work."

"You've had over an hour of peace and silence."

Jesse was shocked at how long had passed, but he could see that she was right. The sun was dipping towards the western hills. Shadows were longer, the heat was heavy and old as a memory, and he shivered as a bead of sweat ran down his back.

"Have faith," Wolf said again, this time from just behind him. Jesse heard the man kneeling in the dust. "But how long, Jesse?"

Jesse glanced down at the apparatus. Dials turned lazy revolutions, a bulb emitted a low illumination. The needles in his arms tingled as they transmitted low power from him into the device and back again, an arcane symbiosis.

"Soon," he said.

"Make it sooner," Wolf said. "Lucy-Anne, don't be an asshole."

Harley lowered the gun but remained squatting close in front of him. There was an ugliness in her eyes that was reflected in Wolf's and Snake's. Maybe violence left its mark in your soul, like blood on dirty money.

"Let me—" Jesse began.

"Just fucking do it!" Wolf's shout was so loud, close and unexpected that Jesse fell forward, almost sprawling across the apparatus. One of the wires tautened and tugged at the needle in his right forearm, and he yelped as a trickle of blood emerged from beneath the tape.

"Okay!" Jesse said. He straightened himself, trying to ease his beating heart. The bulb glowed brighter. The dial span faster. A noise came from the apparatus, like an engine grinding on dirty oil, parts wearing and corroding.

"That mean it's working?" Wolf asked.

"Yes," Jesse said, because to answer any other way would buy him pain—or worse. He looked up to the sky where a grey sheen dulled the deep blue, and the first hint of clouds had begun to form.

How could he tell Wolf the truth?

Did he even want to?

Jesse craved the rains as much as anyone else. This was his art, his living, and each time he attempted to make rain it felt like a treat. Even when he wasn't sure it would work. It didn't always. His was a fickle talent.

"Faster!" Wolf said, flicking the back of Jesse's head.

"Look, boss!" Snake said. Standing off to Jesse's left, surrounded by dead and dying plants, he was looking up at the sky like a kid watching plane trails.

"I see," Wolf said. "Faster! It's working!"

Jesse tried to ignore the pain where the needle entered his right arm, and the fear growing inside at what he had begun here. It was something different from before, something wrong, and the knowledge that there was no going back sat in the pit of his stomach, a hot knot growing, eating. Getting worse.

"Yes!" Harley said. She'd holstered her gun and was also looking up. "It's good, boss. Gonna be good!"

Gonna be good, Jesse thought, and the apparatus ground as its components spun and spat. *I should stop.* Sparks tickled his forearm, dancing from the needles and along the wires. He smelled hair singeing across his skin. *This all feels wrong.* His ears rang with distant thunder, and he knew that it only sounded inside, rolling along The Shore as if announcing something bad.

It had been like this several times before—a feeling of dread, an unknown danger looming from The Shore—and he'd always been able to stop. If he stopped now, he'd end up feeding the poppies with a bullet in his skull.

The first spot of rain struck his forehead and ran down beside his nose.

"You asked for this," Jesse whispered, and he didn't know what *this* was, and wasn't sure that any of them even heard beneath the sudden, sweet sound of falling rain.

Snake started jumping up and down and whooping. Harley stood with her head back and tongue out. Wolf was more restrained, talking on his phone and instructing someone to prepare the rain catchers, ensure the irrigation controls were set, oversee the storage of as much water as they could catch and save.

Jesse waited. The fear, the sickness, had not abated at all, and he knew the storm he had seeded was far from over, and far more than a simple storm. The Shore remained distant but something about it was altered.

Jesse closed his eyes and let his apparatus spin and grind and whirl him back to that place. Until now, anything he'd sensed of The Shore had been a part of him—the soft hush of the sea was his pulse in his ears; the tang of that distant beach was the fresh hint of rain on the air. Now, though, he was more there than he had ever been before. The thick, oily seawater surged, dipping and rising as if something huge was striving to thrust through the thick surface. Where it broke on The Shore the water seemed to become pebbles, rolling black beads washing up the beach. To his right the cliffs loomed, a solid wall that seemed to tug on the whole scene with their gravity. Creatures flitted through the air and scampered across the ground, but they were as vague as memories, so fast and fleeting that he couldn't focus on them.

Far along the beach, in a hazy distance where reality faded to dream, several groups of huddled shapes stretched taller and turned grey faces his way.

He had never noticed The Shore noticing him before. And it was terrible.

As Jesse exerted a huge effort to pull himself back and away from The Shore, Wolf grabbed his shoulder and squeezed, as if they were friends or colleagues. Jesse leaned to the left and vomited, making sure to miss the apparatus where raindrops spattered across its hot surface. Wolf seemed unconcerned. Perhaps he thought puking was just part of the show.

"What the hell?" Snake asked.

Jesse looked to where the man danced between dying plants, scratching at his back with both hands.

"It's rain, you idiot!" Harley called, her voice high with delight.

Something squirmed on the ground in front of Jesse. It scrambled in the dirt before righting itself. A scorpion.

Woken in the dust? Brought up by the rain?

Its legs scraped at the damp, loose soil as if it had never felt ground beneath its feet before, then it darted towards him.

He was shocked, and at the same time not shocked at all.

He lifted the box and apparatus and brought them down on the creature. The needle was tugged from his right arm with a spurt of blood that mixed with the rain, feeding the ground. He vomited again. His head thudded, thunder rolled, and this time he wasn't sure whether it was within or without.

"Woo-hoo!" Harley shouted, splashing in puddles like an excited child. The rain was a deluge now, sheeting down and soaking the ground, the poppy plants, and the climbing shrubs suspended above to camouflage their existence. Some leaves and stems came apart beneath the battering downpour, too dry and decayed to survive. Others seemed to shiver and shimmer in the rain. Dust was washed from leaves, revealing pale green tints that might grow lush once more.

"Ouch!" Snake said. "Motherfucker! What the fuck—?" He slipped and fell. Jesse saw several scampering shapes converging on the fallen man through pooling water.

"Mike?" Harley asked. "Mike?"

Mike screamed.

Jesse stood and unplugged his other arm from the apparatus. Something bounced from his right shoulder, and he saw the scorpion hit the ground. He stepped on it, crushing it into the mud. He snatched up the apparatus and box, wincing as it burned his hands but knowing he could never let go.

Harley was dashing through rows of plants towards her fallen companion.

"What have you done?" Wolf asked behind him.

Jesse turned, bringing the apparatus up before him to fend off any attack. But Wolf was beyond violence. His left hand was fisted around the remains of a scorpion, its sting curled into his knuckles. Another was tangled in his beard. His bottom lip was already swollen, and his eyes were glassy and wet, reflecting the rainy dream he had been living for so long.

"I brought rain," Jesse said.

Wolf took a step forward, right hand raised as if ready to grab him. Jesse stood back as he groaned and fell, then stepped over the twitching man to head back towards the relative safety of the building. Lightning thrashed and thunder rolled.

Between rows of plants he saw a hint of movement, a pale face, and then shadows fell again.

He ran. Water washed dust and sweat from his skin, but some of it was slick and warm, like blood. His forearms bled. Sickness rose in him again, a reaction to what he had done, mourning what he had wanted to do. He'd only ever wished to bring rain. Not anything else. Not this.

Ten metres from the building, as he splashed through mud and saw a pinkish hue to the flowing water, a shape burst from the plant rows beside him. Harley stumbled closer, hand pressed against her neck. She could barely stand.

"Bastard," she said, voice slurred and almost lost to the storm.

"You should have let me do it my way. I told you. I *warned* you."

"Bastard…"

Jesse lifted the wooden box ready to swing at her, but paused with it raised over his shoulder. If he struck her, broke the box and apparatus apart, he might never be able to do this again.

Harley lifted the gun in her other hand and shot him in the face.

Lightning. Thunder.

Darkness.

PART ONE

THE EYE

ASH

In the eye, in the silence, I am almost myself again. I don't know how long I've been lost in the tumult—three days? A week?—and I'm not really sure where I am. A small town, somewhere. A sad, tired place with sad, tired people. A few of them glance at me as I walk along the street, probably because I'm a stranger. I hope it's nothing more. One time, on emerging from the tumult, my face, clothes and knuckles were covered in blood and one of my teeth was loose.

I pause in front of a store window and examine my reflection. I have to shift left and right so that I can see. No blood on my face, at least. My short hair is dirty and heavy with dust. My eyes are deep-set and surrounded by wrinkles from the heat, thirst and hunger, but rarely from laughter. My appearance doesn't seem too bad. Wherever I've been, however long has passed, I've been looking after myself. I've even been applying sunscreen. Soon I'll start to recall some of the recent past as scenes and voices, feelings and thoughts that might not even feel like my own. I'll grab on to what I can and make as much sense of those moments as possible, but there's always a miasma of chaos about the memories that come to me while I'm in the eye. Of course there is. They're tales of my time in the storm.

Reflected in the store window, I watch the street. A few people walk here and there, some of them using umbrellas to shield against the merciless sun. One elderly couple hold hands, and when they pass behind me I see the woman glance at me, frowning. I wonder what she's thinking. Maybe she feels pity. I'd rather that than her be afraid. Many of the towns and farming communities scattered across the dying plains of the Desert are visited by drifters, those looking for work or something to steal, or simply somewhere to live for a while. I've met these wanderers. I'm one of them. None of them hide secrets like mine.

"Hello," I say, turning to the old couple. They pause. The man smiles, the woman's frown remains. "My name's Ash."

"Morning, Ash," the man says. He's tall and gaunt, with folds of skin round his eyes and heavy jowls that hint at a past as a more portly man. "Can we help you?"

"What brings you to Three Rocks?" the woman asks. "Work or charity?"

"Work," I say. I have no idea how long I'll remain in the eye. The shortest time I can recall is mere days; the longest several months, a more settled period when I'd tried to put down roots. But the storms returned, as they always do, and hauled me down into the tumult once again. I work when I can and sometimes, even in those dark times I hardly remember, I manage to hold down a job.

"What're you good at?" the man asks.

"Anything manual."

"You don't look strong," the woman says.

"I'm wiry." I try to smile. I can tell by her reaction that it doesn't work.

"Where're you from?" the man asks. He's kind. I can see that in his eyes, hear it in his voice, and I think his wife must be too. I've experienced many moments of kindness on the road, and the opposite as well. I'm not lying about being wiry and strong, and I can look after myself. One time, in Farzon Gap, I stabbed a man in the arm and shoulder when he wouldn't take no for an answer. I left that place without waiting to see if he'd bleed to death, hiding in the back of a Soaker's wagon for two days while they drove me into darkness. By the time I was in the eye again I was afraid to look online for news of the stabbing. I didn't see my face on any screens. That was good enough for me.

"Massachusetts originally," I said. "But here and there, mostly."

"You got family?" the woman asks.

"No." The lie is quick and easy.

"Poor kid," the man says. "We used to run a farm, me and June. Small, only a couple hundred acres. Our two sons took it over, what now… twenty years back?"

"Twenty-three," June says. She smiles at me at last, thinking of her sons.

"It was bad back then, but nowhere near what it is now," the man says.

"No work on your farm, then?" I ask.

"The boys went west," June says. "Can't blame them. Farm's just a ruin now."

"Fields're a desert," the man says.

"Bruce, friend of ours, runs the store downtown." June nods along the street. "Moore's. Try there. He might not pay much, but he's decent, and lets workers stay in the cabin in his backyard. I hear his last helper left three days back."

"And his wife's a great cook," the man says. June glares at him but he doesn't seem to notice. His gaze has shifted over my shoulder, into the window and a reflection of easier times.

I wonder at the story behind his stare, her glare, but it's not my place to ask.

I'm tired and in need. I've got a hundred bucks in my pocket, a phone with a dead battery, and a backpack full of my worldly belongings.

"Thanks, I'll drop by," I say.

"Good luck," the man says. June only nods at me as she leads him away.

In the distance, past the low buildings at the edge of town, a dust devil dances left and right, sucking up dying plants and spitting them out again, as if taking pleasure at mixing up the past. I watch it for a couple of minutes in case it develops into something more ferocious, but no one seems concerned. The dust falls, and drifts, and the thermal and breeze that formed the tornado breathes its last.

I turn back to the store window, trying to see the old man's past. Looking deeper, through the sheen of sun on grimy glass, I see an old guitar case propped on a stand. There are many other objects around it. They look like the orphans of homes that have been boarded up and cleared out by people like the old couple's sons, eager to move on, to try to find something better. But it's the guitar case that draws my eye.

I catch my breath. An image plays across my mind, sepia and blurred, and I blink rapidly as if to make it move, because I can tell it's a memory of something recent. I'm viewing it through the haze of my recent tumult. The guitar case has inspired it, and my blood turns cold.

The case reminds me so much of the one I used to keep my apparatus in.

Something happened, I think, and between my rapid blinks a series of memories plays like a flipbook.

The small town market, tables shaded beneath huge awnings, families trading unwanted items or selling homemade food and drink.

The table belonging to two young women, loaded down with a selection of strange contraptions.

The odd, old machine that catches my attention.

It wasn't what I thought, and of course that was right. But back then I was in the tumult, confused and adrift. Vulnerable.

Grabbing the trailing wires of the machine and trying to plunge them through the skin of my forearms.

As if it was an old apparatus I could use. But even if it had been an old Rainmaker's device, it could never have been mine.

Me, shouting about rain and drawing attention. People around me flinching back in shock, or watching with interest, and a few of them laughing at this strange woman kneeling in the dust and muttering confused words about storms, and rain, and a place only I knew called Skunksville.

"Oh, no," I say, and my voice echoes back at me from the store window. At least I must have moved on quickly, because this place is not where that happened.

But something about that almost-forgotten experience from days or weeks before has planted a seed, and now seeing the old guitar case has urged it to take root. In the eye for a while, I'm safe to let it bloom.

I wonder if I *can* build it again. I wonder if I *can* get it all back, and the storms inside me will abate and allow me to reconstruct, reimagine, and bring back to life the device I saw crushed beneath my father's boots.

I wonder if I can remain in the eye long enough to make it work, or even if I can stretch that eye forever so that I am all it sees. I feel the storm's potential inside me all the time—soul torn by violent winds, memories diluted and scattered by downfalls the likes of which I never imagined before—and it's always flexing and straining to burst from me, flooding me with madness once more. Always inside instead of outside, because of what my father did.

In these rarest of moments, when the tumult is held at bay and I view the world with my eyes of old, I wonder.

Usually the darkness floods me again and washes my wonder away, but I won't let that happen this time. I fucking won't. Something has taken hold. Skunksville is calling with a louder voice than I have heard in nine years, and I'm going to answer.

The moment I set eyes on the storeowner, I don't like him. I've seen his like before. There are always those willing and eager to prey on the misfortune of others to benefit themselves.

He doesn't speak as I enter the store. He eyes me up and down. He's short, overweight. I shouldn't hold that against him, but with swathes of the country suffering famine, he's not ashamed of his obvious food wealth.

I consider turning around and leaving, finding Moore's to ask for a job. It's only a guitar case.

It might have been my *case.*

The voice is mine, an echo from my past. It's smooth and firm, echoing the confident young woman I'd been before my father poisoned me. Hearing that voice is like listening to an old, supportive friend.

"How much for the guitar case in the window?"

He's obviously been watching me looking in at it. I should have walked away first and come back later.

"Guitar's in it."

"I only want the case."

"You already own a guitar without a case?" He glances at my dusty, dirty clothes. I hate his eyes on me. The knife is in my right jeans pocket, and I rest my thumb on the pocket's edge, feigning being relaxed, but ready.

"Just the case," I say. "Forty bucks?"

"Two hundred. Guitar as well. Comes with the case." He's standing behind the counter, and there's a dirty plate beside him and a can of cool beer. I can smell the cooked chicken, see the moisture beading on the outside of the can.

"I've got a job at Moore's," I say. "I can give you fifty now, fifty at the end of the week."

"Bruce Moore's a prick," he says. From this man I take that as a positive character reference.

I look around the store. "How's business?"

"Up and down."

When I turn back to him I see his eyes flicker up from my body. My heart stutters and I feel the thud of something deep inside, a flash of lightning in dark places.

Not now, my inner voice says. *Don't let him force you away from the eye. Be calm. Take this moment of peace. And… there's that case.*

"You get all this stuff from people moving on," I say. It's not a question.

"Some folks can't take the heat," he says. He's sweating, shirt stuck to his distended belly, even though there are three fans on full blast around his jumbled shop. "I give them good money when they decide to move on. Seed money, so they can start somewhere new. Somewhere it fucking rains, every now and then."

"Nowhere's good," I say.

He shrugs. "So my staying here makes sense."

"I've got eighty here, now, just for the case."

"Eighty and what else?"

I let out a deep, fast sigh. It's almost a snort. I put my hand in my pocket and hold the knife. I don't bring it out, not yet, but he sees the movement. I guess he's been threatened before, and probably over the same thing.

"I've been on the road for years," I say. "There are good people doing their best to get by and help others. I've been to towns where it's all dried up, the mains are cracked and broken, and they'll still spare a glass of water for a stranger."

"Nice if you can get it," he says.

"There are also lots of assholes out there. Scumbags who want to profit from what the world's become." I look around the store at pieces of peoples' lives bought and sold for a song. "Some places, I've seen those people end up dead. In a little place south of Elk City, I saw a man hanged for stealing water from a disabled kid. The mother was dead. Father looked after the girl on his own, doing everything for her, caring for her. The guy's body was left up for three days in that heat. Some places, that's what's left of the law now."

"What's that got to do with me?" His left hand has dropped out of sight behind the counter. I'm not sure whether he has a gun or not. It's a risk, but my whole life is a roll of the dice.

"You're one of the assholes."

He freezes, staring at me. Maybe he's caught a glimpse of the tumult in my eyes.

"Eighty," I say.

He nods.

Without letting go of the knife in my right hand, I reach into my left pocket and pull out all the cash I have. I dump it on the counter and tuck a twenty back in my pocket.

Three minutes later I am walking along the sidewalk towards a large red sign that reads 'Moore's'. The guy in the shop didn't say another thing, and I'm grateful. I feel sick and thirsty, and I sense the storm flickering at my edges like a steer at a gate.

With a room and some food inside me, hopefully I can tease the eye to remain for a little while longer.

I haven't examined the guitar case yet, but carrying it brings alive something inside me. I'm more aware of my surroundings, perhaps because for the first time in a long while I'm thinking of the future, and what it might bring.

Maybe I can build it again.

The weight of the case is a comfort, and an invitation to make it heavier.

I'll start looking for components. Very soon.

Electric cars pass back and forth along the street, and I remember something my dad said when production of gas-powered private vehicles ceased. *Shutting the stable door after the horse has bolted.* I don't like remembering him; it makes me sick and sad and angry all at once. He made me like this when he tried to kill me.

I walk faster. There are gasoline vehicles on the road too, more than usual, mostly trucks. Their engines are loud compared to the soft whisper of electric cars, and the noise inspires a surprising nostalgia in me, for a time when I was a child and more than half the vehicles on the roads still belted out fumes, rattles and growls. *That's how a car's supposed to sound*, my dad said, and he told me about when he was a kid and the whole idea of all cars being electric was still mostly science fiction. I wonder if my nostalgia is really for the cars, or for my dad. I hated those times close to the end when he stopped loving and trusting me. Earlier memories, with him and my mom planting and tending our smallholding, surviving on homegrown food, were mostly good.

There are horses here, too. They're a familiar sight, and most people in small towns like Three Rocks know how to ride. They're easy to master, cheap to keep—if you have the land, and can afford feed for the years when the grasses die right back—and at the worst of times, they can feed a family for weeks.

Three Rocks is trying its best. As many stores are boarded up as remain open, maybe more, and I'm guessing the houses behind and beyond the main street are the same. But those who remain to weather the ongoing years-long storm of heat, drought and famine are trying hard.

I reach Moore's at last and discover the old couple were right. Bruce Moore is a good guy, and he takes me on for an initial four weeks. I'm grateful, though uncertain that the eye will last that long. He gives me a cot in the cabin in his yard behind the store, and though he can't pay me much, he feeds and waters me, and I have daily access to his shower. The water is just a trickle, and it's recycled and filtered again and again, but he has soap to mask the slightly oily smell.

Each night I return to the cabin and spend a while examining the guitar case. It's unremarkable, battered, scarred, yet the empty space within thrums with potential.

I scratch at the knots of scar tissue on my forearms.

I look for components in Moore's store, and find none, but I'll know them when I do. I remember the first apparatus I built, and how the components called to me. I haven't heard that calling yet, other than the case. When I'm working, it calls to me still. Back to the cabin. Back to stare at it, and imagine it filling up.

One morning I hear the patter of rain on the cabin roof. Excited, I scramble to the door and fling it open. Outside it's as dry and arid as ever, and the sun scorches the cloudless sky and hurts my eyes.

That afternoon I feel the eye starting to disappear, and so I decide to move on as the storms swell to smother me once more.

This is my fate. I'm always chasing the eye. This time, though, it's with more purpose than ever before.

When the storm consumes me, it smothers my senses, and my perception of time, and it takes away most of what makes me Ash. Afterwards, in the eye, I can look back and pick out random memories of my time in the tumult. Sometimes they confuse me, other times they come as a shock. I retain enough of myself to push through, and it's like being deeply drunk—basic instincts remain, but memories are washed away.

There was a farmstead, deserted for years and home now to a small group of stragglers abandoned by the world. They were wary of me from the moment I arrived, but one woman took an interest in my guitar case. I carried it everywhere, slept with it, and she must have assumed it contained something precious. When she tried to take it, I swung it at her head. Next thing I recall is slipping down a dusty bank, tripping over rocks, and crawling into a dry culvert in a cracked riverbed beneath a road. I remember blood on my hands. I remember the rattle of a snake warning me away.

Another moment is like one verse of a long song. There was a group of Soakers parked in a circle. I appeared among them, an apparition from the dark, lit by camp fires and walking from the shadows of my memory. One of them asked me to play my guitar for them. I asked for water. They laughed. Whether their wagons were full or empty, they could have spared me a drink. *You'll never meet a poor Soaker*, my mom used to say. I showed one of them my knife and she laughed in my face, and then that verse ended and the song finished without me.

There are other snippets of memory, all of them framed by darkness and upheaval, and the pain of not being able to release the storms that churn me up inside.

A man offering me a floor to sleep on for the night, and I can't remember whether I took it.

A woman showing me an image on her phone of a town in the Midwest destroyed by tornadoes.

A couple dragging their children away from the mad woman in the street.

My life has become a flip-book of images with most of the pages removed.

In the eye once more, the peace, the quiet, comes as a shock. My heart still races as if trying to catch up, and I have a whole new collection of mysteries—a split lip that does not want to heal, a new jacket with a collection of old baseball cards in one pocket, and an ache in my heart. I don't know whether it's cause by grief, loss, or love.

And there's something else. Somewhere in my travels I have found a base board for my new apparatus.

I sit in the shadow of an abandoned truck in a field filled with similar vehicles. The tyres are flat and melted into the ground, cabs have smashed windows and rusted patches blurring old company names. Scrub has grown around and between them, a bramble that has become common in drought-dried areas across the Desert. It's straggly and sharp and is known as devil grass. It grows in places where it hasn't rained for years, and when an occasional storm comes, the devil grass flourishes. It's like a manifestation of nature mocking what we have done to the land, and to ourselves.

The truck graveyard is silent but for the scampering of lizards and the mournful songs of a few lonely birds. Heat haze hangs above the acre of abandoned metal, blurring the world. It's a good place to gather myself, and to examine the board I've found. It's a sheet of hardwood maybe two centimetres thick. Two-thirds of a metre long, as wide as my splayed hand, it's heavily polished and deeply scratched in places. The scratches form dark lines in the wood, filled with dirt compounded over time. Screw holes are bored into the wood at irregular spacings, but none of them go the whole way through. There's a sunken square at one end with a small screw hole at each corner where a metal plaque might once have been affixed. It's a piece of old wood that has forgotten its purpose. I'll give it a new one.

I can't remember where or when I came across the board, but even in my lessened state I recognise it for what it is: the base and foundation of a whole new apparatus.

Touching the wood—turning it in my hands, feeling its contours and tiny terrains—between each blink I see my father's boot crushing the old apparatus I once used. That was the device of a child still finding her way. Now I have lived, and I am no longer a child.

This new creation will be the true tool of a Rainmaker.

"This is my apparatus," my dad said.

"Can I touch it?"

"Of course. But be careful."

"Will it hurt me?"

He offered a strained smile but did not reply. Even though I was barely ten years old, I understood what that meant. *No, but you might hurt it.*

I reached out and touched the shining brass tube on top of the apparatus. It was cold, smooth, somehow mysterious, and one of many separate elements that made up the device. I ran my hand along the surface to the cogged wheels fixed at one end, the bolts holding them there, the rusted washers beneath the bolt heads, the metal frame that was screwed down onto the blocky wooden base, then along to the first of the dials. Its glass cover was missing, and I heard my father's indrawn breath as I delicately touched the dial's white face, its finely embossed Roman numerals, and the hair-fine needle that pointed, sprung and coiled, at the zero.

I had never seen it working. My father had stopped rainmaking just a few years after I was born, though he made sure to tell me all about it. He had to, he said, to ensure I never made the same mistakes he made. I'd asked him a few times what those mistakes were, but he said I was too young to know. He never did tell me.

"I built this over thirty years ago," he said. "You never met my mom, your grandma, but she guided me and taught me how to use it."

"Mom says she died in a big fire."

"That's right. A bush fire in Texas." His voice was measured and guarded. He rubbed at the pale scar on the left side of his face. It reached from the corner of his mouth, along his jawline to just beneath his ear. He sometimes smiled when he realised I was watching him do it, and said he was trying to tune in the metal plates and bolts in his jaw to the local radio station.

"Was she trying to help?" I asked.

"Always. Like her father, my grandfather, and generations of our family before them. And they all made their own apparatus. They're unique to each Rainmaker. It's as much a part of them, as linked to them, as their own heart. And building one can be a long process. I started this one in July of my seventh year, and finished it one hundred and ninety-seven days later. I knew when I was ready to begin." He touched a small, round ball-bearing affixed between two blocks of hard concave rubber, the first component he had found, the one that sang to him. I had mine in my hand. "And I knew when I was done. Here, with this." He picked up one of the coiled wires.

"Do you have my grandma's apparatus?" I asked.

My father lay back on the ground. We were in our backyard, and the lawn was dead. Our vegetable patch and wildflower garden took all the water we could spare, because they fed us and kept the bees alive. Food and bees were important; a nice, neat lawn was not.

"No," he said, looking out of the sky. "It burned with her."

"Oh." He often said shocking things in front of me and told me I shouldn't be shielded from the truth. Sometimes Mom looked angry when he said things, sometimes sad, but she never disagreed. She knew that he was right. The time to hide children from the depressing truth of the world was past. You couldn't pretend things like that weren't happening.

"Even if it hadn't, I'd have broken it into pieces when she died. You can't pass on an apparatus. It isn't meant to be handed down. These are... not normal things."

"Like, abnormal?"

"Maybe."

"Magic?"

He laughed, sat up and ruffled my hair. I liked it when he did something like that, because most of the time he was so damn serious.

"Magic is a word people use to describe things they don't understand." He ran his own hand over the apparatus, from one end to the other, and I noticed he didn't quite touch it. If anything, he seemed a little bit afraid. "So yeah. Definitely magic."

Mom called from the house then, urging us inside to help her make dinner. This was two or three years before things got really bad, and there was still water in the faucet most of the time, and no rationing at the store.

"So, will you help me build mine?" I asked.

"I have to." He tried to keep smiling, though even at that age I could tell he looked troubled. "If I don't, you'll end up building and using it on your own. And you need guidance."

"Will you always help me? After I've made it, and when it's time to use it?" I opened my hand and the small circle of glass I'd carefully removed from a magnifying glass sat there, catching the sun and warming my palm. It was my first component, and it sang to me.

"I will."

And for a while, he did.

There must be a hundred abandoned trucks in the vehicle graveyard. I don't recall arriving, but for now it feels peaceful and quiet and I decide to stay. Besides, something is keeping me here. I recognise the feeling from more than fifteen years ago. Something here is lost and needs me to find it.

With the base board locked away inside the guitar case, I wander between the trucks and cabs, avoiding the devil grass where I can. These were huge gas-guzzling beasts, silent for many years now, yet still the scent of spilled oil hangs in the motionless, hot air. The ground here is marked; I see patches beneath and around the trucks and wagons where the soil is darker, and the plants growing there are ugly and squat, feeding on spilled fuel. Devil grass snags at my jeans and pricks my skin. I wince and pull away, and I see glimmering blood on several long thorns.

I climb into a cab. The door is rusted open, the leather seats brittle and torn by unknown creatures, the elements, and the march of time. As a child I'd been fascinated by the idea of huge trucks traversing the country hauling tons of goods, and the men and women driving them. I'd been most entranced by the idea that the truckers slept in the cabs. The idea had seemed almost exotic, travelling the country with no rules, choosing where and when you'd stop to camp down for the night, and the concept of the cab as both work and home space felt so safe.

There is no romanticism to this truck now. Much of the dashboard has been vandalised and stripped out, plastic and leather cracked and snapped, leaving a fan of wires trailing like dried veins. Switches and knobs have been ripped away, and someone has tried but failed to saw off the steering wheel. The guts of the machine have been tugged out, leaving a sad, useless shell. Behind the front seats is the small area where the driver used to watch TV, cook, and sleep. Something must have crawled in here and died years ago. I can't make out what it was through the mass of matted fur, exposed bones, and leathery skin, but the must of old death is still present. I wait for a while, rooting around in the rotting cab to see if I can find what might be calling to me. I listen for it. I even ask where it might be, my voice surprisingly loud in this confined space. There's no response, so I jump down from the cab and start to walk, weaving between trucks and trailers and watching out for snakes. Rattlers often make devil grass their home.

When I find it, the next component for my apparatus isn't inside any of the vehicles at all. It's on the outside, hanging from the open door of a big rust-red truck by one solitary screw. Moments before I find it a soft wind stirs the graveyard, whistling through rotted sections of chassis and rustling leaves and thorns, and the old wing-mirror arm rattles gently against the metal door. I hear it and see it, and the wind rises again as if in triumph.

The mirror and frame have long gone, leaving behind the metal arm with a small fixing plate at either end. It's as long as my forearm, made from stainless steel that has stained nonetheless. This environment does that, defying human efforts at permanence.

I snap the arm away and weigh it balanced across my palm. It's perfect.

My heart hurries as I think about the new apparatus taking form. I look to the sky, deep and blue and scorched by the endless sun. It's just past midday and I should be sheltering from the heat, but I'm too eager to keep looking. Instead, I pull on my sun hat and slather my face and neck with another layer of cream. There might be a dozen more pieces to find, or two dozen, but the more I search and discover them, the more those unfound will lure me in. I learned as a child that an apparatus will desire to be built.

I slip the guitar case from my right shoulder and unlatch it, placing the rust-spotted metal fixture inside. It sits perfectly against the base, and the screw holes of its fixing plate match old holes in the wood.

Of course they do.

I move on. This is a dangerous place, but also a sad one. The danger lies in the remnants: sharp, rusted metal; shattered glass; rainbows of fuel soaked into the ground. It's contaminated with memory, and therein lies the sadness. These rusted trucks and tattered trailers are an echo of the past. Maybe they weren't better times, but they were more fruitful and less challenged. Back when fossil fuel vehicles roared there was water in every faucet, countless square miles of fertile farmland, and food on every shelf. It was a time and life of excess, and those years seeded what we are living through now.

I push through a low spread of devil grass, lifting my legs high to step past as many of the thorny stems as I can. Something's drawing me this way. I tug my leg free of more clasping thorns, hissing as one of them pricks my calf through my jeans. That's when I hear the singing.

I pause, head tilted to one side, breathing through my mouth so I can hear better. It's a woman's voice, and something about the way she sings makes me believe she doesn't know I'm there. It's free, unconcerned. She's singing to herself.

Turning my head left and right, trying to make out where the voice is coming from, I go to move away but surprise myself by taking a few steps towards the sound. I don't mind interacting with people, and sometimes I actively seek it out, because life on the road can be lonely. But here, now, I'm looking for something in particular.

Maybe she has it.

I pause at that thought. As I pull myself through the last of the devil grass, and errant stems scrape across the lower chassis of a stripped-down trailer, the singing stops.

"Hello?" the voice calls. I smile and wonder why. Maybe it's because there's no fear evident there at all, although anyone travelling alone should surely be cautious. Maybe it's because her talking voice is almost as musical as when she sings.

"Hi," I say. The smile remains, unfamiliar. *Can't trust hunches*, I think. *She might be trouble.* But a hunch brought me here, so I let it lead the way.

A head pops out from an open trailer thirty metres ahead. "Oh, fucking hell, you heard me singing."

"It was really good," I say. "What's the song?"

She ignores the question. "Got a guitar?"

"Er, no." I shrug my shoulder, shifting the guitar case. "It's empty. Mostly."

"What use is an empty guitar case?"

It's my turn to ignore the question. "You alone?"

"With a voice like mine, do you really think I'd sing in company?"

"Weird place to be hanging out," I say, but I understand that maybe it's not that weird at all. I've spent time in stranger places, and I've also become good at identifying fellow travellers. Her short hair is inexpertly cut, her T-shirt is sun-bleached, and despite her cheeriness and open smile I can still sense a distinct wariness. She looks around me, not at me, checking to see if I'm alone. I bet she's already ensured there's more than one exit from the trailer.

"It's not too bad," she says. "Pity the hot tub's not working, though." Seemingly satisfied that I'm alone, she jumps down. Her landing kicks up a shower of dust.

"Nice boots," I say. She's wearing sturdy leather walking boots, worn pale through use.

"Took them from the last man I killed," she says, putting on an exaggerated American drawl. I blink in shock. It took that to make me realise she had a British accent.

"Hope you took his feet out first."

She freezes, eyes wide, then laughs. It's an honest, gushing guffaw, with a snort included, and she bends with her hands on her knees. It's utterly infectious and I laugh as well, and for the next few seconds this graveyard sings with jollity.

"Fuck," she gasps, wiping her eyes. "Fuck! I love someone with a sense of humour. No one has a sense of humour anymore!"

"Can't blame them sometimes," I say.

"Yeah, true, but if you don't laugh, you cry, right?"

I smile.

"My name's Cee," she says.

"As in the ocean?"

"Huh. Never thought of it like that. More like the letter after 'B', but…" She frowns.

"So your name's Celia, or something?"

"Fuck, no! I'd have murdered my parents much sooner if they called me that." She has a knife on her belt, the leather handle as pale and well-used as her boots. It's her second reference to murder in as many minutes.

"Hey, I'm totally fucking with you. Promise."

I breathe an exaggerated sigh. "Phew. Only murdered your father, right?"

She smiles but looks aside. Uncomfortable. "My name's Chelsea," she says. "After the football team, not the politician. From a young age I've fucking hated people shortening it to Chels. So, from the moment I was able to tell people what they should call me, I've been Cee."

"Huh," I say. "I like it." And I do. It goes along with the strong fuck-you attitude she exudes. "In that case you should maybe call me Leigh. Though no one ever has."

She narrows her eyes. "Ash."

"Ash," I say. "So, you got any food in that derelict grocery store food wagon, Cee-not-Chels?"

"Maybe I have," she says. "Tell me you're not a meat eater."

"I eat what I can get," I say, because it feels wrong to lie, and I think she'd know.

"Fair enough," she says. "But try my veggie food and tell me I'm not a demi-god of cheffing." She climbs back up into the trailer, extends a hand down to me and helps me up. "Welcome to my humble abode. The view's shit and it gets cold at night, but the neighbours are great."

"I like what you've done with the place," I say. "Very minimalist."

"Sit down if you like. I was just cooking some soup, and I've got a loaf of bread. The crust's stale but the insides will be fine."

I can smell the soup and it sets my stomach rumbling. Her sleeping bag is laid out along one side wall of the trailer, backpack propped at one end, and a small camping stove is set on a square of wood in front of the sleeping bag. The soup bubbles and steams, and beside it on the wood is a loaf of bread. I realise just how hungry I am.

"Turnip and sweet potato," she says. "I traded for some veg in Melton, and I always carry spices, pepper and salt."

"It smells great."

I sit down and lean back, and Cee kneels and stirs the soup with a spoon.

"Oh. Only got one cup and spoon."

"I'll use mine," I say. I open my pack and delve about inside.

"So what's with the empty guitar case?" she asks, nodding at where I've propped the case against the opposite wall.

"I dunno, just like it. I'm looking for stuff to fill it."

She's silent, stirring, not looking at me.

"Already got a wooden plinth and a metal thing."

"Okay."

"How long have you been here?" I ask.

"Only one night so far."

"Where are you going?"

"Next town. Always the next town."

"How come you're here?"

"You mean in the States, or squatting over a pan of soup in this trailer?"

I shrug.

"I'm over here because of my dad's work. We moved out ten years ago, me and my parents, and my little brother Sammy. Lived in New York for a while, then his work took us to Minneapolis. He led, we followed."

"What sort of work?"

"Pharmaceuticals. He was a salesman, I guess, though he'd give it a dozen grander titles."

"So, successful?"

"As far as it goes." She stirred a little harder, swiping the spoon around the edge of the pan. If there was such a thing as angry stirring, she was doing it.

"So how come you're here now?" I ask.

Cee keeps stirring. Maybe she's considering whether or not to answer.

"Choice," she says. For the first time I notice her arms, as if saying that one word exposes some of the bad choices she's made. She's wearing cargo pants and a Mumford & Sons T-shirt with the sleeves cut off. She's fit, strong, tanned but not burned, but the spiky shadows of old scars and bruises running up and down her forearms tell another story. I try to swallow down the stale disappointment I feel. I've hardly made a startling success of my own life, and even though I blame my father for the pivotal swing in my story that sent me to the here and now, a million decisions of my own edged me towards that moment, and have steered me out the other side.

I should be the last to judge, because I don't want to be judged myself. Not for what I've done, and even less for what I'm going to do.

And I am going to do it, I think, *because it's what I was born to do.* And at that moment I hear a soft whisper and see what I need next. It's close to Cee's pin-pricked history, a simple black strap around her wrist. I've seen them before, even owned one once. It's a fitness and health tracker, GPS equipped, and as I blink I see it stripped down to its basic components and strapped to the board in my guitar case. This is part of my new apparatus, and I have no idea at all how I will be able to take it.

I hold out my battered metal cup and Cee pours us both an equal measure. She's right about the bread being stale, but the inside is still soft and fluffy, and I break it up and drop it into the cup. The soup really is good. We sit side by side on her sleeping bag for several minutes, eating and making appreciative noises, saying nothing.

"You've been travelling a while," she says.

"Oh?" I mop up the dregs of soup with the last of my bread, smiling. People often offer to tell me my story. None of them ever come close.

"Want to know how I know?" She's finished her soup now, and she leans back against the trailer's side. I do the same. It feels comfortable, even though our arms are almost touching. I can smell her, a faint odour of garlic and dust, and the honest sweat of a life on the road.

"Sure," I say.

"I'm pretty good at seeing people's stories."

I laugh. She takes that as a challenge.

"Right, okay then. Maybe this needs some fuelling." She reached into her backpack and pulls out a half bottle of something unlabelled. "Picked this up from a farmer down in South Vale. It'll put hairs on your chest."

"I kinda hope not."

She offers the bottle to me first, and I'm strangely moved by her politeness. I return the kindness by not wiping the open neck before I take a slug.

It hits me like a scorching fist, slamming into my mouth and then opening up, spreading fingers of heat across my tongue and the roof of my mouth, down my throat into my stomach, then setting a match to the spreading fluid and bursting it aflame. My eyes water and my nose starts to run, and just for a moment I'm reminded of how it felt when I was connected to my old apparatus trying to make rain. Not hot or in pain, but slightly stunned and out of control. It feels wonderful.

As my eyes slowly close I see Cee's scar-speckled arms as she takes the bottle from my hand.

"Holy… fuck," I say, my voice soft and high.

"Right?" she says. "I shoulda warned you just to take a sip."

"I… did."

"Oh. Well." Cee takes a good glug of the fluid, swallows, and smacks her lips. Her own eyes water but she doesn't seem in pain, or even uncomfortable.

"So tell me," I say.

"You've been on the road a good few years." She glances sidelong and looks me up and down. It's a blatant appraisal, lingering. "You know how to look after yourself. That knife in your pocket isn't just for decoration. You've used it."

I lean back against the trailer side, looking away from her, not giving anything away. She takes another drink before continuing, offering me the bottle. I shake my head.

"You're mid-twenties, too old to be classed as a runaway now, but I think that's what you were. You ran away from home, still running. You're as lost as me. No one lost would think staying in a place like this is a good idea, so you're looking for something important."

"And you're not?" I ask.

She takes another long drink and offers me the bottle again. She's pretty insistent. It feels rude to turn it down, and I'm thinking about what comes next, later, after Cee has finished the bottle. I press it to my mouth and let the fluid just touch my lips.

"I'm just looking," she says. "Seeing things. Wondering about some, despairing at others. But you, you've got an end point in mind." She nods at my guitar case. "That's something to do with it. Empty, but you're looking for stuff to put in it, and you're not just some hobo filling her shopping cart with a bunch of random shit."

"Kind of you," I say. It's surprising how close she is, but I also wonder if I'm discovering stuff about myself just by listening. Maybe she's moving my story forward by telling it. Or maybe I just want to cling on to something. Either way, she's right about the case, and I hope she hasn't seen me looking at her watch.

"Something else," she says. I must be an enigma because I hear her taking another drink before continuing. Fortifying herself to the challenge, perhaps. "There." She reaches out and touches my inner forearm. Her fingers linger, fingertips moving across the knotted scar tissue beneath my track-marked skin. It's shockingly familiar and judgemental, and I feel a flush of anger.

"Nothing like me," she says, and my anger fades as quickly as it rose. "I shook it three years ago. An old guy called Maxwell helped me, hippy as fuck but he was the wisest man I ever met. Maybe the nicest. He helped more than anyone, ever, and he didn't even try to get in my pants. He helped me start over again, and ever since then it's been the best time of my life. But I'm still an addict at heart, and Maxwell said I always need to think that way. It keeps me sharp. Think you're cured and the disease will come back because it's insidious. But you…" She touches my scars again. "You're not addicted to anything so banal as drugs."

"Why do you say that?" I ask. She's still touching my arm, where the needles from my old apparatus once connected me to my fate.

"Just a feeling," she says. "Your story's more interesting." She takes another drink and this time doesn't offer me the bottle. Perhaps she knows I've been faking.

"Pretty good," I say. "I'm impressed. So what's your story?"

"Boring," Cee says. "I gotta piss." She stands, swaying a little before walking to the rear of the trailer and jumping down. It's almost dusk. While she's away I take a handful of candles from my pack and place them around the sleeping bag, ensuring they're a safe distance away before lighting them. The need to stay here with Cee for the night isn't only because of the draw I feel towards her bracelet, which remains strong. It's also her company I crave. It's been a while since I spent the night sleeping beside someone.

"Romantic," Cee says, climbing back into the trailer. She's rubbing her butt. "Fucking devil grass. You'd think I'd have learnt by now, huh?" She laughs, slumps down beside me, and picks up the bottle again. "So sing me a song."

"What, me?"

"Come on, Ash-not-Leigh. You've heard my voice. I need music, and I don't want to offend the fucking night."

"Okay. A song."

We sit in silence for a while. Maybe she assumes I'm thinking of a song to sing, but in reality I'm wondering how I can get her bracelet. I could ask for it, but if she says no then I'm stuck, and she'll become defensive. She already feels like a friend. It's a strange thought and something I don't want to ruin. The alternative is to steal it, and that's worse.

Her eyes are already drooping. She feels safe with me. I start singing an old pop song my father used to sing when I was a little girl, and it feels sort of nice. The candles barely flicker in the still air, and through the torn canvas roof of the trailer I can see the first stars starting to emerge.

As I sing, Cee leans her head against my shoulder. She still clasps the bottle in one hand, and she draws her legs up and rests her other hand on my knee. My song pauses, but only for a second. It's been a while since I've been close to anyone like this, and I like the intimacy. It's unforced and innocent.

Her hair smells good. Dusty, honest. I feel the heat of her hand through my jeans. She's breathing softly, and as I segue from one song into the next, her breathing lengthens and she starts twitching in her sleep.

I stop singing. I wonder if I can do this. I wish I could leave her a note, a way to apologise. Carefully, still humming, I reach down and unclip the bracelet from her wrist.

That's it, my inner voice says, and I imagine the interior workings of the bracelet affixed to the plinth.

"Sorry," I whisper, as quietly as I can. As I ease her hand from my leg and gently lower her down, I say, "Gotta pee," just in case a small part of her is still conscious and listening.

Bracelet clasped in my right hand, I swing my backpack onto my shoulder, pick up the guitar case, and creep to the rear of the trailer.

I glance back. Cee is still asleep on top of the sleeping bag, candles placed around her and bathing her in a gentle warm glow. I blow them out.

I'll see her again, I think. I drop down from the trailer and run. There are no sounds of pursuit. For the first time ever in the eye, I wish the tumult would fall around me and carry away this guilt.

I'll see her again.

"So you're a troubadour?" the driver of the car asks.

"Huh?"

He nods at the guitar case. "Troubadour. Minstrel. Travelling musician."

"Oh, no," I say. "There's no guitar inside."

"Right." He frowns but smiles as well. He seems friendly, and I've become a fair judge of character. "So where're you headed?"

"Anywhere down the road." It sounds so aimless that I worry it'll scare him off and he'll leave me in the dust. Either that, or he'll give me a condescending grow-up lecture. I've had both.

"Hop in. Some company'd be welcome about now." He looks over my shoulder, then around at the desolate surroundings—truck graveyard, dusty road, a few scattered buildings in the distance marked with gently turning wind turbines. I like him more because he doesn't ask me what I'm doing here.

His name's Mick, and he's a sustainable energy engineer, spending most of his days on the road servicing small community wind farms. He has a wife and two kids back home in Boston. He could make a living doing his job around New England and up and down the East Coast, but he's come to the Desert because he feels driven to help. He's paid, sure, but he also knows that he's providing a service. And the drought affects everyone, Desert-dweller or not.

"There are still good people," I say after he tells me his story. Maybe he's waiting for mine.

"Sure there are. Plenty. The world's got big again, 'specially with towns closing in and trying their best to look after themselves. And the famine's causin' that a lot more and a lot quicker over the past few years."

"I've seen it."

"But there's still good folks, and hope. Wanna know how I know that? I ain't religious at all, but I've seen things on my travels. Saw a field of red birds once, hundreds of thousands of them, and they took off as one and their undersides were as white as Heaven against the sky." He glances at me. "You've got to take hope from that, right?"

I nod and smile. It's nice that he can see the good in things.

Mick drives, the electric car purring along the road, and I can feel his questions backing up like water behind a dam. I feel something else, too, and it doesn't take me long to realise why. It's a large plastic head on his dashboard—an actor whose name I've never known—but it's not the head that sings to me, but the delicate metal spring that allows him to nod and bobble along to the car's movements.

"Can I buy him from you?"

"Casey? You can have him. Never did like that motherfucker." Mick laughs, and it's so free and unselfconscious that I can't help but join in.

I ask him to drop me in a small town called Merran Falls. It's a weird name for a strange place, with one street running perpendicular to the highway for a mile out into the Desert. Maybe when the Desert was grassland and the river wasn't dried up, Merran Falls was a name with meaning.

"You're sure?" Mick asks.

"Thanks for the ride, Mick." I smile and shut the door, and his car whispers away. I've enjoyed his company. He made my day lighter.

I grasp the nodding head of Casey the actor, rip it apart, and examine the spring against the dipping sun.

In Merran Falls I find an old radio set in a motel room, and it sings to me with a song very different from the one being broadcast. I pluck out the circuit board—I don't yet know if I'll use the whole board or just one of the components—and hide the dismantled radio under the bed when I leave.

From there I head out to the plains, where a small aircraft crashed a couple of years before. I heard about the accident in Merran Falls's solitary bar, and from that moment the site called to me. It's a hike from town, and I have to camp out overnight at the crash site, sleeping beneath half a wing that's propped against a rock. I wake in the night to find a snake curled beside me and sharing my warmth. I kill it and cook it for breakfast.

Once the sun rises red and angry on the dust-smeared horizon, I examine the remains of the light aircraft. It's been picked over, yet a lot of its mechanics remain, and I soon find what I seek. I draws me in, zeroing my attention, and I feel the shudder of distant thunder inside as I touch the dial's cracked face. I wonder if the lightning shows in my eyes.

I work the dial free with my knife, saving as much of the wiring and its connecting plugs as I can. Adding it to the growing contents of my guitar case, I sit back on my haunches for a while, the open case shaded in my shadow. If I look from the corner of my eye, I can almost make out how the apparatus will look. It's as if I am catching it unawares.

This feels like something I have been waiting to do forever. The nine years I've spent in the Desert, drifting and living on my own, quite possibly mad, has been a prelude to this time. I'm beginning to sense a true destiny forming in and around me.

Walking back across the parched dead farmland towards the faint echo Merran Falls has become, I feel the eye moving on, and the storms I keep inside rise to smother me once more.

When the eye settles over me again I am in the suburbs of a city, and my case is heavier with parts, and even though I estimate I have been taken by the tumult for only two days or so, I understand that I have been collecting components even in that state. I'm hungry but not thirsty, unkempt but not dirty, and the brief flashes of memory suggest that someone tried to look after me for a while.

I usually avoid the cities, but as I surface from the deluge and rise above the waves I take a moment to look around. I am sitting in a park surrounded on all sides by busy streets and tall buildings. The park is large, and I'm one of many passing time seated on a bench, wandering the paths, or lying down. Some appear to be asleep, and a little way from me beneath a sparse tree canopy there's a spread of tatty tents. Even in places where a good proportion of the population has moved on in search of better times, there is homelessness.

A passer-by pauses close to me, eyeing me up and down. It's a man, short and slight and dressed in a smart business suit, even in this heat. He's young and quite handsome, his face speckled with dark patches of old sunburn. He catches my eye and smiles, and I lift my hat a little and smile back. He seems to take that safe contact as a signal, and he closes the distance between us, places a large coffee on the bench beside me, then digs inside a paper bag he carries in his other hand. He takes out something wrapped in paper. I smell hot toast and butter, and it sets my stomach rumbling.

"Have a good day," he says, and his voice is quiet, almost shy. He's already walking away by the time I call out my thanks.

This small act of kindness makes me feel good, especially in a place displaying obvious signs of the catastrophe plaguing this nation. There are water standpipes in the street with people waiting in long lines to fill large containers. Many shops are closed and boarded up, and I see a couple of grocers with queues leading out the door. Past the far corner of the park I see three Soaker wagons parked in a side street, their loads of fresh water destined for those who can afford it. I wonder if they're part of the Soaker group I came across days or weeks before.

The park itself is marked by drought. Grass is dead. A large pond contains a mere puddle of muddy water, and a few scruffy ducks pad across its oily surface. Hardy trees persist here and there, but planting beds are home only to cacti and a few swathes of invasive devil grass. Even in the city, people are fighting against the painful truth of change. They don't even call it the climate crisis anymore, or global warming, or any other name that might once have been used to urge positive action. Now, this is the norm.

I take a sip of coffee and it's good and strong. I bite into the salty, buttery toast, and close my eyes as I chew and swallow. When I open them again there's a ragged, wild dog standing a dozen steps away. It's lost an ear in a fight, and its fur is patchy and knotted with dirt and dried blood. I wonder what name it once had, called by an owner as it chased a ball, muttered by a child as he or she cuddled the mutt late into the evening.

"Hey dog," I say. It pricks up its one good ear and whines. I throw it the remains of my toast. It snatches the food from the air, swallows without chewing, then wanders over and sniffs around my feet. It pays close attention to the guitar case beside me, then crawls beneath the bench and stretches out in the shade. Its doggy smell hits me. A wistful nostalgia thumps me with surprise, tears coming to my eyes, as I remember Teddy. My father always said a kid should grow up with a dog.

"Let's see what we've got then, eh, Teddy?" I say. The mutt pays no attention as I open the guitar case and take a look inside. After just a couple of minutes examining the contents, I come to a conclusion that is felt in every part of me—I am almost ready to build.

I close the case and look around the park. I'll need to get out of this city, back into the parched Desert, and find somewhere quiet, private and still. I've been collecting components even while far away from the eye, and perhaps it's an act of self-preservation. Maybe if I can't find a way to release the storms locked inside me, they will one day swallow me up, and the eye will pass me by forever.

JESSE

Nowadays, most people wished for rain. Sometimes Jesse did too, in the same abstract way that he wished for his old life back, or that he'd been born normal, or for world peace. But the coming storm was far from normal. He could feel it in his bones. His limbs ached, his shoulders were sore when he moved, and every time he walked uphill his left hip shouted at him to turn around and go the hell back down.

He paid no attention, because he had spent so much time and effort making this place his own, and it was too precious to lose. Yet he had always known that rain would be his downfall.

"What do you reckon, Rocky?" he asked. "Can't see the thunderheads yet, but look at the colour of that sky above the mountains. Pale and fucking angry." He leaned on the heavy timber fence surrounding his vegetable garden, and Rocky cocked her head at him, eyes wide and ears raised. That always reminded him of Ash. She'd loved their dog Teddy, and used to make clicking noises so he tilted his head because it made him look cute. Jesse had berated her for teasing him, telling her that Teddy did that because he was trying to understand. Maybe he'd been projecting himself onto the dog, because he had never really understood Ash. If he had, he wouldn't have killed her.

"Good girl," he whispered, and the dog cocked her head at him again. She whined softly, then trotted away searching for interesting smells.

Jesse stared to the north, his aches and pains settled deep. Karina had been confused that he'd named a female dog Rocky. He hadn't done it to piss her off. Or maybe he had. Fuck it, he didn't regret it, and Rocky didn't give a shit.

It was still only seven in the morning. Usually at this time of day he was cooking breakfast and brewing coffee so strong it required a new symbol on the periodic table. Sometimes, on a Friday, Jenny made the thirty-minute drive from the little town of Blueton to join him for breakfast, bringing groceries if he'd run out. Every now and then she made a joke and said, "I brought you your mail," throwing him nothing, which he always did his best to duck. But today wasn't Friday, and the only company he could expect was the storm forming over the mountains.

Groaning as pain bit his complaining hip, Jesse set to work battening down the hatches. He'd call Jenny later to check she'd done the same , though she lived in a second-floor apartment in town, and she didn't have as much to lose as him. She was almost seventy, had some money from a dead husband and a decent enough teacher's pension, and most of what she treasured was experience. If the storm washed away something she valued, she'd find worth in something else.

Jesse stopped, frozen to the spot. *It's me*, he thought. *Me and my damn life up here, that's what she's most likely to lose.* He laughed out loud at the realisation. Rocky glanced back at him from where she was sniffing around a tree. She was used to him talking to himself. The times when she became twitchy and whiny were those long periods when he sat in silence, staring into space.

That was pretty often.

"Fetch me some tarpaulin from the barn, Rocky?" he called. She made a noise back at him which he translated as, *Get it yourself.* He had to do everything around here.

Somewhere in the distance he heard a low, long rumble of thunder, so quiet that it was almost sub-audible. His skin prickled and a hot knot dropped in his stomach. It was a sound that played background to his nightmares.

Jesse felt protective of the home he'd made. The nearest paved road was three miles east, and the dirt track leading to his place was negotiable only in his rattling four-wheel drive. He'd sought such isolation, but that didn't mean he felt cut off from the world, nor did it lessen the comfort and beauty he'd been eager to create here. Jenny had once called it his little oasis, and he remained proud of her assessment.

There had been three buildings already here when he'd bought the plot for a song—a log cabin, a timber garage, and a sizeable storage barn, all of them tired and run-down. It had once been a hunting cabin, then for a few years it was rented out as a vacation retreat for more adventurous travellers, before falling empty and into disrepair fifteen years before. In just a few short years left untended, extremes of weather had subjected the place Jesse had named Hillside to various assaults of blazing sun, occasional deluges of heavy rain, and even one freak winter when four feet of snow had buried the mountains and hills all around for weeks. Abandonment and the elements had done their work, wearing down Hillside year on year, fading and fracturing the wooden walls and shingle roof, cracking the glass windows, rusting metal hinges, and washing away parts of the cabin's foundations in flash-floods that troubled the region more and more. When Jesse came to buy the place with the few bucks he had left, it was in a poor state of repair, not quite condemned to demolition but slumping to the ground, close to defeat like an old man bearing a heavy weight.

It had been exactly what Jesse sought, a home out of the way and hidden in the hills, and a large refurbishment project to keep him occupied. Making money and exchanging favours doing small building jobs in and around Blueton, he had slowly made the cabin safe, repaired it where necessary, and done what he could to proof it against whatever the increasingly unpredictable climate threw at it. He'd shored up the barn and made it as weatherproof as possible, and he now used it for storage and as a garage for his old truck. The old timber garage had undergone the most extensive transformation. He'd removed much of the outer walling and roof structure and replaced it with heavy double-glazed units incorporating blackout blinds. He'd installed a third-hand cooling plant as well as two large oil heaters, dug an irrigation and watering system, and just outside he'd excavated a compost pit. He had created a growing space for seedlings and fruit in which he could maintain almost complete environmental control. In a world where humankind had comprehensively fucked the climate, in this small space Jesse could still master the seasons.

This place was his small effort to adapt, survive, and face the future prepared and unafraid. And all of this work needed protecting. The looming storm might bring heavy rain and dangerous floods. Sometimes freak hailstorms could swoop down from the mountaintops and drop six inches of hail the size of golf balls in a matter of minutes.

He set to work locking down Hillside, and this was what he loved—working with his hands, outside, with Rocky by his side—because on the best days it took him away for hours. The greenhouse was the most important part of his oasis. He fitted preformed timber shutters to protect the glass walls, hanging them on hooks already screwed into heavy wall struts and locking them closed with chains and padlocks. He used a small stepladder to climb onto the shallow pitched roof and did the same there, weighing down the locked shutters with bricks to give added heft to the protection. He slung rolls of heavy tarpaulin across the wired fence surrounding the vegetable plot, weighing the ends down with more bricks then screwing long planks across the top, spanning the few metres between fence posts on either side. That would in theory keep the wind and rain out of his vegetable garden, but floods were a different matter. His solution had been not only to attempt to redirect any water that flooded down the hillsides, but to retain and store it.

The two large tanks had taken him weeks to dig out, even with the use of the small, tracked excavator he'd borrowed from a builder in town. He'd cast concrete raft footings, then built timber formwork to hold back the dried soil, against which he'd constructed brick-thick walls and an internal coating of thick waterproofing. Finally, another brick wall had completed the buried structures. Topped with a roof of heavy timber planks, the buried reservoirs could hold almost four thousand gallons of water each. It was unclean and untreated, but he had other means to do that when he used it for drinking or cooking.

Using that same excavator, he'd dug a series of drainage trenches all around Hillside, and a good way up the slopes behind. There was no way to stop a truly catastrophic flood, but in most cases he hoped his drainage system should steer enough down-flow around the edges of the property—and some of it into the storage tanks—to avoid catastrophic damage.

With the storm drawing nearer, he inspected the closest drainage channels, pulling out branches that had fallen in, flattening where walls had collapsed, opening them up to increase the flow as much as possible. They were barely half a metre deep and wide, and already nature had started to refill and reclaim its own. He berated himself for not inspecting them more frequently, but there was no time for regrets. They'd handled the several big storms that had hit since he'd been at Hillside; they would handle this one, too.

"You think we'll be okay, Rocky?" he asked. The dog tilted her head and whined. "Yeah, I know what you think. Feed me, play with me, throw me a stick." She froze at that word. "Stick? Stick?" Jesse snatched up a stick and lobbed it long and hard, then watched the dog chase it. He liked having the time to play with her. In his late fifties his life had become less cluttered, and he liked that as well. He made what money he needed odd-jobbing around town and working on the local farms come harvest, when the farmers worked twice as hard to save what crops they could. Some years were better than others, but for Jesse it worked. The shadow of his daughter, dead by his hand, loomed over everything and dulled his world, but he did what he could to move from day to day, year to year. It wasn't moving on. It wasn't living. It was merely existing as time went by.

Wind was starting to gust, whipping up dust. The air had cooled and tasted metallic. He called the dog indoors and closed the door, slumped on the sofa, and reached for the bourbon bottle he'd placed on a side table ready that morning. He'd known what was to come. This was his other way of passing time, and he made no excuses.

It was barely 1 p.m. when he took his first drink, but the clouds rolling down from the mountains and blotting out the sun made it feel like dusk.

———

Jesse knew that he had to stay awake and alert. He should make sure the shutters remained closed, the fire in the wood burner low but alight, and now and then he could peek out to make sure the rest of Hillside was safe. He could see several of the drainage trenches from the back and side of the cabin, and he wanted to check they weren't overflowing. If they did, there wasn't much he could do. But at least he'd know.

By three o'clock the wind was up and he heard the first frantic footsteps of rain across the roof. He rested his head on the back of the sofa with the fifth bourbon in his hand.

I need to stay awake. He probably spoke out loud, because Rocky shifted on the sofa beside him, whining softly and thumping her tail against the cracked leather.

A heavy gust of wind struck the cabin. The timbers groaned and creaked. It sounded like the impacts of something solid, as if the breeze that rolled down the mountainside had picked up a wave of debris along the way.

Jesse closed his eyes in a gentle blink, and when he opened them again the light had changed. Some of the candles he kept burning on the low table in the centre of the room still burned, but three of them were out.

Rocky snored and twitched beside him, chasing dreams.

His gaze rested on a few dozen books piled on the shelved alcove in one corner of the room. He'd read them all twice. He took another glug of bourbon. Also tucked away on the top shelf was the old wooden case containing his apparatus. He hadn't taken any notice of it in a long while, but he saw it now, the thin edge of the case just catching a flicker of candlelight. He recalled the intricate inlaid tree design on the lid and felt a peculiar sense of shock that he hadn't laid eyes on it since he'd first shoved the case up there. It was a shame to hide such beauty away.

I should bring it down and open it again. It was an idea that occasionally haunted his drunken moments. He never pursued it to its end.

Lightning flashed outside, outlining the edges of windows and the door. A few seconds later a roll of thunder came in. It sounded like boulder gods waking and grinding high up on the mountainside.

The trenches will catch them if they roll down here.

Rocky slept on beside him.

He blinked again, and this time when he opened his eyes only one candle still burned, and Rocky stood barking at the door.

The storm thudded and thundered around the house. Lightning burned bright and continuous around the shutters and the closed door. Rocky barked again and Jesse stood from the sofa, wiping his eyes and gathering himself, seeing away the dregs of troubled dreams. Eight months before, Rocky had warned him of a grizzly approaching while Jesse was sitting in a shaded yard chair, reading. He trusted his dog.

The lightning never ended and he realised it was not lightning at all. It was a set of headlights glaring at the cabin.

Someone had come to him through the storm.

KARINA

It's almost like he knows I'm coming, Karina thought. Ever since she'd started up into the hills from Blueton the rain had been falling, the skies darkening, and the sense that she was drawing nearer to Jesse than she had been in over nine years closed in on her like darkness striving to smother a candle. The symbolism of the storm smashing down around her Jeep was so obvious that she chuckled as she drove. Or maybe that was nerves.

The mountains loomed like ragged teeth each time the lightning thrashed. The trees beside the road performed a chaotic dance in time with the wind. Several gusts rocked the Jeep as she followed the rough road sloping up into the foothills, and sheets of rain fought against the headlights, dulling the light and allowing the dark to loom closer. All the way from Blueton, knowing that Jesse was at the end of this journey gave the storm a personality. Angry. Dark. Dangerous.

As she followed the GPS and left the main road for a rutted, flooded lane, she thought, *He can't know I'm coming*. She'd had to ask around in Blueton to find out exactly where Jesse lived, but the reaction from most people had only reinforced her conviction that he had shut himself off from the world.

She wasn't sure whether that made her intentions here easier or even more difficult.

The Jeep jolted across a pothole, tugging the seat belt across her chest and winding her. The track rose suddenly, and in the poor light and pouring rain it gave the impression of an almost vertical wall. The four-wheel drive hauled the vehicle up the slope, dashboard lights illuminating and dimming again in warning, as if the Jeep itself were as worried as her.

Karina wasn't accustomed to this. The places she inhabited now, the landscapes she had travelled through, were dry and arid and dead, cracked ground and ghost-trees witness to the extremes of climate that had devastated swathes of the country over the past couple of decades. They called it the Desert, but that was an ignorant catch-all name for a shattering loss. Some people had left. Others remained, hostages to finance or circumstance and given no chance to make a home elsewhere. Many had died. Society regressed. Place names changed, communities shrank, rules were made and broken. Wider awareness closed in, because sourcing the next meal or drink was all that mattered. Survival pared existence down to its basics. And everything was cooked by the sun, starved by famine. Humanity dehydrated, and wider histories and personal tales turned to sand.

Rain like this was what many people in the Desert might pray, wish and dance for, in the hope that it would bring some reprieve and a return to kinder times.

The trail wound and twisted for what seemed like miles, and Karina began to worry that the GPS had sent her along the wrong track. She was used to sleeping wherever her journey ended for the day—she'd slept in hotels and barns, abandoned houses and broken-down cars, in underpasses and culverts, and sometimes out beneath the stars. She had her backpack in the Jeep, and it contained everything she needed for extended periods on the road. Clothes. Sleeping bag. Food. Money. Her gun.

But the last thing she wanted today was to sleep in this car, in this storm. Moving was fine, because her muttered curses were accompanied by the soft whisper of the electric motor, the breath of the car's heater and demister, and the radio station that dropped in and out of reception. If she got lost and the storm grew worse, she'd have to park and camp down. Then it would be the outside sounds that would accompany her, not those inside.

Such storms had become her nightmare years ago.

A few more minutes passed, and then, as the Jeep mounted a rise and its headlights swept down and ahead, she saw the bulky outline of a building. Steering left to splash the area with light, she realised just how dark it had become since she'd left Blueton. She was not used to seeing a night sky without stars, and the torrent caught in headlights made it seem that a million stars were falling.

"Jesse," she said, and her heart skipped a beat. She hadn't seen him for so long. That had been down to her, and coming here to see him now was also her choice. That should give her a sense of control, and if he didn't know she was coming, all the better.

She drove towards the small scatter of buildings and came to a stop with the headlamps bathing the log cabin. She turned the engine off but left the lights on. She sat there. All this way, all this time, and she didn't have a clue what the fuck came next.

She reached into the backpack on the passenger seat, grabbed the gun, and slipped it into her jacket pocket. It felt ridiculous, but also a comfort. During her years on the road it had become her friend.

The cabin door opened, just wide enough for her to see a faint light from inside, and the silhouette of the man she had once loved. She hated him now, probably.

For another few seconds she remained in the Jeep, keeping herself a mystery, holding on to control. Then she opened the door and jumped out into the rain. She kept her hood down so he could see who she was.

"Karina!" His voice was almost lost to the storm.

Karina hadn't planned this at all, but she gave it to him all at once.

"Hello, Jesse. Ash is still alive. And she's trying to make rain."

JESSE

Jesse had often imagined what it might be like seeing Karina again after so long apart. Sometimes he saw her smiling and raising both arms in greeting, ready to gather him into an embrace. Other times he wondered what would happen if he glimpsed her across the street or behind the window of a cafe, and he caught her eye, and she turned away as if she no longer knew him. Once, sleeping halfway into another bottle of cheap bourbon, he'd dreamed of coming across her close to Hillside, in the woods where a bear prowled and wolves sometimes stalked, and her raising a gun and shooting at him. He woke before the bullet struck. He'd spent that day mourning the past more than usual, and he'd made several calls and surfed the net trying to track her down. All to no avail. The infrequent phone contact they'd had over the past nine years had always been on her terms, not his, and had never been fulfilling. The few times she'd phoned, he'd wondered if she was drunk.

She held no gun now. There was no arm lifted ready to hug him close. But there was news about Ash that tilted his world on its axis.

Ash is alive?

"How did you find me?" he asked.

"Oh, nice," Karina said. "Great to see you, Karina? Would you like a steaming hot coffee, Karina?"

"I'm sorry. Coffee." He headed to the kitchenette, glancing back as she dropped her backpack, shook off her coat, ran her fingers through soaked hair, and wiped water from her face. "She's really—?"

"Coffee. Then we talk."

He took a deep breath, gripping the edge of the work surface. "You look well."

She didn't even look at him. "You don't."

"Thanks. Make yourself at home."

The cabin was split into the open plan living and kitchen area, and his bedroom and bathroom. It was far from grand, but he'd made it home and he was proud of it.

Brewing coffee on the wood burner, he watched as Karina looked around, assessing his life. He remembered that look, even though he hadn't seen it in almost a decade, and prepared himself for whatever was to come.

And all the while his heart thudded and he processed the shock of what she'd said. *Ash is still alive. And she's trying to make rain.* He'd lived with the deep guilt at causing his daughter's death, because what had happened to her, how he'd seen her react after injecting her, had convinced him that she had run away and died. Her friend Jonny had told them both that someone had seen her falling into the river. He'd carried on looking along the course of the river, even after Karina left him and disappeared on her own search, which he had always considered hopeless. But from that first moment he'd been filled with the conviction that Ash was dead, and even though her body had never been found, he had effectively killed her.

It was such guilt for a father to live with, and on a few occasions he'd wondered whether he should continue living. But Rocky and

Hillside nursed him through a dull form of life, and drinking blunted the sharp edges of some realities.

"So this is what you ran away to," Karina said.

"Soon after you left," Jesse said. "I like it. I've made it home."

"I guess this is Rocky." The dog pricked up her ears and Karina gave her a scratch. "You got too comfortable."

"You really believe that?"

Karina looked around the cabin but did not reply.

"You still got the farm?" Jesse asked. Their old home had not come up in their brief, awkward phone conversations.

"Never went back. I sold it years ago."

He found a second mug for her coffee.

"What, you want your share of the money?" she asked.

"I'm doing fine here. Got no needs I can't meet for myself."

"Good. 'Cos there *is* no share. What's left of the money I'm still using to look for her."

"What about our things? Photos. All that."

"I had Jonny put our personal stuff in storage, but I've never gone back for it."

"So where do you live now?"

"Here," Karina said, and she paused long enough for him to pause also, hand halfway to the coffee pot. "There. All over, really. I've been on the road, on and off, for nine years."

"I knew you were travelling," he said. "You never told me much, those few times you rang. But I speak to your dad every Christmas. It's the one time of year he answers when I call."

"I know, I'm sometimes there. He always did like Christmas. He misses spending it with his granddaughter."

"But I never thought you were baseless." He poured coffee, and its warm aroma filled the cabin. He took in a deep breath, letting it flow through him and fend off the fuzziness of his impending hangover. He'd probably measure way over the legal limit if he was tested, but seeing Karina on his doorstep, he'd never felt so sober.

"Looking for my girl is my base, and I've found her at last. She's still alive." Her voice broke a little on that last word, and Jesse wasn't sure whether the moisture on her face was left over from the rain, or new. "I never gave up, even though... you have no idea how difficult it is trying to find someone in the Desert when they don't want to be found. But I always knew she was still out there."

"You hoped," he said. "Everything pointed to her being—"

"Dead," she said. "Everything pointed to you having killed her." That bit in, sharp and cold. It always did.

"We both searched the riverbanks for her."

"You stopped. I've been searching those banks ever since."

Jesse closed his eyes and breathed deeply. Pressure built in his throat. When he opened his eyes again his wife was looking right at him, and he saw no hate. He wasn't sure what he saw.

"None of that matters, Jesse. She's still alive, and she's trying to make rain again. I heard about it on the net, a sighting. Just a few whispers on more obscure sites, rumours passed from mouth to mouth."

"Where is she?"

"Where do you think? The Desert." It was a catch-all name people used to refer to the vast swathes of the Great Plains scorched dry and dead by drought, the places that used to be farms and fields for as far as the eye could see, woodlands and forests, rivers and green valleys. Many people didn't like the name because it implied acceptance and a loss of hope.

"How successful?" he asked. It wasn't his real question. He felt sick with the pressure of what he really wanted to ask. He'd come to a terrible acceptance with the idea that Ash and her ability was dead at his hand, but he'd always been afraid that if he heard news to the contrary, his greatest fears would rise again. His fear of her rainmaking, and what she might bring down.

"Not at all, I don't think. Just a mad young woman, but there are pictures. It's… I'm pretty sure it's her."

Jesse handed her the coffee and sat down on his sofa. Karina sat on a dining chair as far from him as she could.

"You hungry?" he asked.

"I ate in town, trying to find out where you lived."

"Jenny?"

"Yeah, nice woman."

"She's just a friend."

"Do you think I give a fuck if she's more than that?" Karina said. "Me being here is nothing to do with you and me, Jesse. Only Ash."

"So you've been looking for her all this time, and now you think you've found her, you decide to find me too."

"I knew roughly where you were. You told Dad. I've come because I think I'll need your help."

"She probably hates me."

"Yeah, but the only reason I've found her is that she's trying that thing again. *Your* thing."

Jesse rubbed his jaw, stroking the artificial bone through the stubble and skin.

"Something I never told you," he said. "I didn't want you to think I was trying to justify what I did. She was the most powerful Rainmaker. Much more than me, my mom, and her father and great-uncle before her. Even young, with her first apparatus, the energy in her was… staggering. I think that made it even harder for her to control and master, and when she started to go wrong—"

"That was all you."

"No! It wasn't me. I'm not sure what started it, though I have ideas. For a while I thought I was guiding her the right way, but when she started bringing down those things, so early and at such a young age, and what happened to Teddy… it made me terrified of what else might come. What if it got much, much worse than anything I was ever capable of? What if she did that in a city?"

"You could have taught her to control it."

"I tried! I told you at the time, I've tried to tell you *so many* times. None of it was about me. She would have gathered the parts and built her own apparatus without me laying a hand on it, and done her own rainmaking. After what happened to me, I was doing my best to make sure she dealt with it safely."

"She's your flesh and blood."

"Her talent isn't. That's all her own."

"Talent?" Karina said. She didn't quite spit it.

"Want of a better word," Jesse said. "It was the fear of what she might end up doing. I killed three people when I brought down a few dozen scorpions."

"Drug dealers."

"Imagine if I'd left her," he said. "Imagine if she'd grown, built more apparatus, lost control and got worse and worse."

"You could have given her a chance."

"I did."

Karina blinked at him over her coffee.

"She was far more dangerous than me, even at that young age. What happened to me was worse than anything my mother brought down, and her father before her. It's a pattern, a degeneration that seems to follow what's happened here to the climate. The effect we've had on the world. I believe it was reflected in my place, The

Shore. Maybe Ash's Skunksville is even more affected. And *no one* can control that."

She blew on her coffee and took a sip.

Jesse went quiet, because vocalising these fears of long ago had seeded new ones. A chill went through him, an infusion of ice injected into his heart. It reminded him of being plugged into his own device—the addictive rush, and then the fear. His vision swam and pulsed, and he felt his looming hangover surfacing again.

"But you stopped all that," Karina said. "That stuff you gave her, you said it'd stop it once and for all."

"I thought so, too," he said. "I'd researched it as best I could, took advice, bought the drug online. It looks like it worked, for a while at least. She's been missing for nine years with no sign of rainmaking. But nothing about that day went as I'd thought. What if, in the long run, I've made her worse?"

Karina glanced around the room, her eyes resting on the highest shelf of the bookcase. She looked back down at Jesse, cup halfway to her mouth.

"I haven't touched it since…"

"Still kept it, though."

Jesse took a drink of steaming coffee without replying and they sat in silence for a while.

"Storm's getting bad," Karina said after a minute of awkward silence.

"We've got to find her, and help her, or stop her trying again."

"That's why I came to you."

"Now."

"In this?" She nodded at the ceiling. The cabin creaked and groaned with each howl of wind, and the windows and door surround flashed with a fusillade of lightning. Thunder rolled directly overhead. Even Rocky whined, and Rocky was a dog of the mountains, familiar with blazing days, sudden storms, and flash floods.

"We'll dodge the floods," he said, standing and draining his coffee. He paused, looked at Karina's wide-eyed expression. "You're not used to this."

"Of course not."

"We'll be safe. Let's get ready. We'll take my Land Rover. It's old but looked after."

"Can you drive?" She nodded at the half-empty bourbon bottle.

"I'll be fine." Jesse turned away before she could pass more comment on the liquor. He started moving around, thinking about what he should take, what must be done to lock up the cabin for a while. He could contact Jenny and ask her to tend the place, water his crops after the storm had passed, make sure Hillside was secure. And he'd take Rocky with him.

Karina used the bathroom while he gathered his stuff, and as he heard the toilet flush his eyes rested on his apparatus. It was the one thing that linked him to everything happening today—Karina arriving with the storm, Ash, and the storm itself. He took down the case and placed it on the low coffee table. The inlaid tree design, though faded and with missing parts, was as striking as ever. He passed his hand across the surface, sweeping a clear path through the collected dust of years lost to grief, guilt, and the bottle.

He noticed Karina standing in the bedroom doorway, looking at the case. Despite everything that had happened and the distance that had grown between them, he loved her. He always had, always would, and his love was a solid centre to his world, anchoring him in the storm that had buffeted and bashed him his whole life.

"Hey," he said.

"Hey," she said, and he could have sworn he saw the ghost of a smile.

"I didn't kill our little girl."

"So let's go find her."

KARINA

While Jesse prepared to leave the cabin, Karina placed both of their backpacks beside the door, ready to be loaded into the Land Rover. She worried about leaving her rented Jeep behind but saw the sense in it. The storm was growing louder and more violent by the minute, and Jesse was used to moving in these conditions. Though even he appeared slightly unnerved by the ferocity of the wind and rain.

"Rocky's lead is hanging with the coats," he said. At the sound of her name Rocky's ears pricked up, and she trotted across and prodded Karina's hand with her nose.

"You're sure?" Karina asked.

"Sure." The weight of the world was hammering down on the cabin, but though it was late afternoon he still wanted to venture out in this and start their journey. She was glad of his sense of urgency, but it couldn't cancel out the years he'd spent here, doing nothing. She watched as he closed off the air to the wood burner, blew out candles, shut the bathroom door, and generally tended his home, preparing to leave it for however long he might be away. He cared about this place, and it must be nice having somewhere like this to return to. She'd been on the road for so long and had met so many wanderers, some like her with a purpose driving them, most simply adrift. The happiest people she met were always those who had roots, however far from those roots they might have travelled. A base or home gave the world a centre. She'd meant it when she'd told Jesse that she was not baseless, but in selling their farm she had made herself homeless.

She envied Jesse this place, but it was also strange seeing him at home somewhere she did not know.

Rocky nuzzled her hand again and looked up at the coat rack beside the door. She rummaged beneath a couple of jackets and found her leash.

"She need this on?" she asked.

"Just roll it up and put it with my stuff. There's a bag of dog food in the cabinet under the sink." Jesse was in his bedroom, messing with an open box on the wall that might have contained fuses and a distribution board for the cabin's limited electricity.

"Right," she muttered. "I'll get your dog's food then." As Rocky followed her into the kitchen, a burst of wind struck the cabin, rattling shutters, creaking timbers. Karina froze by the small table.

"Woah," Jesse said from the bedroom doorway. "That was a big one."

"You're sure we should be travelling in this? You're used to this, right?"

"Haven't seen a storm like this in three, maybe four years," he said. He gave a lopsided, nervous smile. "But we'll be fine. This might be in for a couple of days. We can't wait that long."

Karina nodded her agreement. The trail to Ash was cool when she'd found it and was growing colder, and just by diverting here to find Jesse she'd wasted more time. Maybe coming here hadn't been one of her best ideas after all. She should have gone after Ash on her own, because alone was how she'd been searching for the past nine years.

Karina picked up Rocky's food and followed Jesse to the front door. They had never legally divorced, but she had stopped thinking of Jesse as her husband years before. He was the father of her child, but there was so much more to being a partner than that. She didn't know him anymore. He looked different. He'd lost weight, his hair was greying rather than brown. His eyes were haunted by the past and the memories conjured by his last bottle of liquor. He hid the drinking well, but there were signs he could not disguise—the eyes, the lethargy, the weary way he bore his own weight. His short beard might have been a sign of being comfortable in himself, but she thought it more likely an attempt to be someone else. Even Jesse didn't like who he'd been back then. He smelled different, too. He smelled of the wild, the woods, and the food he grew and ate out here had changed his physique to slim and gnarly. He even sounded different, his voice lower and gruffer, as if time weighed heavy.

But she had changed more. If he looked different to her, she must have been like a stranger to him.

At the front door he paused, looked down at his bag and kit ready to load into the car, and he turned back to the sofa and coffee table.

"I didn't want to touch that," Karina said.

"That's okay." He picked up his apparatus and held it beneath his left arm.

"Why do you even need it?"

He shrugged. The box moved beneath his arm as if containing something alive. "It connects me," he said. "To Ash, to this. To everything."

Karina nodded and opened the door, and the storm came inside. It snatched the door from her hand and slammed it back against the wall. The gale blasted rain against her face, stinging darts against her skin and eyes. She squinted and covered her face. The noise, the sensation, and the smell of the storm were overpowering, and she took a few deep breaths, reversing back into the cabin. She bumped into Jesse. He squeezed her shoulder, and she realised it was the first physical contact there'd been between them since she'd arrived.

"It's okay!" he said. "Straight over to the barn, my Land Rover's inside. Come on, Rocky!"

Rocky barked once and edged outside ahead of them, looking left and right as if expecting something to come at them out of the storm. Karina followed the dog, then she heard the cabin door slam closed behind her. Jesse locked the door and pocketed the keys, and Karina thought, *This is harder for him than it is for me.* He pointed past her at the barn.

The feel of cold fresh water on her skin was amazing. The breath of the storm, its violence and fury, started to excite rather than frighten her. *If only I could take this to the Desert.* She'd been in countless places over the years that would have welcomed such a downpour. Even a haze of rain became the talking point in some places for weeks. But this…

…this was, she realised, as much a part of things now as the Desert. This was no normal storm. One tree was already down, leaning drunkenly in the woods to the east of Jesse's home, rocking back and forth as if eager to continue its final journey to the ground. Its creaking was audible even above the rain. Streams flowed across the gravelled yard, carving new routes where too much surface water coursed down from the hillsides above. A tarpaulin had come loose, snapping in the wind like a series of gunshots.

"It'll be fine," Karina shouted.

"Doubt it," Jesse said. "But we can't fight the weather, even if we made it."

By the time she reached the barn, Karina was soaked. They entered through the large open front door.

"Isn't that what you Rainmakers have always done?" Maybe that was harsh. She didn't care. Years in the Desert had knocked all the niceties out of her.

"Let's get the stuff in the car," he said. "Longer we leave it, the harder it'll be to get to Blueton."

"Harder?"

"Trees down, mudslides, new streams. Subsoil's weakened and lots of the topsoil's already been washed away. The wild forests here have changed, become more dangerous."

"You really don't think we should wait it out?"

"How long ago was this sighting of Ash?"

"I saw it two days ago, and it was posted a few days before that."

"Then no," Jesse said. "No time. You got more stuff to get from your car?"

Karina touched her backpack's strap, saying nothing.

"Travelling light," Jesse said. Rocky jumped into the Land Rover's rear seat, and he shut the door behind her. "I know these woods. We'll be fine." More lightning flashed and thunder rolled overhead, and Karina thought it might have been the wild objecting to Jesse's misplaced confidence.

They climbed into the vehicle, and for a few seconds there was relative peace and silence as Jesse strapped himself in and readied to drive out. Neither of them spoke. As he drove past Karina's rental, he threw another concerned look back at his home.

Karina couldn't feel sorry for him. Her home, and his *real* home, was wherever Ash was now, and they were on their way.

The windshield wipers flicked back and forth at top speed, sweeping aside torrents of rain and revealing blurred snapshots of the surroundings. Headlights cut shimmering patterns through the downpour. It was late afternoon, but the storm gave the impression of twilight. Shapes danced and jigged in the beams as wind surged through it, making waves in the water before it even hit the ground. The gale struck the Land Rover, and Karina felt the impact and saw Jesse gripping the wheel as he aimed the vehicle between the first of the trees.

The track down to the surfaced road was so different from when she'd driven up just an hour previously that Karina wondered if Jesse had taken a different route. Water flowed across it in many places, carrying leaves, twigs and branches, filthy brown sludge moving like thick soup. The vehicle jerked left and right as it bounced over water-filled potholes. Jesse veered back and forth across the track, concentrating, avoiding the rough areas he knew about and finding new ones.

"You sure this thing'll hold together?" she asked. The vehicle was old, the dashboard cracked in places where the leather had dried out, seats creaking.

"I look after it well," he said. "So what have you heard about Ash?"

"It's like I told you. Online whispers. Rumours on a few obscure websites. There's one about you."

He snorted.

"There's so much bullshit to trawl through online. Conspiracy theories, all that sort of crap, you know?"

Jesse didn't answer. He *didn't* know, she realised. He'd cut himself off from the world and everything he had done and been, existing without the internet. His phone was basic, not smart, almost a museum piece. Most of the time when he needed something he drove down into town, or sometimes he hiked. He liked to fill his days, his friend Jenny had said. From Hillside to town and back again was almost eighteen miles of tough terrain, enough of a challenge even in a car.

"So what did the whispers say?"

"It was a photo. A young woman in a Desert town trying to plug some old device into her arms. Reports said she was ranting about bringing down rain. And it was Ash. Some of those dark sites picked it up and ran with it, and that's how I got to see it."

"It's been so long, how would anyone even remember?" Jesse asked.

"The internet is really fucking deep," Karina said.

"What do you mean?"

"There are websites dedicated to the Rainmakers. I wasn't joking when I said there was one about you. Old photos, stories, myths. You, your mom, her father, her great-uncle. Other sites just talk about rainmaking in general. Military, scientific, all the stuff you never wanted to be compared to."

"Because there is no comparison," Jesse said. "We don't seed clouds. We don't spray chemicals."

"But you do kill people."

He didn't answer that, and Karina felt almost sorry for saying it. Almost.

"So where was this photo taken?"

"Place called Collier, in Utah."

Jesse tapped at the GPS, keying in a few letters, and eyed it as it calculated.

"We're twenty hours away," he said.

"She won't be there anymore, it was six days ago at least."

"So you've got other reports? Other sightings?"

She shook her head.

"Then it's where we start." Jesse grunted. "Tree."

Through the rain-washed windshield, Karina saw the tree that had fallen across the road. It was thin and dead, but still too high to drive over.

Jesse skidded to a halt. "You taking care of yourself?"

"Huh?"

"You're strong. You always were."

"Hardly."

"Come on. I've got a chainsaw in the back, much quicker if I cut and you shift."

Jesse jumped from the car, and Karina pulled up her hood and followed.

JESSE

Jesse enjoyed the feel of the chainsaw buzzing in his hand, the way it sliced through the dead tree with ease, and the roar it made, smothering out all the other sounds. He welcomed the hammering rain and the wind screaming through the trees, shaking the canopy in a random dance. He loved this place, loved the outdoors, and for a minute or two while he worked on the tree, he might have been alone. But one thought kept intruding, echoed in the buzzing of the saw and the vibrations travelling up his arms.

Ash is still alive.

His girl was still alive, and he hadn't killed her after all. It should have come as a staggering relief, but he needed to see her with his own eyes to fully believe it. The decade-old guilt of what he'd done was still buried deep in his soul.

He wasn't sure he could trust everything Karina said. He glanced at her as she hauled away cut portions of the tumbled tree. She was thinner than he remembered, worn by time and grief, and marked by the years she had left on the road, but still Karina. Yet there was something deeper that troubled him, and he couldn't quite put his finger on it. Their estrangement had always hurt, though they had both made their own decisions—him to accept Ash's death at his hand; her to chase what he thought of as a ghost. Though her fury at him was still evident, there was something to her now that he no longer recognised. It had been nine years since they had been together, and perceiving this change in his wife—this unknown strangeness—was unsettling. Perhaps it was the wildness instilled by her years on the road, a toughness born of having to look after herself and survive while travelling through unknown, sometimes dangerous places. She must have so many stories to tell, and he hoped she might impart at least some of them during their long road trip to Utah. But perhaps she needed to remain something of a stranger to him. She hadn't returned to get to know him again, she'd come back to ask for his help in finding Ash. Her tales of life on the road might well remain her own.

"That'll do," he said. He turned off the chainsaw as Karina hauled the last chunk of chopped tree aside. The track was waterlogged. Torrential rains flowed across ground hardened by weeks of intense heat and sunlight, picking up surface dust and turning it into an inches-deep soup. He'd driven up and down here countless times, but usually when a storm like this hit he'd be in his cabin with the hatches shut, the fire lit, and a bottle of bourbon alight with the flickering flame.

Back in the Land Rover, Rocky welcomed him by licking water from his hair and ear.

"Okay, girl, lie down," Jesse said. "It's going to get bumpy." He started the car and drove past the remains of the fallen tree.

"So much rain," Karina said, and he knew what she was really saying. *So much water.*

"This isn't normal," he said. "Climate here's complex. Hills and mountains to the north, plains further south, but the drought has hit us too. Thirty per cent of the trees are dead or dying, so they say. I reckon it's more. And that's just in the forests that haven't been cut down by illegal loggers since the preservation laws were passed fifteen years ago. The one we just had to chop up to get past might not be the last, and any local knows when there's winds like this, you stay out of the forest."

"And we're driving right through it," Karina said.

"Like I said, storm might be in for days. And I've cleared quite a few of the dead trees along the track over the years. Chop them and use them for firewood. Curing timber to burn's not such a problem now so much of it is dead."

"Your compound looked pretty prepped for weather like this."

"Compound?" Jesse asked, raising an eyebrow. "You make it sound like I'm some kind of survivalist nut."

"Aren't you?"

He didn't answer that. For every sentence spoken that sounded like her old self, there was one where he heard the taint of hate in her words. Maybe even derision, which was worse.

"You've cut yourself off up here. No net, self-powered electric. Assume you've got food growing under those tarps."

"It's not a compound. It's my home. I don't have much, don't need much."

"Right. Well, it still looked ready for the storm."

"Because I've made it that way. Got to protect what you…" He trailed off, felt Karina glaring at him. "It's just as fucked here as everywhere else."

"How would you know about everywhere else?"

Another fallen tree. Two wheels went into the ditch beside the track, and Jesse guided them around.

"I've been out there, seen it all," Karina said.

So tell me, Jesse thought, but he didn't say it, in case pushing her made her clam up completely.

"How long to town?" she asked after a couple of minutes' silence.

"Half an hour if we don't find another tree down, or the track's not washed away."

Karina turned on the radio, tuned in to some rock and roll, zoned out.

ASH

Even as I place them, I cannot name the parts. This is pure instinct, and I could do it in the dark, or with my eyes closed, just as I'm doing it now in the tumult. My memories are stormy. My present is a bench in a quiet, small park in a town whose name I can't remember. I have a screwdriver and a pair of pliers, and set out before me on the bench are all the components I've collected.

I'm putting things together while the tumult rages. The storms seem excited at what's happening. I can't blame them, as hopefully soon I'll get to set them free.

"Let them out," I say, and the idea is glorious. Perhaps by venting the pressures, the violence inside, I'll be able to bring on the eye myself.

Time passes. The apparatus grows, and its coming together looks so smooth, so perfect, that it resembles a filmed deconstruction played in reverse. Every piece knows its place. I attach each part without error.

I close my eyes and keep building by touch. It's as if I have done this a hundred times before.

When I open my eyes, a tall woman with wild hair is looking at me from across a planting bed that's gone to dust. Her eyes fix on mine, and everything else about her seems to blur.

I've seen Hotbloods before, but never this close. Everything I know about them urges me to keep my distance.

She glances down at what I'm doing, and for a moment the world around me comes into focus again, and I think to myself, *Here's trouble, come to find me at last.* I place the rest of the loose parts inside the case and close it.

When I look up the woman is still staring at me, and those strangest of eyes pin me to the world.

JIMI

Jimi Chastain hadn't seen a deer this big in seven, maybe eight years, and watching it now reminded him of his parents. He'd grown up in a nice house on Vancouver Island, but from a young age he was aware that things were changing. Food sometimes became scarce, and one year the trees on the island started dying from blight. That changed home forever. His father started shooting deer when he saw them in the woods behind their house, saying he was worried they'd come into the fields and damage the crop. His mother was outside sometimes too, hoping to scare the creatures away before his Papa put a bullet in their hearts. He always said they were good for food and he could sell their skins. His mother said they were beautiful creatures who deserved more of a chance at survival than stupid humans. Jimi and his sister Mel were usually caught in the middle, smiling and nodding at their father while secretly agreeing with their mother. So she chased them from the woods, he shot them, and as the refuse pile at the bottom of their yard filled with unsold pelts and hooves and bones, so the relationship between them—and between them and their two teenaged children—began to change. Jimi supposed they'd transferred their troubles onto him and Mel. Papa had grown more distant and unpredictable. His mother had chased the deer away. In the end it was Papa and

Jimi who had left, his Papa chasing dark, violent dreams and dragging his son along.

Jimi didn't know what sort of deer this was. White-tailed, maybe, though there weren't many of them left in the wild. Pretty thing, innocent, unaware of the change to the world, it represented beauty in this harsh place. It was a gift to be able to watch it. Jimi waited until it dipped its head to the water before squeezing the trigger, and it was down and dead before the shot echoed away across the valley.

He stood, shouldered the rifle, and walked out from the shadow of his tanker. He'd been there for several hours already, and he guessed that was why the deer had felt safe enough to make its way down to the water's edge. The wagon's pump was a steady background grumble, and the vehicle had become part of the landscape. He shielded his eyes and looked around. The shot would have scared away any other animals looking to come take a drink, but it might also attract the sort of company he didn't want. Jimi spent enough time in his own company to enjoy it, and he was lucky enough to be able to pick and choose when he interacted with other people. He'd left Mosey behind a little over a week ago, and since then he'd only spoken with people at roadside diners. They knew Soakers better than anyone, and most of them appreciated what they did well enough not to give Jimi a hard time. Some even claimed to like them. Back in Mosey he'd passed a couple of days spending the money he made from his latest load, got drunk, ate some good local steak, got a blowjob from the motel owner, then left town before he outstayed his welcome.

That time always came, too. Soakers were used to it. When your wagon ran dry people tended not to like you so much.

He walked down towards the remains of the reservoir to drag the dead deer away from the water. He probably wouldn't eat it—

skinning and butchering it would be too much of a ball-ache, and he still had plenty of dried food he'd picked up in Mosey—but it had been drinking his water. He'd leave its corpse out in the sun, and carrion creatures would pick its bones clean.

It took him a couple of minutes to reach the edge of the sad pool of water. He'd parked the wagon up on the road that had once skirted the old reservoir's edge. It was unlikely he'd get bogged down—the cracked ground was hard as rock—but he'd heard tales of Soakers refilling from old reservoirs and losing their wagons to vast sinkholes beneath the dried-out beds. Some of these dammed and flooded valleys had been inhabited once, and beneath the landscape of dried silt there might be old walls, sunken roads, and buildings buried deep in the past. Jimi imagined he was walking across an abandoned town, flooded and buried beneath decades of silt. Maybe its old inhabitants remained there as ghosts, trapped in place and reliving their final moments again and again.

He followed the pipe that ran from his wagon to the water. It was an old hose, and it had kinks and splits he'd patched up over the years. He passed one place where water misted from a tiny hole in the plastic under high pressure, spraying into the air and disappearing in the heat. A few flies flitted back and forth in the hazy cloud, finding temporary solace from the sun. Closer to the lake was a larger dark patch in the dust where water spurted from a new crack in the pipe. It wasn't one of the areas he'd fixed before, so at least it meant it wasn't his fault. But the fact it was a new split meant that the hose was degrading faster than ever. He'd have to get a new one.

Sighing, he stood again, adjusted the rifle on his shoulder, then walked the last fifty metres to the fallen deer. The bullet had entered its heart, and the animal had been dead before it hit the ground. Papa would have been proud. One glassy eye stared up at him, already buzzed by flies. It had fallen with its hindquarters in the edge of the water, and Jimi's boots started to slowly sink in the mud as he bent to grab its head and pull it out.

He paused, head tilted to one side. "What the fuck was that?" He was sure he'd heard the crumple of wheels on gravel.

He dropped the deer's head and stood, shielding his eyes from the sun and turning a slow circle. He looked back towards the wagon, which still stood alone on the old road two hundred metres up the gently sloping bed of the dried reservoir. The road to the right was deserted where it curved around the reservoir's edge and disappeared along the parched river valley. To the left it eventually crossed the earth and rock dam that closed the valley off at that end, and it was from that direction that he heard the noise again. There was still nothing visible through the shimmering heat haze, but by turning his head left and right he made out the distant sound from across the reservoir, where the other end of the dam merged with the valley side.

A flash of sunlight on glass and metal, and then the vehicle appeared on the road crossing the dam. Jimi cursed the fact that he'd left his binoculars in the cab. It was too small to be another Soaker come to take their fill from the reservoir, but it might have been cops from the local town, investigating who was draining their paltry supply.

Whoever it was, he had to assume they were watching him closer than he could watch them, so he bent and started dragging the deer's corpse from the water. That would explain the rifle on his shoulder. It wasn't often that Soakers worked and travelled on their own, but when they did it wasn't unusual for them to live off the land.

The car moved across the dam. Maybe it was just passing through, heading up into the hills towards communities he didn't know about, but Jimi was ever cautious. Soakers were seen to ride the fine line between either side of the law, and that meant he'd developed a healthy suspicion of other people. It was self-preservation. Some didn't like their water being collected for someone else's profit. Others didn't trust those who were seen to be preying on victims of the drought, or taking advantage of the millions who had no desire or means to leave the Desert. And there were also bandits who existed foul of the law and who knew that most Soakers worked for barter—food, valuables, or cold hard cash.

As it neared the wagon, the car started to speed up. When it reached the end of the dam and turned onto the road, Jimi let go of the deer and stood with one hand resting on the rifle strap. He was still down the gentle slope from the wagon, on the old reservoir bed. If he ran for the truck, his movement would raise the stakes. He thought he was pretty good at reading situations like this, viewing the lie of the land. And out here in the open, he had a full field of vision if anything kicked off.

As it closed on the wagon, Jimi made out some more details about the car. It was a BMW, an old gas model that had been converted to electric, its chassis bumped and scarred from decades of use. It was dusty from travel, windows glazed with sunlight, and there was no indication that it was here for him. It was driven casually—not too fast, not too slow—and the passenger window was open, the passenger's elbow resting on the sill.

What about air-con? he thought. No one would choose to drive with windows down unless they had to.

He curled his thumb beneath the rifle strap, ready to slip it from his shoulder. As the car disappeared behind his truck and water wagon, he took a few rapid steps to one side. He'd been shot at three times before, and never hit. He wasn't keen on staining his clean sheet.

Instead of passing behind the wagon and emerging again, he heard the violent grind of wheels locking and tyres scraping across the gravelly road as the car braked to a halt. A cloud of dust drifted to the left, and Jimi squinted, trying to see beneath the chassis and between the four sets of wheels to the car beyond. He could make out nothing.

He crouched, shrugging the rifle from his shoulder and into his hands at the same time. Moments later, when a flower of flame bloomed between his truck and the water wagon, he was primed and ready to shoot.

Fuckers!

The flames spread, carried by flowing, blazing fluids, and he'd seen enough truck fires to know already that his vehicle could not be saved. His clothes were in the truck, his cell phone, almost everything he owned. A minute ago he'd been worried about buying a new hose.

Fuckers!

He levelled the rifle and let off a shot aimed beneath the water wagon. He couldn't see anything because of the smoke and dust, but there was still a chance that he'd strike metal or flesh.

The fire crackled as it fingered its way into the cab, and windows cracked and popped. He could still hear the low rumble of the pump... and then the sudden growl of spinning tyres spraying stones.

He aimed at the rear of the wagon just as the car powered out from behind. His first shot ricocheted from metal as the car skimmed right, its wing scraping around the back of the wagon and severing the hose. Water sprayed and splashed across the BMW's windshield. As the wipers flipped on, Jimi aimed at them and squeezed off a second shot. He saw it spark from the car's roof as its nose dipped, dropping with a loud crunch from the road and down onto the edge of the reservoir's dried, cracked bed. As its wheels gripped and the vehicle accelerated right at him, Jimi realised he only had three, maybe four seconds in which to act. Its rear end shimmied as the tyres skidded on loose dust and hard-baked ground. He squeezed off another shot that starred the windshield high up, then another that shattered the glass. A fist punched through.

Jimi rolled left, squeezing the trigger at the same time and hoping for a lucky shot. He kept rolling, trying to see the car, hearing it bearing down on him. He heard the grind of brakes, then a sickening crunch as it passed over the dead deer.

He went up on one elbow and tried to bring the rifle to bear, but the car was too close now, skidding sidelong towards him. The passenger door opened, and though Jimi flinched to one side, its leading edge caught him across the right shoulder. He grunted and dropped the rifle, flipping over onto his back and landing heavily. Shock pulsed through him, stealing all sensation. Gritty dust pricked at his eyes and coated his mouth, and when he inhaled it filled his throat, a ragged cough pulling him over onto his side. Pain screamed in, scorching his shoulder and arm.

"Get the fuck up," a voice said. Male. Gruff. And familiar.

Jimi wiped his eyes with his good hand.

"Get the fuck—"

"He's hurt," another voice cut in. A woman. "But watch him."

Jimi pushed himself up into a sitting position, still wiping at his eyes. Dust burned. He coughed. His shoulder ached, pain scorching in when he moved, but he could still make a fist with his right hand.

"Son of a bitch," the man said. Jimi tensed, ready for a punch or kick, but none came.

"Who…?" he asked.

"Forgotten us already?" the woman asked. "Take our money, poison our kids, then forget us?"

Mosey, he thought. *That's where I know them from.*

"Alison," he said. He looked up at them standing beside the BMW and towering over him. She held a metal pipe in both hands. The man's two heavy fists were clasped at his sides like clubs. "Josh."

"We've been looking for you," Josh said.

"You tried to run me over."

"No," Josh said. "If she'd wanted to do that, you'd look like the deer."

Jimi glanced at the deer's mangled remains.

"So, what?" Jimi asked.

"You sold us dirty water," Alison said.

"No. I always treat it."

"You going to treat the shit you're pumping up from here too?" Josh asked. "It's stagnant. Rancid."

"Good enough for the deer," Jimi said. "And yes, I'm loading up first, but it's always treated in the wagon, and filtered when it's drawn out." He looked past them and their car at the wagon. The truck was ablaze now, the scarred paintwork on the water wagon blistering and bubbling. The big batteries contained down behind the engine would probably blow soon. They were far enough away to avoid any acid burns, he hoped. But he wasn't sure that meant he'd survive the day.

"Half the town has been sick," Josh said. "We lost three people."

"People die," Jimi said. "It's a sign of the times."

Josh swung one of those big club-like fists. It slammed into Jimi's head and he fell away, trying to ease the blow.

"Maggie McCourt," Alison said. "She was an actress back in the day, then a farmer, and had two kids. She was my friend."

Jimi didn't remember the name.

"Kevin Boone," she continued. "Used to be a paramedic, helped rescue thirty kids from a bus during the LA 'quake. He was my friend, too."

"Old people's names," Jimi said. "Old people die from heat, hunger, thirst, the blight. Our world's full of stuff that'll kill old people."

"Jenny Pearce. She didn't have a job because she was eleven years old."

Jimi sat up, vision swimming. "I'm sorry. I treat the water. It's filtered. I've been doing this for a long time."

"Yeah, so you told us," Josh said. "And on your own for a long time, too, since no other Soakers will work with you. We've been tracking you. Following." He knelt so that they were face to face, and Jimi saw fury in the man's eyes. It scared him. Very little scared him nowadays.

"You're a cruel piece of shit," Josh said.

"I provide water."

"They said you were callous," Alison said. "Brutal. Lots of Soakers started doing what they do to help people, bypass efforts by the authorities to buy water where there is none. They make money from it, but they bring the good stuff. The convoy of Soakers we caught up with know you—and know your ways."

"Why should you listen to them?" Jimi asked.

"We sure as hell didn't come to listen to you," Josh said, and then it came, the fists and the pipe and the hate, and there wasn't a single fucking thing Jimi could do about it.

———

Afterwards, senses as pummelled and confused as his body, Jimi heard Alison's heavy breathing and smelled her sweat. The tang of blood was thick in his mouth, gritty with the sharpness of a shattered tooth. Every breath was a knife in his side; he'd broken ribs before and guessed at least two were fractured. Blood pulsed behind his closed eyes, his heartbeat boomed in his head, irregular and uncertain.

Somewhere, sometime during the beating, he'd heard a deep thump, felt it through the ground. He smelled burning, acidic and rich on the still air. He heard glass cracking and the screech of metal warping. A satisfied grunt from Josh told him that they'd done what they came here to do. Jimi was still alive, but there was small comfort there. His truck was burning, water boiling in the wagon, wheels melting. Not only had they taken his livelihood, they had destroyed his home.

Groaning, Jimi risked opening his eyes. He was lying on his back, and the afternoon sun strived to melt them into the back of his skull.

"Motherfucker," Alison said. She was leaning against the BMW, breathing hard, metal pipe still in her hand. It glinted with Jimi's blood.

"Come on," Josh said. "We can go home now."

"Maybe I haven't finished yet."

"Ali."

She stared at Jimi.

"You're not a murderer, Ali."

"It wouldn't be murder," she said. "It'd be mercy."

Josh walked into Jimi's field of vision and held Alison's arm. "We've a long way to go home. And we've gotta find a new windshield first."

Jimi averted his eyes when they looked down at him. It was a strange feeling, being stared at by someone who wanted him dead. Unsettling. Thrilling. *The rifle*, he thought. *I dropped it, they don't have it, if I can—*

"One more thing," she said. She moved, and Josh braced himself for another impact from the bar. Perhaps this would be directly into his skull rather than his arm, his hip, his torso. He'd seen his father die. He'd heard his screams, witnessed his agony. *At least this will be faster*, he thought.

But Alison did not strike him again. Instead, she disappeared behind him, and he heard something being dragged across the dry ground. At first, when the wet thing landed across his face, he thought she was dropping the ripped remains of the deer onto him, one final indignity before leaving him to fend for himself. Then she knelt and forced his mouth open. He cried out at the pain from battered jaw and broken teeth—and hated the fact that he made any noise at all—then felt thick, slick water flowing into his mouth.

"Drink," she said.

Jimi retched. It was warm and dirty, sandy with sediment, and as the water dribbled from the hose she'd sliced through, he felt a sense of unfairness. He tried not to swallow. *I was going to sterilise it!* He retched again, but his throat worked and he took the water down. *I always clean it!* He spat and bucked, and finally she let him onto his side, spitting, wiping the back of his hand across his mouth. Blood and filthy water smeared his face.

He usually dropped a kilo of steriliser into the wagon. Eight, maybe ten kilos would have made the water safe. But it cost money, and he was never one to linger once he'd pumped water into the buyers' tanks and containers.

He guessed he'd been lucky up to now.

He looked around for his rifle and found it propped against their car, barrel stomped and bent. They must have done that after they'd beaten him, while his senses were still reeling.

"Fuck him," Josh said. "Come on, Ali."

"Yeah. Fuck him. His kind's extinct anyway, now there's a Rainmaker."

Ali glanced at Josh, who pulled an amused face. *Eh?*

Jimi froze on his side, drooling and seeping pain from every pore.

Rainmaker?

Josh slumped into the car, exhausted.

"See you again, I'll kill you," Alison said. She glanced at the blazing truck, then sank into the BMW's driver's seat.

Rainmaker! Jimi thought, and something coursed through him, a strength that seemed to lessen his pain and reinvigorate his battered muscles. He went to stand, swaying, wobbling, but upright.

The BMW was already heading slowly back towards the road, at an angle towards the dam that avoided the burning truck.

Jimi took a single step towards the flames, then broke into a run. Every part of him screamed to stop—pounding head, torn muscles, stabbing ribs, the pains and agonies planted in him by the beating he'd just undergone. But he moved with one purpose, and with one word at the forefront of his mind: *Rainmaker.*

After his father's murder, Jimi had gone searching, but the Rainmaker had melted away into the shadows. He became more of a rumour than ever—awed whispers within groups of believers, amused jokes among those who doubted. Jimi believed, but not with awe. His belief was born of hatred.

The heat from the burning truck increased in intensity with every step, but he wasn't heading that way. It was the rear of the wagon that held what he sought, an insurance policy he'd almost forgotten about. Once he was behind the water wagon, its bulk hid him from some of the fire. He plunged his hand past the various faucets and spigots at the massive tank's rear, delving around until he found what he was seeking. His hand curled around the pistol's handle and he tugged. It didn't shift. *Two years?* he wondered. *Three, since I even looked at it?* He could feel the grease and filth around the gun, and doubted it would work even if he could release it; but when he leaned to his left and saw the BMW, that gave him the kick he needed to pull harder.

They must have seen him running for his burning truck. They'd stopped, watching to see what he did. He was pretty sure he could hear Alison laughing, even past the noise of the blaze.

His battered shoulder screamed as he gave one final hard tug, and then the gun was in his hand. He stepped out from behind the wagon and fired two shots, startled that the gun still worked. He ran directly at them and fired three more. He saw Josh's head flip back and blood splash inside the car, and he aimed lower at the front tyres, firing three more times as he drew close. The tyres didn't deflate but it didn't matter. Alison was driving nowhere.

Standing beside the car, Jimi tried to catch his breath as he looked at what he had done. He'd seen people killed before—had witnessed his father hacking someone apart with an axe when he was eleven, his father's people shooting three thieves, and he'd watched his Papa die—but he had only ever killed one other person himself.

He'd often dreamed about killing. Not these people, but they were a start.

It didn't feel bad. It felt *good*. Seemed to Jimi that his father had been right. After the first, it got a whole lot easier.

Alison was pressed back in her seat, one hand clasped hard

against the side of her face. Blood pissed through her fingers and down her arm, and her eyes were wide and white against their wet red background. Jimi leaned into the car and pressed the gun beneath Alison's chin as he looked across at Josh. He'd caught a bullet in his neck, ripping out most of his throat. He still quivered as he bled out, but Jimi thought he was probably already dead.

"Rainmaker," Jimi said. "Tell me about him."

Alison frowned, and blood beaded in the creases across her forehead. Jimi thought she didn't have very long left.

"Just… stupid rumour… don't really believe—"

"Tell me about him!"

"Not him," Alison said, eyes wide. Maybe she thought telling the truth might save her life, but she was dying anyway. Jimi could see that.

"Not him what?" he asked, confused. He lifted Alison's chin with the pistol's barrel.

"Not him. Her."

KARINA

She hadn't seen him for years, but Karina could still tell when Jesse was nervous. He blinked faster than usual and stroked the left side of his face, running his thumb along the jawline that had been shattered by a bullet and then rebuilt with half a dozen surgeries performed by inexperienced backstreet surgeons.

"Roebuck Road's flooded," Jenny said. She took a sip of beer and glanced at Karina for the hundredth time. "Your Land Rover might get through, but I wouldn't lay odds on it."

"What about Baxter's?" Jesse asked.

"You really wanna go through there? After last time?" She laughed and rolled her eyes. Karina couldn't help liking the woman.

"What happened last time?" Karina asked.

Jenny leant forward over the table. The bar was bustling and buzzing with the sort of manic excitement and borderline hysteria that came with disruptive events like this storm.

"Baxter's farm." Jenny smiled and pointed at Jesse with her bottle. "He and Baxter are friends. Weird, 'cos Baster's a contrary old bastard with odd ideas of civility. So, even though he and Jesse are friends, he still charges a toll for crossing his land. Fair enough, I say. He owns a lot of land round here and he farms it as well as he can, got some serious irrigation infrastructure going on, government paid for some of it back in the day, but he's extended and experimented and... well, whatever. He charges to cross his land, even his friends." She pointed at Jesse with her bottle again. "And even when his friends claim not to have crossed at all."

"He says I owe him a hundred bucks," Jesse said. "He saw a Land Rover take out some of his crops and reckons it was me, but it wasn't."

"A hundred bucks?" Karina asked.

"From four months ago," Jenny said.

"Friends that fall out over a hundred bucks can't be friends at all," Karina said.

"Right," Jenny said. "Right! Kyle, three more beers over here!"

"Not for us," Karina said. "We've got to move."

"In this?" Jenny had asked that before, and Jesse had told her who Karina was, and that it was important. He hadn't mentioned Ash. "Well, I guess you *could* ask Baxter. He and his people will be all over their water collecting systems, making the most of this."

"It's set to continue for a day at least," Jesse said. "They'll be busy trying to divert floods rather than save water."

"Feast or famine," Jenny said. Her cheery demeanour dropped for a moment and Karina caught a glimpse of what she thought was probably the true Jenny, a sadder, older woman doing her best to make her way through this tougher world. Karina reckoned she was seventy, maybe older, so she'd have good, rich memories of how things had been before everything had gone to hell. Karina's memories of that time were vaguer, caught up in young childhood and adolescence. When the 2029 hurricane season devastated the Gulf of Mexico and much of the eastern seaboard, Karina was dealing with her first relationship and finding her way in the wider world. She remembered the events as background news, even though the hurricanes had signalled the start of the First Great Drought, which had seared much of the USA and set in the seed of decline that led to where they were today. Jenny had seen and lived through all of that in her middle years, and had probably been touched by it personally. Karina guessed she had many stories to tell.

"We'll be fine," Jesse said. "I know those roads."

"You do? Since when? When's the last time you drove anywhere more than a few miles from Hillside or Blueton?"

"Doesn't matter," Jesse said, rubbing his jaw again. "So you'll look after the place for me?"

"Sure I will. Might even make some improvements. Plenty of ideas to make it a bit more homely."

"I've told you before, no curtains."

"No curtains." She smiled at Karina again. "He always had so little taste?"

"Always," Karina said. She wondered what Jesse had told Jenny about her, and found that she didn't care. Over the years she had been searching for Ash, she'd stopped giving a flying fuck about what anyone thought of her. She couldn't afford the headspace, and she was rarely anywhere long enough for it to matter.

"You sure you need to take Rocky with you?" Jenny asked. At mention of her name, the dog whined a little from where she was lying beneath the table.

"Yeah," Jesse said. "Sorry, I know how much you love my girl."

"I'm thinking about how much the poor mutt loves me."

"She'll survive."

"Will you?" Jenny asked. It threw an awkward pause into their stilted conversation, almost as if she'd forgotten Karina was there.

"I'll be fine," Jesse said. "You know I will."

Jenny nodded, raised her bottle in a silent salute, then drained it in one gulp. As she did so she looked at Karina and her eyes sought a dozen promises. *Look after him* was the first and foremost. There was suspicion too, and doubt. However much Karina found herself liking this woman, she didn't have time for any of it.

"Good to meet you," Karina said, standing. "And he'll be fine. He's always been good at looking after himself. Jesse, I'll meet you outside."

She walked from the bar without glancing back. It felt like a thousand other places she'd walked out of over the years. This time she was no longer alone.

JESSE

The road out of Blueton was quiet. Despite his assurances to Karina, Jesse knew that few people were foolish enough to travel in the dark in weather like this. Once he'd paid their toll—including an agreed split of what Baxter believed was owed—negotiated the tracks across Baxter's property, and hit the main highway heading south, he saw only very occasional headlamps passing the other way. The ongoing deluge dispersed the light and made the vehicles look like ghosts in the dark, and he would appear the same to them.

It was a good while since he'd been this far out from town. Jenny had been right about that, though Karina hadn't mentioned it, and he'd volunteered nothing once they left the tavern. But his nervousness surprised him. He'd never really seen himself as a hermit, shut off from the world, but he guessed that was as good a description as any. Hillside was his home, Hillside and Blueton his world, and over the years since arriving he'd shown less and less interest in what was happening beyond. The world had shot him in the face and torn out his heart, and at Hillside he'd let his simple, ignorant existence tend those wounds, even though he knew none of them could ever be truly healed. Especially those that were self-inflicted.

Karina was browsing the news sites on her phone, its soft glow reflecting from the windshield. Wipers swept at full speed, but still his view of the road ahead was obscured. The phone's light did little to help, but he slowed down rather than ask Karina to turn it off. She was looking for Ash.

She had been lost to Jesse these last nine years. If dead, as he'd always believed, he had been responsible. If alive, she would be in pain, mad in herself and at him, a person he no longer knew. She'd left him no choice. He should have tried other ways. He'd done it to save her. He'd done it for himself. He dreamed about it while asleep and agonised while awake, and though his life at Hillside and deep in a bottle were distractions, he was never at peace with what he'd done.

"Anything?" he asked. She hadn't spoken since they'd exchanged a few sparse words while driving across Baxter's land, and his attempts at a few light-hearted comments had elicited no response. Rocky lay sleeping on the back seat. The radio splurged some bland new music he'd never heard before. The atmosphere was thick with unsaid things.

"Huh?"

"Ash."

"Nothing new. I'm looking at the news." She fell silent again, tapping and scrolling.

He slowed when he saw the headlamps reflected from a deep, smooth darkness beyond. The flood spanned the road, and he dropped down a couple of gears and ploughed through the deep water. It rose and splashed up on either side, washing across windows and wing mirrors. Karina didn't even look up.

"So, what's the news?" he asked after a couple more minutes of silence.

Karina sighed. "More drone strikes in Rio."

"What's going on in Rio?"

"Seriously?"

He glanced across and she was staring at him, face lit by the ghostly phone glow. She looked back at her phone without explaining anything about Rio.

"More food riots south in Omaha. The Mars crew have signed a joint book and multimedia deal worth a quarter of a billion dollars. The bush fires in California are even worse than last year, and spreading north and east."

Jesse absorbed the headlines. He wasn't completely ignorant of the major news events, because Jenny often filled him in, and when he went into town he'd catch snippets of conversation and sometimes see stuff on the TVs in the tavern. Mostly it didn't much interest or concern him. That was depressing, but it was also survival. He'd drawn his world in to Hillside—anything beyond would only bring pain to his already tortured mind. Jenny called his attitude ignorance. He called it self-preservation.

"You do know we landed on Mars, right?"

"Of course."

"And you know some of what's going on in the world?"

"Sure."

"So?"

Jesse almost smiled but feared it would infuriate her, drive her back into silence and her phone. He could tell she was exasperated with him, but that was better than driving with no conversation at all.

"So, yeah, we landed on Mars."

"Four years ago."

"Yeah. Joint mission, Europe and Russia and India, and one of our astronauts hitched a ride."

"Good. Great. Nice to know you're au fait with one of the biggest news stories in history, ever."

"Sure I am." He paused, and this time he couldn't hold back a smile. "Jenny told me."

Karina muttered something and carried on scrolling.

"Didn't know about the fires, though."

"You're still bullshitting," Karina said.

"Nope. I knew there were more fires in Texas a couple of years back, ten thousand square miles scorched." He remembered how useless that had made him feel. If only his talent had been contained, refined. Maybe he could have done something for them down there.

"The fires in California have been raging for three months," Karina said. "There are fifty main blazes, maybe more. Biggest fires in its history. Years of drought, and now high winds and record temperatures are making them ten times worse."

"Damn."

"Whole neighbourhoods wiped out. Hundreds have died. A school bus was caught in a flash fire six weeks ago. It's terrible."

"Yeah."

"I can't believe you've shut yourself off this much, Jesse. Not you."

Jesse felt the twinge of something bitter and sweet. *It almost sounds like she cares.*

"It makes life easier," he said, and he expected her to tell him that he'd always just thought of himself. But however much she hated him, she knew that wasn't really true. And it didn't make life easier at all. His guilt at what he'd done haunted every sober or drunken day.

Jesse drove them through the storm, and the night swallowed his hangover. Karina put down her phone and reclined her seat, closing her eyes and ending their conversation. In the back seat, Rocky whined and yelped as she chased shadows in her sleep. Jesse had never found that a comforting sound. He wondered if he shouted as he dreamed of his own shadows.

CEE

In the Desert, Cee rarely went looking for anyone but herself. For the three years since Maxwell had helped her get clean, she had been on the move. That first move was leaving Maxwell, and though she remembered his satisfaction as he watched the new woman leaving his home, she also sometimes recalled the sadness there, too. She thought about Maxwell a lot. He was old, and wise, had seen lots of shit, and had spent most of his life preparing for the clusterfuck the world had become.

He knew why she'd left, and whenever she started to wonder how much time and distance exaggerated that glint of sadness she'd seen in his eyes, her one certainty was that he knew she'd had no choice. He'd helped her shift and bury the addiction, but she wasn't cured. She was an addict, and there was no way she could put down roots and allow the old habits to find her again, stalking her tender moments and shadowy thoughts until they started to whisper to her with dreaded, irresistible insistence.

To stay ahead of her past, Cee had to move. And she'd been moving forward ever since, even during those days or occasional longer periods when she ended up pausing in one place. Moving, always moving. She didn't trust time to do it for her, because though she was still young, she knew that time could deceive.

She was on the run, and she'd always strived to stay ahead

of that dreadful fucking puppet master that once held her in its grasp. Sometimes her forearms ached as if the strings were still attached, and she'd scratch and rub until the scar tissue bled. *At least it's clean blood*, she'd tell herself, even though she'd be left with new wounds healing all over again. That was when time fucked with her. People looked at those fresh scabs and saw all the wrong things.

Lately something had changed. Ash-not-Leigh had caused the change. And now, for the first time since Maxwell, the thing that Cee was looking for smothered much of the threat of what she ran from. She guessed that was why she thought of Ash more and more with every moment that passed.

She was good at finding things. Her time in the Desert had shown her that. And just two days after waking to see that Ash had stolen her bracelet and run, Cee found her again.

The town was called Kenworthy, and Cee had been there before. Deep in the Desert, it was home to misfits and hope, and it existed beneath a familiar miasma of sun-scorched, low-level madness. Once a farming town, its trade was now in vehicle modification; with a series of low hills to the south, its wind farms provided for over two hundred charging points for electric vehicles. No one visited unless they were passing through. And that's just what Cee would have done, if she hadn't heard the muted conversation at the charging point. Leaving her bike plugged in, she wandered closer to the elderly couple charging their truck, pretending to look at the refurbished and converted cars she would never afford.

"Not often you see them in town," the woman said.

"Only if they're looking to steal something," the man said. "Damn scum, every one of them."

"They can't help being Hotbloods," she said.

"Maybe not. I don't understand much of it myself. But you can decide whether you end up thieving, whatever disease you have."

"I feel sorry for the kid with them. She looks lost. You seen her?"

"Dixton never did mind where his trade came from, nor whether their money was clean or dirty."

"Lost, and maybe something else, I thought. Confused. Not scared, but not really all there. You seen her? Them?"

"No!" the elderly man snapped. "I told you, I stay away from Hotbloods." He caught sight of Cee then, watching. She glanced away, but he'd already seen.

"Keep to your own business," the man said harshly, and there was a tone in his voice that reminded her of her father. She thought this man enjoyed being cruel.

"I'm just waiting for my bike to charge," she said.

"Yeah, then on your way, I'm sure," the man said. His skin was leathered by the sun, face speckled with a dozen dark growths. He exuded anger at a world he'd never wished for and didn't understand. Everyone had their own way of dealing with the clusterfuck.

"I might stay a while, actually," Cee said, and the man grunted. She looked at the woman, not sure whether there was anything more welcoming in her expression. "Which way to Dixton's?"

"You're not a Hotblood," the woman said.

"Not last time I checked."

"You'd do well not to mix with them." The old woman's face wasn't exactly kind, but bore a concern that might once have been for someone else. Everyone had lost someone or something, and the cruel reality was that pain and loss was inevitable. Some people dealt with it better than others. Some projected their loss outward, onto people or situations they knew little about.

"I've fucked more Hotbloods than you've got teeth in your head," Cee said. The woman's eyes went wide, the man's narrowed with anger. "Both of you, combined."

It wasn't true. Cee had never slept with a Hotblood and never would, because she had met them enough times to know to stay the hell away. But she resented this couple offering her bitter advice from the confines of a dying town they probably hardly ever left. She'd been out there for three years, travelling the Desert and doing her best to stay one step ahead of her history. She'd moved from state to state, town to town, breathing in the dust of dead fields and forgotten dreams, and feeling her skin stretch and burn when she couldn't afford or find sunscreen. She'd seen people wretched and thin from hunger. She'd once found a family huddled in the shadow of a broken car, mad from thirst and dying, the shrivelled body of a child nursed between them. She knew the Desert, and the wild. She was aware of Hotbloods and other cruel people out there who were a threat, the same as she knew about the kindness of strangers.

"Dixton's?" Cee asked again. It was the man who nodded across the street to a narrow side alley. That surprised her, and she felt a pang of regret at how she'd treated them. The world had made them that way.

She smiled her thanks as she disconnected her bike and wheeled it along the sidewalk.

"Just watch out," the woman said.

"She can look after herself," the man said, and Cee felt a pang of pride.

I can, she thought. *I have before, and I will again.*

————

She smelled Dixton's before she saw the diner's frontage and dusty window, the ratty chairs and tables set along one side of the wide alleyway. It was the same aroma that hung around a hundred diners in a hundred different towns: grease and burnt fat, singed bacon, and stale coffee. The sense of hopelessness that hung around the diner was only partly due to this familiar scent. The tables outside held ashtrays overflowing with cigarette butts, and a few empty plates being pecked at by a scruffy bird. A string of coloured bulbs hung above the door and front window, but half of them were smashed, and the others were dulled with dust. A woman sat in one chair with a large coffee mug on the table before her. Both hands rested in her lap. She was staring across the alley at the boarded windows of the premises opposite. It had once been a bookstore, and a few old volumes were still scattered from a broken display rack in front of the nailed-up door, as if the erstwhile owners had put out the last of their stock before leaving. No one had bothered taking them. Their covers were faded, loose pages dried and brittle.

Cee liked books. They took her away from the world, and however terrible the fictional worlds were, more often than not she wished she could stay.

"Pie's good," the woman said without looking at Cee. "Dixton makes it himself. His coffee's tar, though."

"Thanks for the recommendation," Cee said. The woman looked her up and down, rolled her eyes, and returned to her silent, motionless stare. Her full coffee mug had a cool skin across the surface.

Cee shouldered her pack and leaned her bike against the wall, then approached the door and tried to look inside. The diner was gloomy, and even in the sheltered alley, sunlight glared from the windows. She pressed her face to the door, just as a shadow approached and someone opened it from the inside.

Cee stumbled through the door and into the person who'd opened it, and as she stepped to the side and away from them she felt the heat exuding from their body, and thought, *Hotblood*.

The man was shorter than her, and so thin she wondered how he didn't break. That was a familiar trait of the Hotbloods, as was the sun- and wind-burnt skin, the head of wild hair, and the startling eyes. They jittered and vibrated in their sockets, tiny pinprick pupils shifting back and forth and up and down, several millimetres at a time. They should have blurred, but they gave the disconcerting impression that the rest of the Hotblood's face was shifting, and the eyes themselves were fixed.

Perspiration speckled his nose and forehead in large, greasy-looking pearls. She'd once heard that you could catch the Hotblood affliction simply by having some of their sweat touch your own skin. She'd also heard that it was not a physiological condition at all, but a psychological one. She had come across a few packs during her time in the Desert, and she avoided them wherever she could. Unstable, unpredictable, and mostly uncaring, they were always bad news. They valued life as much as sand.

"Desert girl," the Hotblood said, staring at her with his spooky eyes.

Cee pushed past him and entered the diner. She spotted Ash immediately, sat in a booth with three more Hotbloods blocking her in. Her guitar case was propped on the seat beside her. Cee wondered if her bracelet was inside.

"Ash!" Cee said, smiling as she approached the table. She read the situation quickly. She was good at that, and it had got her out of trouble a few times over the years. Helped her cause trouble for others, too.

Ash looked at her, eyes blank, not even a flicker of a smile. Cee glanced from one Hotblood to the next—at their hands, the table before them, the mugs and plates and crumbs scattered across its surface. There was no sign of any drug usage, and Hotbloods were never concerned with hiding their habits.

"What the fuck do you want?" asked a tall, thin Hotblood. She was thirty, or maybe sixty, her grey hair long and frazzled as if subjected to intense heat. She sat closest to Cee, with Ash beside her pressed to the booth wall, and two others opposite. The Hotblood she'd met at the door must have been perched on the stool at the end of the table. Cee shifted her right foot so that it rested against one of the stool's legs.

"Just to see my friend. Right, Ash?"

Ash tapped a glass on the table before her, a ring on her thumb making a regular *plink plink*, and she looked at Cee with interest but no real recognition.

Cee wondered if she was sending her a sign, but thought not. This was something different. Ash really didn't know her.

"But this is *our* friend," the Hotblood said. "Ash. Ash is *our* friend." Cee thought she looked like a dandelion with her craze of grey hair and stick-like limbs and body.

"You didn't even know her name," Cee said. She was tense, wired, ready. Danger hung like heat haze, and for a moment she questioned herself and her motives for coming here, doing this. But only for a moment.

Ash was vulnerable, and these Hotbloods were a pack of fucking wolves. There were rumours that they sometimes ate people. That wasn't the worst she'd heard.

"What's in a name?" Dandelion asked. "We're getting on just fine. We're friends to her and she's feeling safe and protected. Until you came along and…" She waved a hand, and Cee saw her shimmering gaze flit towards the door behind her. The Hotblood she'd met at the diner door had never left.

"I don't take any shit in my diner!" a man said. Dixton, Cee assumed. He stood behind the counter with a big mug of coffee in one hand, the other resting on the countertop.

"No trouble from me," Cee said.

"No trouble," Dandelion echoed, eyes flickering left and right. She giggled. Sweat ran down beside her nose and rested on her top lip. Her tongue snaked out and flicked at it, and it was grey and pasty. The woman looked sick. Some Hotbloods took drugs to keep themselves upright and forever driving forward, dooming themselves to an early grave and a fast, frantic time getting there. Others relied on a constant intake of any type of calories they could find—meat, roadkill, wild and domesticated animals, scrubby plants, old leather dried in the sun, anything they could chew and swallow without it killing them. Drugs or food, their metabolism struggled to keep pace with their affliction. Cee had once seen a pack of Hotbloods camped around the carcass of a horse in the Desert. She'd moved on quickly, wondering how long they'd take to consume every scrap of the creature's remains.

Dandelion tried to smile. Cracked lips. Blackened teeth.

"She's not for you," Cee said.

"Not for me?" Dandelion asked, and Cee knew she'd been right in her supposition that the woman was the pack's leader. That might make what came next easier. She pressed her right hand against her hip. Her left hand rested on the table's edge, close to the left leg pocket of her cargo pants. The weight of the small pistol she kept there was never more obvious, more comforting.

Cee sensed movement behind her. Ash's eyes shifted that way and she frowned. The fourth Hotblood was getting into position. Cee looked at the two across the table, assessing the threat, preparing herself, reading as much as she could into their body language and strange, haunting eyes.

"No trouble," Cee said, quieter. "Do yourselves a favour."

Dandelion laughed, a throaty cackle.

"Seriously," Cee said. "She's my friend, and whatever you want of her, she *doesn't* want."

"You're speaking for her?" Dandelion asked.

"She can't speak for herself." Cee took a chance saying it, planting ideas she wasn't sure were valid or true.

"Got my case," Ash said, tapping the guitar case propped on the seat beside her. "Filling it up."

"She's filling it up," Dandelion said. "And she's something special."

"She sure is," Cee said, troubled by the Hotblood's words. It was said that in their madness, some Hotbloods possessed a wider, enhanced perception. Cee had always attributed that to the drugs, or the accelerated speed of their chaotic metabolism. She'd never seen evidence of anything else.

"You don't know," Dandelion said. "She's not your friend at all."

"Turnip and potato soup," Cee said, and Ash's eyes opened wide. She went from slumped to sitting bolt upright, a smile splitting her face. She went from not there at all, to *there*.

"Fucking devil grass!" Ash said, and Cee remembered leaving the wagon for a leak and getting stung.

Ash's waking changed everything, and Cee's coiled, taut muscles reacted instantly.

Dandelion's left hand reached for whatever weapon she nursed in her lap. Cee didn't let it get that far. She plucked the knife from her belt and slammed it down through Dandelion's hand, pinning it to the table. At the same time she dug into her pocket with her other hand and produced the pistol, lifting it to aim at the two Hotbloods across the table. She wasn't quite fast enough. The man was sliding off the end of the booth's bench, reaching for her with hands that seemed far too large for the rest of his body.

Shifting her weight to the right, Cee shoved her boot against the stool and scraped it across the floor. The man went sprawling, his grasping hands slashing past her arm, long fingernails scratching the skin in several places. As he hit the floor, Cee aimed the pistol at the other Hotblood on that side, an older woman with greasy sweat beaded on her dark skin like a hundred stud piercings.

"Still!" Cee shouted. "You behind me, stand back!"

The diner whispered with a dozen startled movements and indrawn breaths, like a heavy breeze huffing through a tree canopy before fading once again to silence. Cee saw Ash's eyes flit from her to the Hotblood behind her, and she twisted the knife in Dandelion's hand.

The woman grunted, a sound ending in a high whine. "Do as she says," she hissed, and Cee was impressed with her pain threshold. Another thing Hotbloods were renowned for. That, and their tendency towards violence.

"I will shoot you," she said to the older Hotblood. "Every one of you."

"I took your bracelet," Ash said.

"Don't worry about it."

"I'm sorry. But I had to take it. Sometime soon I'm going to make rain, almost ready to try. Built it already. Want to see if it works."

Make rain? What the fuck?

"Special," Dandelion said, spittle dropping from her lips. She was tense, all her attention focussed on the blade pinning her hand to the table. Cee felt the grind of bones transmitted through the knife handle. That meant she'd probably have to leave it behind. That made her sad. It was a good knife.

"Now then," Dixton said, and he started around the end of his counter. He held a baseball bat in one hand.

"Just leaving," Cee said. "Please, Mr Dixton, stay where you are 'til we're gone."

"I'm going with you?" Ash asked, and Cee saw something so innocent in her eyes, so confused and sad.

"Yeah, Ash."

"More soup."

"Sure." Cee looked from Dandelion to the older Hotblood, then the one still sprawled on the floor. "This is over," she said. "Doesn't have to be any more than this. Just a little bit of tension, a little splash of blood, and an adventure we can all tell our grandkids." Her heart hammered, but her senses were alight and alert. Clear.

"Dovey won't have grandkids," Dandelion said. "She's only got weeks to live."

Dovey, the older woman, tilted her head to one side. She didn't quite smile, but her expression said, *Do you think I'm afraid of your gun.*

"Let's not make it seconds," Cee said. She shifted her aim slightly, from Dovey's face to her stomach. No one wants a bullet in the belly. "Okay Dovey, you slide across the seat and set your arse on the floor beside your dummy friend."

"You know 'dummy' isn't a politically correct term," Dandelion said.

Cee ignored her as Dovey started moving, slowly, hands drifting along the table as she went as if playing a piano.

"And talking of friends... dickhead behind me, you get down too." Cee looked at Ash. She glanced past Cee, then nodded. She seemed to be more present, though she was still twitchy, as if waking from a disturbing dream she had yet to forget.

"Over the table and slide out this way," Cee said to Ash.

Ash went to move. Dandelion grabbed the guitar case handle and held it back, and Ash's eyes went wide. She shouted, "I need it!" and Cee leaned on the knife, hearing the table's Formica crack and feeling Dandelion's bones grind against unforgiving metal.

Cee caught a shimmer of movement with her left eye and aimed the pistol that way. She'd killed before, but maybe that made it harder. Crouching, glancing left, she put a bullet in the floor between the two Hotbloods.

The shot cracked through the diner and echoed away, freezing everything in place.

"Next one's in your belly," she said to Dovey. "Ash. Come on."

Ash tugged the guitar case and Dandelion let it go. She climbed over the table and slid off its end, pulling the case behind her, a scatter of mugs and cutlery falling around Cee's feet. A glass smashed. A mug bounced, spilling coffee like dark blood.

"You can keep the knife," Cee said to Dandelion.

"Get the fuck out of my diner," Dixton said, but his voice held a tremor that made Cee feel bad. She didn't like scaring people who didn't deserve it. But she wasn't about to apologise. She didn't want to betray even a glimmer of weakness.

"I'll give the knife back to you one day," Dandelion said. "I'll put it in your friend's face first, though."

"See, now you've said that, I'm going to have to kill you all." Cee swung the gun around and pressed it into Dandelion's cheek. The Hotblood leaned back, wincing as her hand pulled against the knife.

The diner held its breath. Cee didn't. Though her heart was hammering, she breathed slow and deep, not wanting to display a single moment of fear or doubt. She had control, and knew her life, and Ash's, depended on maintaining it. Dandelion had to believe with every fucked-up element of herself that Cee was

ready to put a bullet through her cheek. If Cee couldn't convince
the Hotblood of that, she'd just have to shoot her anyway.

"We should go," Ash said. "Storm's on its way again. I'm always
in the tumult."

"We're going," Cee said. She shoved the gun harder, pushing
Dandelion back in her seat and eliciting a groan as her hand was
split some more by the knife. She could smell fear, beneath the
Hotblood's dusty, warm stench. That was good. Fear might just
help her and Ash get away.

"Chance," Cee said. "Just 'cos I like this diner, and I don't want
the nice people to have to see your brains. But if I see any of you
ever again, that's your chance card played."

She eased the gun out of Dandelion's cheek and backed away
from the table.

"What now?" Ash asked. Her voice sounded more distant than
before, almost as if she was going to sleep.

"Now we go outside," Cee said. "You first."

Ash left the diner, guitar case slung over her shoulder, backpack
in her other hand.

"Sorry," Cee said to Dixton as she backed up to the door, gun
still raised. "You shouldn't serve them."

"I serve who the hell I want," Dixton said.

"I won't be coming back," Cee said.

"True. You're barred."

Cee kept the gun aimed at the Hotbloods as she backed
through the door into the wide alley. Outside, the woman still sat
in her seat, looking at Cee and Ash with only mild interest. Ash
was leaning against the wall, staring into space.

"What the hell's wrong with you?" Cee asked.

"I'm lost in the storm," Ash said. "I'm holding on to you,
though. As hard as I can. If I don't, maybe I'll drown."

Cee glanced at her electric bike but dismissed it. It would take both of them, but not far, and not very fast.

"What now?" Ash asked.

Cee kept hold of her gun as she clasped the strange young woman's arm with her other hand.

"Now we find our way to—" *The edge of town*, she was going to say. To get a lift with someone, or steal a car, or maybe just walk out into the Desert. Cee had survived fine out there on her own, but something told her that being out there with Ash would be different. Everything about Ash was different, and maybe the Hotblood was right. Maybe something about her *was* special. But she didn't have the chance to suggest any of this, because the diner door creaked open with a breath of spilled blood and coffee, and as Cee turned and raised the gun she hoped to see anyone but Dandelion standing there framed in the doorway. But of course it was Dandelion, one hand dripping blood and the knife in her other hand.

Cee might have let her live, even then, if she hadn't raised the bloodied knife, pointed it at Ash's face, and taken a rapid step forward.

Cee squeezed the trigger as she brought the gun up and put a bullet through Dandelion's face. Her left cheek imploded, her shaking eye flooded red, and she took a couple of stumbling steps back into the diner. The door swung closed on a startled scream and the scrape of chairs.

Cee stepped towards the door and kicked it open, Ash muttering, "No," behind her, but she couldn't stop now. She was not a woman of half measures. Leaving something like this unfinished was like only part-cleaning and sealing a wound. Infection would take root, insidious and unrelenting, and the wound would get worse and result in more pain, greater heartache.

Hotbloods were driven and unrelenting. She had made enemies of them, and she would have to face them again now, or further down the trail.

"No," Ash said again from behind her, louder, but Cee was already standing in the open door, aiming at the Hotbloods crouched and kneeling around their fallen leader.

Dovey came at her, fast for someone so close to the end. Cee shot her in the chest and she went down, falling across Dandelion's body. The other two stood, one of them grasping up Dandelion's dropped knife, and darted in opposite directions, attempting to confuse Cee's aim before attacking. She squeezed off two quick, careful shots, aiming for each Hotblood's centre of mass. One of them danced backwards and tripped over the stool again, falling and squirming on the floor. The other slumped onto the end of the table they'd been sat around, trying to breathe. Blood bubbled at his mouth. He stared at Cee, eyes wide and vibrating in his skull, oily sweat beading on his face like colourless blood.

Cee held the gun ready. The cafe was silent, but for the laboured breathing of a dying man. She crouched and picked up her knife. It had Hotblood blood on its blade. She would clean it later.

No one spoke as she backed out of the door. Her bullets had killed their words.

"Not the first Hotblood I've seen dead in this place," the woman sitting at the table outside said. She looked Cee up and down and rolled her eyes again, before reaching for the small phone propped against her coffee mug on the table. "So I gotta call the law. But Sheriff Wilson's slower than he used to be, on account of losing his dog three weeks ago. He really loved that dog. They're probably calling him from inside, too, but the Sheriff and I've got history." The woman waved her hand as if Cee had asked about that history, shoving it away. "So, get moving. I'm not one to put more value on one life than another, but the Hotbloods meant ill of your friend there. That I know. They mean ill of most folks, and I've had words with Dixton about them before. But Dixton's not making much money no more, and Sheriff Wilson's lost his dog, and now…" She picked up her mug and sniffed at the contents. "…now my coffee's gone cold." She looked from Cee to the phone in her hand as she started dialling.

"Come on," Cee said.

"What about the others?" Ash asked.

"Other what?"

"The other Hotbloods."

"Inside looking after each other."

"Oh."

Cee grabbed her hand and pulled her away, glancing back until they reached the end of the alley and turned onto the sidewalk. She didn't want Dixton or any of the others to come out after them. This was more than enough for one day.

"What's in the case?" Cee asked.

"Stuff. Your watch. More."

"Okay."

"I… not now," Ash said. She shook her head as they walked, as if to spring droplets from her hair.

"Not now," Cee agreed. "Now, we need to get away from here."

"Out into the storm," Ash said.

Cee looked up at the sky. It was a clear, cloudless blue, the sun a familiar furnace, a blazing mouth into Hell, high above and just starting to scorch its way west towards the Desert it continued to bake day after day, month after month. It hurt Cee's eyes to look.

It hurt her mind to remember, Hotbloods or not. Killing was easy in the moment, but the deaths got harder in retrospect, as if the memories of them were implanted in her soul to sprout and grow cruel, angry spikes that grabbed on and never let go.

"Sure," Cee said. "Out into the storm."

JESSE

It took them three hours to outdrive the storm. Rocky slept in the back seat, yipping occasionally as she dreamed of life in and around Hillside. Jesse liked to think the dog was sad that they'd left, but when she woke she'd probably hardly even remember. She lived for the moment—food, chasing rabbits and rats and windblown leaves, a scritch from Jesse whenever she came close, then lounging in front of the fire when night fell. It was a dog's life, and one that Jesse had perhaps tried to make his own. Simpler, slower, more focused on the moment than what might have passed, or what was to come. Sometimes he thought he'd succeeded, but the feeling never lasted for long. Some mornings it was an hour or two after he woke before he thought of Ash, but those days were rare. Most mornings he woke knowing he'd dreamt of her, even if those dreams were already fading like teardrops in a storm.

The car's wipers stopped sweeping back and forth, and just a few drops speckled the glass. Vibrant autumn colours dawned across the eastern horizon, red skies providing a dramatic, late warning. The landscape was smoother than Jesse was used to, calmer, more wide open. He liked his world close and narrow, the distances shielded by hills and trees, the future hidden away within the embrace of a familiar rugged landscape. He could see further here, where rolling hills and long roads hinted at the flatter plains to the south and west. It felt more dangerous. The future was more open to view, and he didn't like what he could see. The horizons were fire and fury, and the skies bled. Jesse had always hated the sight of blood.

Karina stirred in the passenger seat, stretching and then snapping awake. She sat up and looked around, and Jesse glanced at her. He smiled. She didn't.

"How long have I been asleep?"

"Couple of hours."

"How far have we come? Where are we?"

Jesse glanced at the heads-up GPS display. "Just north of Baystown."

"That's north of the Desert."

"It is."

"So we've come a hundred and fifty miles, maybe more."

"Yep."

"Too slow. Too slow."

"I'm going as fast as I can. The roads have been bad, flooded, trees and branches down. We're just coming out of it now."

"So we can speed up."

"Yeah. Need a break soon though, rest stop up ahead. Let's hope it's open."

"We can't stop," Karina said. She hadn't woken rested. She was twitchy, wired.

"I need a piss," he said. "Rocky will want one too. And from what I remember you don't have the best bladder control ever. The number of times we had to stop by the roadside so you could dash behind a tree." He glanced across but she gave him no reaction at all. "And I need to recharge the car and top up the backup tank. And I dunno about you, but I could do with a coffee." She nodded then but didn't look at him.

"We can't stop for long."

"We won't. Fast as a helicopter." It was something Ash used to say when she was a little girl, and Jesse had no idea where it had come from. It just came out. The phrase hung between them, and for a few moments he saw his daughter as she'd been as a child, heard her laughter, smelled her hair. It startled him and brought a lump to his throat.

The heads-up told him that the rest stop was three miles ahead, and he counted down every silent minute it took them to get there. It emerged from the distance as a splash of lights set just off the roadside. Jesse breathed a sigh of relief, and as he slowed the car Rocky came awake in the back seat and started to whine. It seemed to Jesse that the stop had come just in time for them all.

"Something to eat?" he asked.

"I'll get it. You take Rocky to do her business."

He parked the Land Rover beside the gas pump and charging point, then switched off the engine. Karina was out of the door in seconds, heading across the forecourt towards the restrooms to one side of the main building. It was the first chance he'd had to really look at her since she'd turned up the previous night, without her glaring back at him. Her walk was familiar, jarring memories as powerfully as a smell or music, the scent of her hair, a song shared. Her hair was shorter than he remembered and roughly cut, peppered with grey in parts, the rest bleached by the sun. There was a tiredness to her movements, and he thought it was more than the fact she'd just woken up. Her years in the sun had bleached more than her hair. The Desert had changed her, eroding the texture of her quirks and uniqueness so that Karina became a more streamlined, focused version of herself. It wasn't just a lack of love he felt from her now, but a denuded sense of what had made her the woman he loved. Much of her had gone to dust and been swept away by unrelenting winds. Karina was simply Parent now, and Daughter was the sum of all her parts. That made Jesse sad. It also made him afraid.

In the chill dawn he walked Rocky to an area of scrubby grass behind the rest stop, where several old trucks rusted into the ground and other scrap was scattered amongst the stiff, spiky undergrowth. Rocky went off and did her business, then Jesse walked around the building to the restrooms. He was hoping he might meet Karina coming out, ask her to hold Rocky while he went to use the bathroom. But he could already see her through the shop window, browsing the shelves while a young woman sat behind the counter surfing her phone.

"Wait, girl," Jesse said to Rocky. The dog lay down against the wall.

By the time he'd finished in the restroom, Karina was back at the car, standing in front of the grille with coffee cups and paper bags of pastries resting on the hood.

"Want me to drive?" she asked.

"No, I'm good. Got a few hours in me yet."

"Let's get going then. Girl in there said the weather's clear south of here, no rain for weeks, so the roads will be safer."

Jesse realised she'd wanted to drive so they could move more quickly. It wasn't out of concern for him.

"Okay, but you stay awake and keep me company. We can talk."

"About what?" Karina asked.

Ash, he thought, but there would be plenty of time for that. He wanted words that might bring them closer together, so they could face the trip and whatever it might bring as a unit in the present, rather than two separate souls orbiting the ruins of the past.

"About you," Jesse said. "What you've been doing all these years."

"You're sure?" she asked.

"Sure I'm sure." He lifted his coffee from the hood and took a swig. Double shot. He smiled, remembering how he'd always despaired at how she liked her coffee so strong. She smiled too, and for a second he thought they might finally have shared a moment.

"Are you sure you can take it?" she asked. And as her smile grew he saw no real joy there, nothing that touched her eyes, and he knew she wasn't talking about the coffee at all.

ASH

The thunder echoes in my mind, ricocheting back and forth as if seeking escape but unable to find any way out. I open my mouth and mutter useless words, hoping the thunder will drift away and give them meaning. I look into the hot blurred sky in the vain hope that the constant reminders of the tumult might also drift away. It belongs there, but much of the time it seems to live in me.

The sound is constant, and though I feel sun on my skin and the sandy heat of the Desert, between blinks I am subsumed by rain and wind, a storm so powerful that it seeks to sweep away everything that I am. Once, I saw a house washed away when a river broke its banks, the flash-flood so powerful across dried, concrete-hard ground that nothing in its path stood a chance. I remember seeing the ground around the building crumbling, and turning the already muddy water that much darker, the house dipping to one side as the water took it; and though timber walls cracked and split and windows and doors smashed and popped open, the main structure maintained its integrity for minutes as the deluge carried it away. I wondered whether there were people left inside, and what they were thinking, and how they spent their final moments before four familiar walls gave way to violence and a watery demise.

In the tumult I feel like the occupants of that house in those final few seconds, suspended in the moment as the storm tugs and pulls at me, threatening to tear away everything I know and expose me to the true fury of what lies outside and beyond, the vast truth of things. It picks and grinds at my foundations. It erodes my will, seeking my soul. Even though I understand part of where and what I am without the tumult, I feel so little control.

The hand in mine is the greatest help I have ever found. And I don't understand why.

"I've been looking for you," Cee, the soup girl, says. We're on a bus. Kenworthy is behind us, and soon Cee says we'll get off and catch another bus, or find a car. When she says 'find' a car I think she means steal, but that's fine. I've stolen cars before, but have never been very good at it. Something tells me Cee will be.

"I'm sorry I took your bracelet."

"Yeah, that's why I've been tracking you. I really want it back." She looks at me and grins. The hand holding mine feels kind and caring, but behind the smile is a stranger who once gave me soup, and who just shot someone in the face.

My father was shot in the face when I was young. I remember touching my child's finger to the rugged, rough line of his reconstructed jaw and the thunder sings in again.

"You're Cee," I say. "I'm remembering you."

From the corner of my eye I see her staring at me. She's probably wondering who I really am, why I'm so vague and dislocated. There's so much I could tell her, but not here and now. I feel the danger stalking us, as if gunshots have replaced thunder.

"I'm… not always here," I say.

"You're further away than I remember, that's for sure."

It's hot on the bus, and we're sharing a double seat, even though there aren't many other people on board. It's even hotter outside.

Dead fields flit by. There's a car on its roof beside the road, and it's been there a long time. Its tyres are melted. I wonder how long has passed and how far we've come, and by Cee's manner I think it's been a while since Kenworthy. She seems calm.

I wish I was.

"It's not me. It's the tumult. It sweeps me along, and I've no control over where it takes me. But I'm almost ready to take control." I see her looking up at the clear blue sky. "When I'm in the eye… when it lets me go…" I trail off.

"Then what?"

The guitar case is propped between my legs, and I make sure the strap is wound tightly in my fist. I rebuilt the apparatus in the tumult. It was instinctive.

"Then there's something I need to do."

I feel Cee gripping my hand tighter, and it's like an indrawn breath.

"I saw that you're special. It's why I came after you. It's not been easy. But there are only so many women crossing the land with a guitar case on their back."

I squeeze her hand, holding tight. I don't really know Cee, but I sense kindness in her, as well as the terrifying coldness that has just saved me from those Hotbloods.

She killed them.

I don't know what they intended doing with me, but I'm sure it was nothing good.

She shot that one in the face.

I'm in the Desert. I've already seen so much death.

The storm growls, as if my thought of death makes it hungry. It grins with teeth of lightning and thunders around my heart.

"I'm glad you found me."

"Me too. So, tell me. Tell me everything."

The bus rumbles and rocks, and for the first time in years I put my trust in someone other than myself to keep me safe.

I remember the day my father tried to kill me.

I was up in the hills behind our small farm. He'd told me to stop, ease back, have a rest before trying again. I knew what he really wanted. He didn't think I should do it at all, and he was thinking of a way to destroy my apparatus, and still keep me as his daughter. It would never be that easy.

So I'd run, and now I was on my own.

I held my apparatus close to my chest. It was built on a plastic base, its components light and fragile. I felt the same way. My head was throbbing, my limbs sore, my forearms scarred, scabbed and infected from the many times I'd plugged myself in. My mother and father argued about that. She hated to see me hurting myself. He said I had to do it.

I was beyond that now. Because of the things I'd brought down along with the rain, and what they had done to our dog Teddy.

I walked faster, glancing back every few steps, telling myself it wasn't my fault. I hated being afraid of my father. I loved him and he scared me, and that was all wrong. He wanted me to stop because of something that had happened to *him* a long time ago, not because of what was happening to *me*. He told me he'd brought down things in his storm that had made people die. I hated that idea because my father was a caring, loving soul, and he'd never do anything to hurt anyone. I felt sorry for him, and my mother told me it haunted him day and night, and that he'd never used his apparatus since.

Yet he'd still helped me build my own device and guided me in its use. He told me he didn't want me trying it on my own. He wanted to coach me, and advise, and hopefully then I wouldn't make the same mistakes he'd made. He never realised how naive that idea was, and how dismissive of the hold our family talent had over us both.

The very first time I tried it had taken me to that other place I'd named Skunksville, because the air there stank, and my father had been shocked. *I've never smelled it*, he said. *Hardly even felt I was there.* I'd said no more, because I could smell the stench of that strange beach, feel the cool rain against my face, and if I stuck my tongue out it tasted like metal and cold meat. Even that first time it was almost as real to me as home.

I heard a whine, a soft bark, and I froze, looking around for the source of the sound. "Teddy?" I whispered, but of course it could not be Teddy.

Teddy running around, never still, sniffing out wonders in the dried, parched soil, and looking up startled as the first drops of rain pattered down across his back. Teddy celebrating the sudden downpour as much as me, as much as my father and, yes, even my mother, though I could see the way she looked at the blood running down my forearms being diluted by the rain, dripping to the ground, absorbed. The smell of fresh rain, so clean and pure and healthy. Teddy running circles around our yard so quickly that he kicked up mud to spatter across the barn door like nature's morse code. My delight as I looked up into skies that I mastered and controlled, just for those few moments. I was back from Skunksville to witness my success.

Rain pattering across my face and into my eyes, my mouth falling open and tongue protruding, and... it didn't taste quite right.

Wet thuds as other things splashed down.

Teddy's excited barking changing from delight to fear, or warning.

The snakes squirming in the mud around my dog. They were small. He yapped at them, snapped at them, but they were much faster and much, much more deadly.

Teddy lasted until the rains ceased and the ground started to steam beneath the unforgiving sun. Then he died, in pain and with the three of us trying to provide comfort where there was none to be had.

Not my fault, I thought. But deep inside I knew that it was. His terrible whines as he breathed his last would haunt me forever, yet I still wouldn't let my father dictate my future. He'd chosen to turn aside from the unique gift carried by his family's bloodline rather than attempt to tame and master it. I wasn't ready to do the same. The land was suffering too much for me to abandon it now, and I thought that on my own, given peace and calm, I would be able to correct the faults in my rainmaking. I would make that strange shoreline of Skunksville my own.

Pure thoughts, my father told me I needed. A clear mind. Tranquillity, to speak to the skies and hear their response. He inferred that his own thoughts were far from tranquil, his mind cluttered and angry.

Where did those snakes come from? I thought, but I walked on. They weren't the first creatures I'd brought down with my rains—during earlier attempts there had been ants, a few small spiders, and one memorable downfall of worms which had struggled to burrow into the cracked earth in pursuit of the feeble moisture it had already sucked in. They had died, many of them providing a meal for a flock of blackbirds that had appeared from out of nowhere.

I hurried on, looking for somewhere secret where I could hide the apparatus. I wouldn't try rainmaking again today, and probably not tomorrow, but soon I'd come up here again. Away from my father, and on my own at last. Perhaps that was all I needed to make it successful—to make rain free from his tension and anxiety.

"Ash!" My father was shockingly close. I ducked down, hugging the apparatus tight while being careful not to damage it. My arms still hurt from where the needles had been inserted just the day before.

Then I ran. Thanks to my mom, I knew the hills well. She loved hiking, and she'd brought me up here a hundred times or more, exploring the trails and tracks and a few places where old dwellings had started to crumble down into the land. More folks had lived here a decade before, but as the Great Drought consumed the place many of them left, and some died.

I followed the trails, and soon my dad's voice fell behind and began to fade away. My heart was hammering and I was afraid, but I wouldn't let that stop me. This was a defining moment in my life.

And even though it didn't go as planned, it still is a defining moment, because the terrible thing that happened next made me what I am today.

When I thought I was safe and had enough time, I veered off the trail and pushed my way through a spread of wild gorse until I reached an outcropping of rock. I ducked down beside it and waited for a while, calming, letting my breathing and beating heart settle. I needed to be at peace when I started. I'd decided to try again right away, not hide the apparatus. Prove him wrong. He would see the rain, see what I could do, and be okay with it.

I plugged myself into the apparatus and looked to the sky.

Sparks tingled across my skin, and their touch calmed the pain in my forearms. My blood flowed to, through, and from the apparatus, and I heard the soft clicking and creaking of the arcane device getting to work.

Something about this time felt different. Up to now I had always attached and initiated the apparatus beneath my dad's gaze, and he would always be close by to watch and guide me. This was my ninth time, and all eight times before had been with him. Perhaps that was why things had been going so wrong. They had gone wrong for *him*, so maybe his presence was making them fail for me as well.

As clouds gathered and the first drops of rain pattered down onto my upturned forehead, I closed my eyes and became lost.

The tug and rip of the needles from my arms brought me back to a terrible reality. Rain was pouring down, lightning flashed, and my dad stood before me, drenched and mad and with my apparatus held in one hand. His other hand was fisted around the wires, and the needles swung back and forth, my dripping blood adding to the deluge. I wanted to reach out and snatch it back from him, but I could hardly move. Blood poured from the wounds on my arms. He looked at me, looked at the blood, and right then I didn't know who he was or what he might do.

He dropped the apparatus and stomped it into the ground. For a moment it felt like he was stomping on me, the crackle of snapping plastic echoed in the crunch of bones. Water splashed, my device broke apart, and I thought I heard him shout out loud—or maybe it was a sob.

The rains lessened only a little, and rainbow colours manifested and faded again across the hillside. The peace I'd been feeling inside broke apart.

He came at me with a knife.

I held up my hands and fell back, winded with terror as he reached towards my face. The blade glimmered, flashed, and I felt it tug through my hair.

Something dropped to the ground beside me. A spider almost as big as my hand, its body punctured by the blade, hairs glimmering with a thousand diamond droplets. My father crushed it beneath his boot. I didn't even know if it was dangerous, but he assumed it was. He thought everything I did was dangerous, because he viewed me through his own failures.

He dropped the knife, knelt beside me, and lifted me up, nursing me in his arms. I felt sick, unsettled, once in rhythm with the elements and now ripped away. I was weakened, and when he brought a small syringe close to my right arm, I had no strength to resist.

"I'm sorry," he said, and he slid the needle into my arm where he'd ripped another out. I still don't know what he injected me with, but it changed me forever. I felt an acidic surge through my arm, and then further. I shook as a burst of heat pulsed through me like lightning flooding my veins. I jerked, spasmed, and he held me tight.

The storms I had externalised drew back in. They filled me with their violence and fury, and Skunksville screamed in pain, or rage. The weather across that landscape, over there, turned to chaos. And then Skunksville drew back as a great distance grew. It became a dream, a fading memory, and then nothing at all.

That was all I knew until a while later—days, I think, though I don't know how many—when I came to thirty miles away, on my own for the first time, and forever. I had run without knowing it, and when I realised what had happened, I ran some more. I never once considered going back.

Ever since then, the storm raging inside me—the tumult—has been my life. It's only moments like this, when I'm in the eye, that I really know who I am.

"Holy fuck," Cee says. She had let me speak, start to finish, without interrupting.

I laugh.

After a minute spent staring from the window, she says, "I believe every word."

"How can you?"

When she looks at me, I see someone open to strangeness and wonder. It's another reason I'm so glad that I found Cee, and she found and rescued me.

"You're not alone," she says. "I'm here."

"I don't even know you."

"Does that matter?"

I go to answer, but I'm not sure what the answer is.

"He can't hurt you anymore," Cee says. "You're a strange person, Ash, who says strange things. But I've been out here too long, been through too much, seen too much weird shit to be afraid."

I look out at the views. I'm here with Cee, my new friend, and everything that's happening to me is my choice.

"And I want to know," Cee says. "The rain. Your device. I knew you were special from the first moment we met, knew there was something odd and wonderful about you. And those fucking Hotbloods knew it, too. You *exude* it. I feel like I've been waiting all my life to find you, and now you're free to do whatever you want, because I'm here to look after you."

Maybe she's right. Maybe I'm more free here than I have ever been before. I rest my hand on the guitar case. Thinking of the thing I've built inside, I wonder if what I'm doing will divest me of that newfound freedom all over again.

"I think I'll soon be ready to try again," I say.

KARINA

The fire in her eyes kept me searching. I can still feel it sometimes, burning away inside me like a dying star. It swallowed most of what made me me. You'll find very little left, and I know you're thinking of looking.

Don't bother.

I've thought a lot over the years about what I saw when she ran. At the time I thought it was agony, because you'd injected her with your poison and she was burning up from the inside out. But they weren't her eyes. That wasn't her fire. I'd seen the heat of her own desires and ambitions—she only ever wanted to help—but this was different. This was uncontrollable.

It drove me to follow her, filled with dread, led by hope. From the moment I left you, I never looked back. Only forward, towards where Ash might still be. I saw her running down from Peter's Field, that place we used to picnic when she was young, and her arms were still bleeding, and she was wet from the final rains she'd brought down, and the blood. Her eyes also bled.

I pressed on the gas, because I wanted to reach her before she hit the highway. I was afraid she'd get there, put out her thumb and run from us forever. After what you'd done to her, she'd need me more than ever before. That's what I thought. It seems such an innocent hope now, that our tortured, mad girl would need her mother. I'm not so naive anymore. It's me who always needed her.

I locked eyes with her from maybe thirty metres away, and that's when the front wheel struck a rock and the steering wheel jumped in my hands, and the car slewed into the ditch.

I blacked out for a few seconds. Everything went away—the noise of the engine running high where the electric motor hadn't cut out, the smell of spilled coolant water, the taste of blood from where I'd slammed my nose against the wheel—and when it slowly faded back in, I was living in a different world. There was me before the crash, a mom and a wife, someone who loved you despite everything, someone who would die for the people she loved. And then there was me after the crash. The person I am now.

I grabbed what I could from the wrecked car—the gun from the glove box, a half empty bottle of water, my phone—and ran. Blood flowed down my face from my busted nose. My chest hurt, and I was afraid I'd cracked some ribs. They only stopped hurting a year later.

When I reached the highway there was no sign of Ash, other than a few speckles of blood in the dust on the hard shoulder. They looked like spotted oil. They ended beside a set of wheel tracks, and I imagined my girl, my whole world, bleeding in a stranger's car.

So I tucked the gun into the waistband of my jeans, covered it with my shirt, wiped blood from my face as well as I could, and stuck out my thumb.

I never once looked back, because our family was already broken long before then. There were fractures between us, and what you did widened them and made them permanent. I didn't want you with me looking for Ash. I was afraid of what more you might do, so you and the farm were already in my past. The urgent present was the heat glaring up at me from the road, the scent of softened asphalt, the taste of blood on my teeth.

The future was Ash.

I hitched to town and saw Jonny, and he told me about seeing her, bleeding and sick, fall into the river. From the beginning I wasn't sure I trusted him—he'd lied for Ash before, and he never quite caught my eye. But I spent a day looking for her along the riverbanks, and soon realised that was wasted time. She was already far gone. I've often wondered whether this was an exit strategy she'd prepared with Jonny, even before all that happened.

Three days later I'd gone further into the Desert, because I was pretty sure that was where Ash would have gone, if she was still alive. She always wanted to help. Bringing down rain was never about profit for her. I hitched to begin with, then halfway through the third day, in a little pissant town called Clayton Creek, a guy offered me a ride outside a gas station. I'd cleaned myself up by then, and we still had some cash in the bank, and you hadn't frozen the account. So I had new clothes, heavy walking boots and jeans, tough work shirt. Stuff for the trail, not for home. I was future proofing myself without really thinking about the future, I guess.

So this guy picked me up in his Prius, and I should have known, even back then. This was the fourth ride I'd had, and it's fucking ironic, 'cos the first guy was decent and kind, and he told me to watch out because one in four single guys on the road sees a single woman hitching and they think only one thing. Second ride was with two women, sisters who said they always travelled together, never alone, and they were always packing. Third ride was an old dude, Clinton, a lovely man who didn't stop talking and took me home for dinner with his wife and five kids. "Had eight once," he told me. I guess I'd have been around the age of his oldest, who died in one of the first big tornado seasons back in '32.

So I got into the fourth guy's car. His name was Duke, and as we cruised down a straight highway I held the phone out and said I was looking for my daughter, and his hand sleazed across and grabbed the top of my thigh.

I froze, even though part of me had been expecting it. He was the one in four.

We were doing fifty, maybe sixty miles an hour, straight wide highway, a few other cars and trucks around, and I didn't think about what I did next. I slammed the edge of the phone back into his face and pulled my gun and pushed it against his belly.

It felt good. I was squeezing that trigger, not scared, but fucking *furious*. I reckon I had four pounds of pressure on a five-pound trigger, and if we'd gone over a bump in the road that fuck Duke would've had a bullet in his gut. But suddenly Duke was a careful and responsible driver. He cruised to a stop on the hard shoulder, and when I told him to get out he did it like a well-trained dog.

I slid across into the driver's seat and told him to kneel by the roadside, still aiming the gun at his belly. He pissed himself. Glad he waited 'til he was out of the car.

I drove that Prius for the rest of the day, another hundred miles, stopping in towns and rest stops to show Ash's picture around. Then another day later—or two, or three, I've sorta lost track—someone in a convenience store claimed they might have seen her. She wasn't sure, but she thought Ash was one of the young people working a local beet farmer's fields and irrigation systems. That was enough for me.

I followed the woman's directions, and even as I approached the farm I knew it was a bad place. No matter how many times you hear about the Way Farms, the shock of seeing one for the first time really hits home.

The main farm building wasn't palatial, but it was far from a ruin. There were two young women exercising on mats on the dead lawn beside the house. The most bizarre sight. Across the yard, in front of the several big barns dotted around the main farm compound, Way workers were unloading beets from handcarts and stacking them in wooden crates inside the barns. Not one of them could have been older than their mid-twenties, most much younger. These were kids who should have been in school or college but who had fallen through the cracks. They stop, work for a few days, move on. I guess hope stays alive in some of them.

I couldn't see Ash anywhere, and as I approached and opened my phone to show her photo, the farm owner arrived on a quad bike.

I didn't like him from the first moment I saw him. He offered to let me charge the Prius while we talked, asked if I needed a drink of water, and he was genuinely curious about why I was there. I don't think he believed he had anything to hide—he wasn't worried, or suspicious of me. And that's why I disliked him. To his left, two attractive women worked out close to what was obviously the farmer's home. To his right, a dozen casual labourers worked hard to make him a profit. One of the young men had a horrible rash on his face. Flies buzzed around him. One of the women was shaking with fever as she stacked beets, her clothing stuck to her body by sweat.

"My daughter," I said, and I showed him the photo.

"Don't know her," he said. He hadn't even glanced at the picture.

"Mind if I look around?"

He pushed his hat back on his head. The two exercising women had stopped to watch.

"Well, it's a busy time on the farm," he said.

"Looks like they could do with a five-minute break." The Way workers were still unloading, but they'd slowed a little, glancing across the parched yard at my exchange with the farmer.

"They break at one for lunch," he said. "It's still in the a.m. Now, you're welcome to sit in your car while it charges, and maybe show your picture around when they stop for lunch. That's a little over an hour."

I held up the phone again, higher, and waited that way until he looked at it properly.

"She's got your eyes."

"So have you seen her?"

"Don't think so."

"Maybe your daughters have?"

He smiled, but there was a change about him. It was a tired smile, one that said, *I've had enough of this.*

"They're not my daughters," he said. He looked at the photo again. "Maybe she'd be not my daughter, too. If I'd seen her. But I haven't."

"I'm going to ask them." I nodded at the workers.

"I'm telling you—"

I lifted my shirt and put my hand on the gun in my belt.

Everything paused. Even the Way workers loading the beets. Even the two not-daughters raising drinks to their lips. The only movement was my thumping heart, and I was the centre of everything.

"Five minutes of their time," I said.

He blinked slowly, then smiled. "I'll take it from their lunch break. But I'm telling you lady, your daughter isn't here."

I backed away from him towards the Way workers. I held up my phone without looking away from the farmer, but he'd already lost interest. He fired up his quad bike and disappeared along a trail between fields in a cloud of dust.

"Have any of you seen my daughter?" I asked.

A few of the workers shuffled closer to look. I could smell sweat and desperation. I think some of it was my own.

None of them had seen Ash, and I believed them because they had no reason to lie. I wanted to say more, but I also wanted to be gone. If she wasn't there then she was somewhere else, and the longer I remained where she wasn't, the less chance I'd have of finding where she was.

I walked back to the car. The tension in the farmyard had abated, drifting away like the slowly wafting cloud of dust that followed the quad bike. The two women were performing yoga on the mats again, and behind me I heard the gentle thud of beets being unloaded from the handcarts. It was as if everyone on the farm had already forgotten about me.

I skidded a fast circle in the farmyard, accelerating away along the trail that led to the highway, throwing up a cloud of dust that obscured everything in the rear-view mirror.

That was just the first week after I went looking for her. I've been searching ever since, and I've seen some things. In Finnistown, I found a small place where they prayed to a dead wolf stuffed with the corpses of three stillborn babies. In a rest stop south of Wichita, I saw a mother set fire to her car and lock herself inside with her two children. In Keeper's Canyon, I found a preacher who fed his congregation spoonfuls of his blood, telling them it would help them survive the Desert because his was the blood of Christ. On a farm in Wisconsin, I met a man digging holes in search of water that had long since dried away, and we fucked under the stars, out in the open, in the Desert.

You can't judge me.

I killed a man in Sableton. He told me he'd seen Ash, and he led me out to a commune where he said she was building her own home. He claimed it was a place where everyone was preparing for the future with a bright eye. I put a bullet in his throat when he tried to assault me, left him to die in the company of others like him. There was not one bright eye among them.

Don't you dare judge me. Not out loud, and not quietly, to yourself, because you don't know me anymore. You stopped knowing me the day I went looking for Ash and you settled into the wretched comfort of believing she was dead. Now I know for sure that she's alive, I've brought you out into the world to help me find her.

You deserve everything that's yet to come.

ASH

Cee might be the strangest person I've ever known, but over the short period we've been together, I've grown to trust her. I analysed this trust as best I could, because I am always, always cautious around other people. When I'm in the eye, at least. When the tumult falls, that caution is lost to the wind, like when the Hotbloods took me. My memories of that time are like one frame in fifty from an old movie—bizarre, banal, troubling, and violent. I don't like to think that I'm already dependent on Cee, nor the other way around. Our relationship is too new. There's no lust in my gut or fear in my heart. There is no duty or need. There's only a strange, unfamiliar affection, as if two pieces have come together and clicked to make one. That link and connection is holding me in the eye, firmer and more grounded than I have been for as long as I can remember.

Which is why I feel that now is the time to try rainmaking again.

"You level me," I say. I startle Cee from some brief reverie and she glances at me, the corner of her mouth lifting. "You hold me in the eye. You're my anchor in the storm. That's why I'm going to try."

She glances down at the guitar case. "Only if you're sure. You've got to be ready. It has to be safe, for you." Cee's voice is smooth, her British accent all curved edges and soft pronunciation.

We're sitting behind a hotel on the edge of a small town called Abbey Springs. The hotel looks like it's been closed for years, but there are several handwritten signs pointing travellers from the highway to a small area of scattered furniture and a wooden shack selling water and food. The shack was once a hut marking the beginning of the hotel's nine-hole golf course, and there's still an eighteen-foot-tall timber golfer standing beside the shack, like some strange modern-day totem to waste. The golfer has several closely spaced bullet holes in his faded timber head, and his torso is peppered with buckshot. He was once brightly painted, but now he's gone back in time to monochrome.

The golf course beyond the shack is a landscaped wasteland with one sad, forgotten flag in the middle distance.

I pick up my glass of water and swill it around, holding it up to the sun. Bits swirl and dance, suspended in the brownish solution. It might have looked better if they served it in opaque containers, but it would still taste of dust.

"I like Abbey Springs," I say. We arrived the previous day and spent an hour walking around the town, before finding our way to the abandoned hotel. Lots of travellers had done so before us, but we managed to find a room that wasn't too filthy, and we dragged some seat cushions up from the forgotten dining room to make a comfortable bed. During the night we heard wolves in the distance and the sounds of lovemaking echoing along empty corridors. We slept close, arms touching. I fell asleep to the scent of gun oil. I wonder if Cee always sleeps with her gun close to one hand, but I'm not yet ready to ask. It doesn't seem fair, knowing some of what she's been through.

"I like it too."

"I think this is the right place," I say. "It would welcome my help." I pick up the guitar case from beside my chair, lay it across my knees, and open it wide.

Cee looks startled, glancing around in case anyone is taking a special interest. I laugh. They won't, not yet, not until they see what this thing can do. What *I* can do.

"Here?"

"Not here." I look down at the finished apparatus. It's beautiful, an integral and powerful part of me. It's like looking at myself opened-up, viewing my own insides and how I'm put together. The apparatus is so much more than a sum of its parts. I touch the individual pieces, one by one, and with each touch I remember where I found them, not only those I discovered in the eye but also the components that called to me within the tumult. I was always destined to find them and build this. I'm no slave to destiny, nor a fool to fate, but sitting here with Cee, the apparatus open on my lap, feels more right than anything I've ever done.

"Somewhere close," I say. "Sometime soon."

Cee looks up at the sky. It's blue, stark, scorched pale by the sun. The woman selling water from the shack told us there's been no rain in Abbey Springs for over seventeen months. This is the petrified heart of the Desert, and on the way into town we saw where this Desert had burned. It was a wonder the whole place hadn't gone up.

"Out there," I say, smiling. "At the Burn."

Cee nods, seeing sense in my choice. I'll bring down rain on the part of town it might have saved.

The various components that go to make up my new apparatus are warming from their exposure to the unrelenting sun. It's a much simpler, more adult apparatus than the one my father crushed into the ground. That had been the construct of a child, overcomplicated and clumsy, too open to breakages and malfunctions. As a child I'd viewed what I carried in my blood as confusing and mysterious, and something that necessitated a complex device to channel. Now, I've found my way to building this new, simpler apparatus, and it looks beautiful. The fixings are more sure, and the thought that went into building it was far, far more certain. That younger apparatus had been built out of expectation, because it was what I was meant to do. This one is constructed from desire.

Cee is confused by it because she doesn't understand how I can do what I do simply by plugging myself into this machine of random parts. But I am also a part of the apparatus; its battery, its drive, and its fuel.

I hear it clicking and ticking as it expands in the heat.

I whisper back.

It's past midday when we reach the western part of town. It's hot enough to burn unprotected skin in a few minutes, cook food on bare concrete or the metal of abandoned vehicles, and I feel myself wilting like a dying flower. But inside I'm more alive than I've been for some time. The eye is firm and solid around me, so established that the walls of tumult that mark its edges feel too far away to recall. Cee and I are wearing wide-brimmed hats and our exposed limbs are coated in a layer of barrier cream she bought from the town's drugstore. It's thick and gloopy and years out of date, and it doesn't soak into our skin, but it'll keep us safe for a while.

Most other people have good sense and have found cover. Instead, we've found the Burn.

From comments around town, I've gleaned the basics of what happened to Abbey Springs the previous summer. It's the same sad story related again and again all across the Desert, and in other drought zones around our poor planet. Abbey Springs seems to have got off more lightly than some.

The fire raged across the Desert after starting in scrubland. There are a thousand ways for such a blaze to begin: sun shining through a shard of broken glass onto a scatter of dried plants; sparks from a passing vehicle; a clumsily discarded cigarette butt. Sometimes, it's intentional. On a landscape fried dry by terrible drought and baked day after day by a merciless sun, fire was a demon that stalked from place to place, searching for where to settle its blazing roots.

The residents of Abbey Springs saw the smoke and dust, and as the conflagration approached they saw the flames as well, a grinning smile of fire closing on the town's western extremes. They were prepared for such an event, with wide streets designed to slow or halt a fire's spread. There was precious little water to fight the flames, so when they recognised the size and fury of the bush fire the town set about bulldozing buildings to provide even larger firebreaks.

It still took out a quarter of the town over the space of a day and night. Seven farms beyond the town limits went first, along with a dozen farmers and all their remaining heads of cattle. Two hundred homes, stores, several manufacturing units, and the town's small school were also destroyed, and five townsfolk lost their lives fighting the firestorm.

I heard pride in the voices of those who told us snippets of their tale, because they had prevented the whole town from burning to the ground. They call the ruins 'the Burn', and they provide frightening evidence of the dangers faced by anyone living in the Desert that so much of America has become.

The western edge of town is now a barren area scattered with the remains of burned buildings and melted asphalt. The structures on one side of the street have facades scorched by the conflagration. Organic spreads of melted glass reflect the day in soot-tinged monochrome. Timber cladding is warped and discoloured, doors are cracked, roof shingles blown, exposed wooden support posts split and splintered. What I can see inside these buildings, through broken windows and doors, suggests that the interiors were also touched by fire. Beyond, the Burn is a wasteland. The fire came last summer, but the weather since has brought little to smooth the memory of its touch. There has been no rain to wash away the soot, and dry winds have drifted ash against tumbled walls. Charred trees stand in skeletal testament to the fury of the fires, most branches burnt to fragile ash, leaving only scared trunks pointing to the skies. No buildings remain standing. Most construction in the town is timber, and here and there in the Burn a single brick wall or chimney breast is all that remains of a once-large building, the masonry cracked and powdered from the heat. Several metal doors still stand in solitary frames, warped security between nothing and nowhere. Where the structure has burnt down to blackened remains, the twisted wreckage of the building's skeleton are left behind: metal furniture, deformed cookers and other kitchen goods, cracked toilet pans, the exploded screens of TV units, all of them crushed and dead. Everything is black and grey, although here and there rust has taken hold of the exposed metals, even in the baking sun and arid atmosphere of the Desert. It gives a colour palette of startling oranges to the desolate scene.

There is one large splash of colour. Many of the ruined buildings had basements, and most of them are filled with the charred detritus of the structures that once stood above them. One basement, though, has a wide wall facing the road, and someone has taken time to paint a mural. It's a woman's face, expertly wrought. Her eyes, crying tears of soot, stare accusingly into mine, and her mouth is half open in an attempt to draw breath against the flames that destroyed this place, and against the heat and polluted air that seek to finish what those flames began. I look across the road and into her eyes as if she is someone real, and perhaps she is. Perhaps she is everyone in Abbey Springs and beyond.

"Spooky," Cee says.

"I think it's beautiful." I start across the road, kicking through debris lightened and lessened by fire. Cee follows me as I know she always will, even after knowing her for only a few days. She followed me across the Desert and found me again, and she will follow me into the Burn, until I find somewhere suitable to kneel and open the guitar case and attach myself to the apparatus, and bring rain to wash away the painted woman's tears.

CEE

Ash looked confident and in control. Calm as she found a concrete slab to kneel on, measured as she set the apparatus down before her, slow and methodical as she sterilised thin needles and pushed them into her arms. Cee felt a brief pang at this, but only fleeting, and it was a memory that tasted stale and raw.

Ash's needs, she knew, were nowhere so base and basic as her own had once been.

Cee stood some distance from Ash, giving her space and peace. She hadn't asked for it, but Cee sensed it was the right thing to do. She needed no distractions. Out here in the Burn, in the remains of a place that had once been home to many but was now a wasteland, silence hung heavy, like a drape of heat and stillness. Cee held her breath.

She had been holding her breath for a long time, since leaving Maxwell three years before and heading into the Desert, forever staying one step ahead of the wraith of addiction and dependency stalking just a few steps behind her. Always afraid that the strings would reattach themselves to her arms, she had been searching for something new, fresh, and all-encompassing. Cee had been looking for her new addiction.

In the Desert, she had found so much to distract. She had killed six people, including the four Hotbloods who'd taken

Ash. The first was a woman who called herself Princess, who led a small caravan of RVs and trucks across the Desert. She'd been trading in young kids. Cee didn't realise until the middle of the first night she spent camped with them, when a car pulled up and four men got out. She'd seen something of the truth in their eyes. She'd heard more of the truth in the cries coming from the RVs, and when she confronted Princess she laughed and pulled a knife and asked Cee what the hell she expected of this world.

As if pain and suffering was inevitable. As if the only route to take in life was the way of wretchedness, adding more suffering and heartache to an already-tortured world.

Cee had fought with her, taken that knife, and stuck it into Princess's throat. The dying woman had still been hacking blood when a caravan door opened and a naked, sweating man asked her what the fuck the noise was.

Cee didn't remember much more about that night. Only the warm blood covering her, turning her into a demon that scared the men so much they fled. It scared the kids too, and they'd run into the night, crying and screaming at the things they had seen, scarred forever.

Princess was the first, but she had not broken Cee's held breath, nor stalled her flight ahead of the memory of the addiction.

The second was a man who had offered her drugs. They'd agreed to share a cheap motel room, and when he took out the Ice paraphernalia and prepared to shoot up, she'd told him no.

If he'd left it at that she would have just walked away. But he was an addict, his blood already cold, and he came across the bed at her with a loaded syringe. She met him with the knife that had finished Princess. He tried to squirm away from her as she held the knife stuck in his chest, following him on her knees to make sure. His eyes were wide and glassy from the Ice. She didn't understand how she'd not seen it before.

When the first splashes of rain pattered down around Ash, Cee felt her held breath beginning to ease. She closed her eyes and turned her face to the sky; everything she had been through those past three years flitted through her mind's eye, casting shadows and plays of light like sunlight through a moving tree canopy. They were memories both bad and good, but mostly indifferent. Her forearms no longer itched. Her mind was clear, her conscience settled. As the first drops of Ash's new rain splashed on her forehead and cheeks and her closed eyelids—as if seeking entry and encouraging her to watch—Cee gasped in a huge, fresh breath and knew that this was the beginning of her future.

Dandelion had been more right than she could have possibly known. Ash *was* special.

She's doing it! Cee thought. *She's actually doing it, and everything she told me was true.*

Cee would help and protect her with every breath she had, with the bloodied knife in her right pocket, the blooded gun in her left. This wasn't just rain coming down from clouds coalescing from a clear blue sky. This was hope and a promise for the future, and everything Cee had been waiting for.

She opened her eyes and breathed deeply, drawing in the fresh taint of new rain from sunburned air. And there she was, Ash, arms spread wide as if to gather in all the water she was bringing down.

Cee's new addiction.

The rain was warm but it smelled fresh and clean, as if it fell from purer skies. Cee remembered a rainstorm a year before, its greasy feel like rank fuel falling from a plane. It had started burning her exposed skin, the smell singeing the insides of her nostrils, stinging her eyes. Others around her had sought shelter after the initial delight at rain falling for the first time in months, and one woman crouched with her hands on her knees, puking in the middle of the street. The flash floods that flowed down concrete-hard streambeds to the south of the town swept away cars and people, and left behind a toxic sludge that drowned cattle and stray animals for the following three days. It was poisoned rain, returning to earth the toxic chemicals pumped into the skies from there and further afield over many decades. She'd heard of these instances of acid rain, a rare but deadly confluence of meteorological factors and the human stain. That was the first time she'd witnessed it for herself.

Ash's rain washed away those memories, freshening the images in her mind and giving a purity to the fire-blackened surroundings. She breathed in beauty, tasted water like none she had ever tasted before, and even the sound of raindrops hitting the ground seemed celebratory. It was as if the rains Ash now conjured from fleeting skeins of new clouds fell from somewhere in the deep, distant past, before humanity started imprinting its toxicity on the world. These raindrops might have been falling for three hundred years, from a height and distance beyond Cee's understanding.

She started to cry, and for the first time her tears felt as pure as the rain.

"Amazing!" Cee shouted, and Ash glanced across at her, startled. Cee froze, worried that she'd disturbed Ash. She looked up, waiting for the rain to stop, but it continued falling, if anything heavier than before. Ash smiled and looked up again, eyes closed and arms spread wide to welcome the downpour.

She forgot I was here, but she was happy when she remembered, Cee thought. She ran across the Burn, splashing through dirty

puddles, careful not to trip over scattered debris. She circled Ash,
trying to ascertain the limits of the rainfall. Back at the wide road
dividing the Burn from the rest of Abbey Springs, the ground
only showed a spatter of drops. Deeper into the Burn, closer to
where the edge of town had once stood, there was no rain at all.
She skipped from concrete slab to road to bare ground, kicking
through soggy and sloppy debris, and felt it splashing up her
shins, a gloopy mess that stuck to her like glue. This was localised
to Ash. Looking up, Cee saw the hazy light grey clouds forming
above her new friend and the Burn, and there was no real air
movement to disperse them. It was amazing. It was impossible.
It was beautiful.

Cee didn't know how this was happening, or where this fresh,
welcome rain fell from. That didn't matter right now. All that
mattered was the grin on her friend's face.

She was still crying, and she wished that her friend Maxwell
could see her now. He'd saved her, and she liked to think it had
all been for this.

Cee wiped her hands across her face and back through her
short hair. It felt like a cleanse. She did it again, and again, and
each time her hair felt cleaner, her face less scarred and marked
by the years in the Desert. She hoped the rain would never stop.

"Don't stop!" she shouted, and Ash grinned at her. The smile
was open and warm and unselfconscious, an expression of pure
joy, not marred nor tempered by doubts.

This is what I was saved for, Cee thought, *but this is what Ash
was born for.*

"Don't stop!" she shouted again. Water flowed across bare
concrete slabs, washing away ash and soot. It gurgled in growing
streams along shallow ditches. It pinged off a metal door still
standing upright in a half-tumbled wall to her left, and played

jazz on a tangle of blackened metal framework. Cee rubbed her hair again, and each time her fingers seemed to pass through easier, as if this clear clean water—

—from somewhere else—

—was washing away years of accumulated dirt, dread, and dust from the Desert.

She ran again, leaping from a rise of six concrete steps and splashing down in a puddle in what was once someone's backyard. It took her back many years to when she was a little girl splashing in puddles in the village where she grew up, and the pure unalloyed joy was the same. She jumped and did it again, and again, and each time the dirty brown water splashing up her bare legs left streaks of sticky wet mess on her shins. But it felt cleaner.

She ran back up the steps and onto the concrete slab, arms outstretched and spinning slowly around, face turned to the sky. She opened her mouth and stuck out her tongue, and the rain didn't taste like here and now. It tasted of something and somewhere better. She started dancing, pulled her T-shirt up over her head, tugged down her shorts and underwear, and stood naked in the rain. It was glorious. She wiped her hands down across her stomach and legs, washing away dirt and filth and years of desperation and despair. The water sloughing from her body and mixing with that on the ground looked red with the spilled blood of those she'd killed, carrying away the subconscious dregs of guilt she'd always carried. It was brown with the uncut drugs she used to buy and put into her body however she could—up her nose, down her throat, into her veins. It was black from years of memories. She wiped again and again, bathing in the downpour and stomping on her shed clothing, swilling the material around with her feet to cleanse them as well. The feeling of fresh rainwater falling onto her body was freeing, cooling, calming. She revelled in the sense of freedom and freshening, and even when she saw the first townsfolk emerging from between charred buildings, she did not feel embarrassed. Some of them glanced at her, and some did not. But even those who looked did not look for long.

They all looked up to the sky, from where impossible rain was falling. And then some of them looked at Ash, still alone where she knelt on the concrete slab, because even though nobody knew what was happening here, Ash was so obviously the centre of things. She was the origin of the rain and its locus, and the people who now walked out into the Burn—six of them, then ten, then twenty, adults and kids alike—all seemed to understand that.

A middle-aged man on his own approached Cee, walking a pathway between two destroyed buildings. The rain plastered the hair to his balding scalp and made his T-shirt and shorts dark and heavy, but it could not wash away his shocked smile. He looked her up and down briefly, then turn his face to the sky, then he stared to where Ash knelt thirty metres away.

When he looked at Cee again he barely seemed to notice her nakedness. "You two came in together yesterday."

"We did."

"She your sister?"

"Friend," Cee said. "She's my good friend."

"Rainmaker," the man said, and that single word was loaded with knowledge and history.

"Yeah," Cee said. "I guess she is."

"I thought they were all gone." He looked at Cee again, sticking his tongue out to taste the rain.

"She thought so, too."

"I saw one once," the man said as he walked away, climbing onto a fallen wall, standing and staring at Ash with his tongue out to taste the rain.

Some people kept in small, huddled groups, families or friends together to experience the unexpected, unexplained downpour. A few dashed around trying to collect rain in containers. Several children ran like joyous lambs, climbing piles of debris, splashing in muddy puddles shouting and laughing. Others became focused on Ash in the centre of the storm, and Cee saw a few of them holding up their phones as they filmed the event. A woman around her age with long braided hair, and a scatter of tattoos down her neck and across one shoulder, panned her phone back and forth across the Burn. She settled on Ash for a moment, then caught sight of Cee and shifted her focus to her. Beneath the gaze of strangers Cee had felt unabashed at her nakedness. It was celebratory, revelling in the life-affirming touch of unexpected rain. But in the glare of a stranger's phone camera she felt suddenly vulnerable and exposed. She pressed an arm across her chest and her other hand covered her crotch, but the young woman did not avert her gaze. Cee turned her back on the camera and searched for her discarded clothing, finding her shorts in a soaked pile and her T-shirt caught in a tangle of rusted metal. She dressed, pulling on the soaked clothing, and when she turned back to the woman, she was stepping slowly across the Burn's uneven, ruined landscape towards Ash.

Cee felt a rush of concern for her friend. Ash seemed unaware of the townsfolk around her and scattered across the rain-soaked Burn, her face still upturned, arms resting on her knees as she knelt before her apparatus. Cee had been exposed in her innocent nakedness, but Ash was so much more vulnerable.

She dashed across to Ash, splashing through puddles, tripping on a ridge of concrete hidden beneath the splashing surface water. She went down on her hands and knees, grazing her knees and skinning her palms. She wondered what dirt and germs might infect her from the filthy mud. She wondered also what might be in the rain. It smelled and tasted pure and fresh, but where did it come from?

Just where the actual fuck?

Cee stood and made her way to Ash, more carefully this time. She stepped in front of the woman's phone and faced her, trying to smile but blinking as water washed stinging sweat into her eyes.

"Please stop," she said.

"Are you kidding?"

"Please. Leave her."

"After this? Are you fucking crazy?"

You don't know the half of it, Cee thought. She felt the bulge of the gun in her soaked shorts pocket, the shape of the folded knife.

"She isn't doing this for—"

"She's making it fucking *rain!*" the woman said. The tattoos on her neck and shoulder seemed to flex and squirm in the rain hammering down across them, as if they too were dancing in delight. Others were. Men and women, kids, all reacting to the deluge in versions of joy and disbelief, and did Cee really have a right to ask them to stop, divert their attention from this amazing, miraculous young woman? She reached for the phone, but the tattooed woman stepped back and to the side, continuing to walk crablike as she circled Ash so that she could zoom in on her face, the needles in her arms, and the strange apparatus she was plugged into.

Sparks of light spat from the needles. Rain striking the apparatus turned to steam. Blood washed from where the needles entered her arms, giving a pinkish hue to her pale skin.

Cee knelt by her friend's side. The noise of the downpour was so loud now that Cee could no longer hear the excited banter from the townsfolk who had come to see. Rain fell so heavy that it drew shimmering curtains across their surroundings. *Maybe this is what being in the eye feels like for her all the time*, Cee thought, because the only peace was her and Ash close enough to touch.

She reached out and laid her hand on Ash's upper arm, and the Rainmaker opened her eyes.

She was there and not there at all, and Cee saw something in her eyes that she had once seen in her own, each time she passed a store window or looked in a mirror.

A hunger. A need. An addiction.

"Ash, stop," she said, and for a few moments Ash didn't see her, didn't seem to know she was there. Her mouth hung open, jaw slack, skin pale and smooth and greasy beneath the rain. Water flowed into her eyes, and she did not blink or wince as her vision was blurred. It was like looking into the eyes of a corpse, and Cee grasped Ash's upper arms, ready to throw her to the ground and give her mouth to mouth, heart massage, anything to bring her back.

Ash grinned, and it brought her face to life.

"It's beautiful!" she said. "It's all so beautiful!"

"Ash, you've done it, but you have to stop now."

"Stop?"

Cee looked up at the woman still filming them, and the other people circling the scene. She and Ash were the focus, the centre of things. The eye of this storm.

"It's too much," Cee said into her ear. Blood was leaking more freely from where the needles entered Ash's forearms, the water on her arms flowing red. Around them, a spatter of heavy raindrops also turned red. Cee froze, then looked up, squinting, into the deluge. She tasted the unmistakeable tang of blood as it ran into her mouth.

What the fuck?

"Ash, it's taking too much from you," she said, crouching and grasping her friend tight. This was beyond her, but she understood enough to know that. *It was taking too much!* She reached for the needles and trailing wires, but Ash shrank away.

"No!" she shouted. "You don't understand this! You don't get to touch!"

"I'm thinking of *you*!" Cee said. Ash was fully back with her, but her eyes were still wide, pupils dilated and empty with that ravenous need that Cee recognised so well.

Rosettes of blood splashed down with the rain, dispersing in puddles, carried with the flow. Cee sensed the mood in the townsfolk gathered across the Burn changing, from one of celebration to disquiet. People drew together. Others moved away, hurrying back towards the undamaged town where the rains had yet to touch. Some of them saw or sensed blood, perhaps, but it was also the sheer volume of the downpour that troubled them. Everyone in the Desert feared flash floods when rains eventually came.

Water flowed black from sludgy ash and red with blood, bubbling and roaring from concrete slabs in dark filthy waterfalls.

The sky's bleeding. Blood in the rain, from somewhere else.

Cee saw an old woman slip and fall onto her back, swept down into a fast-flowing stream, arms held up and out as her head went beneath the surface. A man jumped in after her, slipping but managing to keep his feet as he grabbed her arm and pulled her to the edge.

"Ash!" Cee shouted. "I'm going to stop it if you don't. It's too much. And you're *bleeding*!"

Ash looked down at her arms, now streaming blood. Silver-blue sparks danced around the needles and along the wires connecting them to the apparatus. Steam rose from its components, and a couple of the metal braces and screws glowed red, water and blood hissing and bubbling when it touched.

Cee went for the needles in her friend's arms.

Behind her, from somewhere across the Burn, hidden behind curtains of torrential rain, someone screamed.

Something splashed in the water close to Cee's left foot. It was a toad, fat and green, and it struggled to its feet and hopped away.

Cee froze. *What?*

Other shapes fell. Two, four, then a shower of things that should not be. A small purple snake like Cee had never seen before, squirming and disappearing beneath the violent water. A fish as large as her hand with spines sprouting between its dorsal fins, needle teeth in its gaping mouth. A bird of paradise, dead when it hit the ground. A spider as big as any she had ever seen, black with a bright yellow splotch on its back in the shape of a butterfly. It actually shook rain from its hairy legs after it landed, then scampered towards the fallen bird and clasped itself around the creature's chest.

"Ash—what the fucking fuck?" Cee gasped.

The woman was still filming, mouth open and phone almost forgotten. A small creature hit her shoulder and bounced into the water. She aimed the phone at it, crouching, but it was already beneath the surface. Something larger hit the woman on the back of the neck and she screamed, waving her free hand behind her to brush it away.

Cee didn't want to see what it was. She grasped Ash's left forearm, turned it upward, and gripped the needle between thumb and forefinger. It was scorching hot but she kept hold.

Ash cried out a long, low groan that sent a chill through Cee as she pulled the needle out.

Blood gushed from Ash's arm, merging with the rain, and Cee worried that she'd torn the artery wall by wrenching the needle out. Ash fell onto her back, tugging the apparatus with her where it was still plugged into her right arm.

Cee crouched over her fallen friend, and a pulse of power thrummed into her, a heavy thud hammering through her body from where she still gripped the blood-slick needle, wire trailing to the apparatus. It was electric shock except slower, somehow more deliberate. It was like nails scraping hard up along her arm from fingers to armpit, except inside too, delving along nerves and through flesh, grinding across her bones. She stood shaking, staring at Ash and trying to move, staring, but seeing something else in flashes, bursts of bright light in the hazy wet darkness.

A landscape like none she had ever seen before. Boiling red clouds. An ocean of thick water. Drifting veils of mist. There were hints of these and ideas of other, sharper features, but the flashes were so brief that they were more suggestion. With each pulse of energy pushed through her body she became more aware of this place, as if repeated exposure was imprinting it on her consciousness.

Let go, a voice said, and she wasn't sure what it meant. Between flashes she saw nothing, only a glimmering darkness as if she was underwater.

Let go.

She was worried that if she let go she would be cast adrift.

You have to let go.

Cee felt a tug on her hand, and then she dropped to her knees, splashing down in warm water as the shocking reality of the Burn hit home once more. She gasped and drew in rain, coughing and spluttering.

"Cee," Ash said, her voice weak. She had pulled the needle from her own right arm and tugged the other needle from Cee's grip, and now she bled over her apparatus. The blood merged with water, cooling glowing parts. The wires trailed in the water.

"Okay," Cee said. "It's okay." She looked around, trying to shake the feeling that she'd been gone from this place for days, not mere seconds. The woman with the phone was crouched twenty metres away, filming something that slapped and flipped in a confused tangle of metal. A shape swooped through the air, passing with a low, shrill call and leaving rain spinning in its wake.

"What the fuck's happening?" Cee asked. "You said you had control, that this wouldn't—"

"We should go," Ash said. "Help me." She started folding away the apparatus.

"Leave it, we can—"

"*No!*" Ash's shout was loud, bursting through the storm like lightning.

"Okay," Cee said. "Let me help." But she didn't help. She stood close while Ash folded and locked away her apparatus. She was afraid to touch those wires again, afraid to feel that thud through her body and experience that fleeting, thundering flash.

Within that flash, somewhere in the strange landscape that had been constructed in her mind's eye by a succession of brief glimpses, like a flip-book behind her eyes, she had felt something growing aware of her being there. Something watching.

She shivered in the warm rain, retching as she smelled and tasted blood. When she held out one hand the drops hitting her palm were clear, clear, and then red. She heard things splashing and saw shapes falling from the corner of her eye, but she remained focused on Ash.

Another scream from somewhere beyond the rain. A voice responded, "Get back from it, get away! It's got teeth!"

Ash stood with the closed guitar case in one hand and blood dripping from her fingertips, and Cee had never seen anyone looking so much like her. But this was the her of several years before: hollow, glassy eyes; pale skin; scars on her arms, bleeding. In her expression a horrible need, and a wretched guilt.

"It wasn't supposed to happen," Ash said. She looked around at the creatures that had fallen with her rains, scampering and crawling, or lying injured or dead where they had hit. "I made it new, made it fresh. The parts called out for me." She looked at Cee. "Your bracelet. It should have all been okay."

Someone else shouted, a man this time. "Get it off me! Get it the fuck *off me*!" A shape ran by them, slapping at his back with both hands but unable to reach whatever was troubling him.

"You need to stop it," Cee said.

"This isn't me anymore. Next time I'll make it better." Ash started walking away, eyes wide in shock, or disbelief, or perhaps despair.

Cee followed. Ash looked weak and vulnerable, and Cee hoped that if the rains stopped, or they reached the extremes of the shower, and the sun touched her skin once more, she would be away from the gaze of whatever strange presence had been watching her.

But it wasn't an eye in this storm. She realised as she followed her strange friend that what she had seen in those brief, terrifying flashes, and what she had sensed, was in Ash.

PART TWO

THE TUMULT

JIMI

Jimi Chastain dumped the shot-up, bloodstained, windshield-less BMW at the edge of the nearest town. He'd driven past the place on his way up the valley towards the dam, and back then he'd taken no notice of the town's name. It was somewhere else to bypass, and nowhere he'd ever go. A place so close to the reservoir, denuded and filthy though it was, would never have need of a Soaker.

Now he had need of the town, and as he hobbled down the exit ramp he had time to concoct his story.

His car had blown a tyre, sending him skidding from the road and into the ditch. He'd smashed his face on the steering wheel and broken two teeth, split his nose, blackened his eyes. The seat belt had tightened and cracked two ribs as the car rolled, and he'd received his other injuries from smashed glass. By the time anyone started to question his story—and found the car where he'd abandoned it a mile beyond town on a gravel track, and seen the bullet holes, and the blood-spattered upholstery—he'd be long gone. He rarely stayed anywhere for long, and now that he had one of the Rainmakers on his mind and in his sights, he'd never stop until he found them. *Her*, the dying Alison had said, and Jimi could only assume that meant the daughter was still alive. If that were the case, one way or another she might lead Jimi to *him*.

For years wandering the Desert as a Soaker, and other jobs before that, it was what had inspired him. His driving force. His reason.

The Rainmaker beneath his boot, squirming and dying in the dust, just as Jimi's Papa had squirmed and died.

The tang of burning still stung his nostrils—rubber, plastic, metal, fuel, and the acidic stench of his wagon's exploding batteries. He could smell it on his clothes and in his hair, taste it on his tongue. He had blood on his hands and arms, but though some of it was not his, no one would have reason to think that. The heat was dizzying, bouncing up from the cracked road to burn his exposed skin. He'd never been so broken, but he'd never felt so good. Soon he would find and kill the man who had murdered his Papa.

Jimi was fifteen years old when he watched his Papa die.

Hidden in the dying crop, far enough away that his father couldn't see him—they called him Wolf, but Jimi only ever knew him as Papa—but close enough that Jimi could see and hear, he watched as the strange man knelt in the dust. Mike and Lucy-Anne were out there with Papa, and that in itself had convinced Jimi that this was something worth watching. Maybe they'd end up killing the man—Jimi had seen that before—but he thought not. This was something stranger.

And yet, despite his patience and conviction that this was something unusual, Jimi fell asleep. The heat lulled him, and the sun speckling through the canopy of failed and failing plants was almost hypnotic, easing him down from sweaty, uncomfortable reality into troubled dreams.

His mother was a deer. Beautiful, innocent, and vulnerable, she was in terrible danger from her husband's rifle, and Jimi wanted to shoo her away before Papa knew she was there.

Papa was telling him how the first time you kill someone is the hardest.

You mean a deer? Jimi asked.

Papa looked at him like he was an idiot. Then with pity.

Yeah, just like a deer, Papa said. *One shot to the heart.*

Jimi snapped awake. He drew in a sharp breath and he was instantly there, in the hot dusty present lying amid the crumbled remnants of his father's failing crop. *I haven't slept for long*, he thought. His dreams were mist and memory, receding with the dainty tap of a deer's hooves. Jimi reached up and touched an itch on his face, then looked at his hand. Moisture. It was raining.

He drew in a breath to shout in delight, but then other shouts came in, and he knew that something had gone terribly wrong.

Lightning flashed and thunder rolled, and more and more rain came down, and through the wooden supports and stalks of dead plants, and curtains of strengthening rain, Jimi saw Papa standing before the strange man. The man had blood leaking from his arms and a long box held across his chest. He could see from Papa's stance that he could hardly stand. Something was tangled in his beard.

"I brought rain," the man said, and then he took one step back as Papa reached for him and fell flat on his face.

The man ran into the rain and out of sight. Jimi ran for Papa, focusing only on his motionless body. He looked to his right as he ran, in case the man with the box and bloody arms returned to do to him whatever he had done to Papa. He was wet and warm, yet chilled by what he saw happening all around. Jimi didn't understand any of this.

Just before he reached Papa, something skittered across the framework above him. Jimi glanced up and saw the scorpion hanging by a couple of spiky legs. It was small and bright yellow.

He'd never seen a scorpion here before. There were more on Papa, one in his hair, another knotted in his beard, with bright red streaks on the ends of its legs. Its sting was curled over and stuck in Papa's top lip, and it was bracing its legs against his chin and lower cheek, tugging, trying to extract the sting and pulling his mouth into a pout. It gave his face the semblance of movement, and planted hope in Jimi that he was still alive.

But rain fell into Papa's open eyes, brimming like tears.

Jimi knelt in the mud, reached out, held back. His father had never been a tactile man, nor an emotional one, offering love in gruffness and advice rather than kind words or contact. Jimi could not remember the last time either of them had even touched.

"Papa," he said, his voice lost in the storm. The rains were what his Papa had been desperate for these past six months, as irrigation efforts failed and contracts with Soakers fell through. Jimi didn't understand the business or politics, and he tried not to dwell on the darker, more violent aspects of what his father and his associates did. He was sheltered in that respect, and much of that sheltering had been enforced by Papa. "I know you'll never be like me," Papa had once told him, and Jimi could never work out whether he'd spoken with regret or pride.

"Papa!" he said again, a little more desperate this time, and more scared. Shapes wriggled and scuttled and crawled in the mud, and he knew it wasn't the man who had killed Papa. Not directly, at least. But whatever he had been doing, plugged into the box, arms wide and bleeding, face turned to the sky as it changed and became heavy and dark and wet... *that* was what had killed him.

The man had brought rain, and other things besides.

He reached out again, and when he touched his father's arm, the scorpion on his face extracted its stinger and scurried away.

Jimi heard voices. Distant, quiet, from one of the huts hidden from view. He froze and half stood, head tilted to one side to hear. Mike and Lucy-Anne? Why hadn't they protected Papa when that was their job?

"Rainmaker," he heard Lucy-Anne say, and as he took a step towards her voice a gunshot rang out, shockingly loud in the gathering quiet, and Jimi ran in the other direction. He spared one last glance for his dead Papa, then fear carried him, and moments later he tripped over Mike's body. He was contorted in agony, and a large spider was crouched in the hollow of his throat, long legs clasping into his skin as its head pressed against his neck.

Jimi almost cried out in shock, but he held it in.

Rainmaker.

He knelt beside Mike's body. He'd dropped his gun and it had come to rest against one of the timber support legs for the suspended plant grid.

Rainmaker, Lucy-Anne had said, and then the gunshot. Papa was dead. Mike was dead. And now maybe Lucy-Anne was dead as well, and the mysterious Rainmaker had done it all.

Jimi picked up the gun and ran. It was heavy in his hand, so he tucked it into the waistband of his shorts. The weapon was just as heavy there, weighted by the promise of revenge.

"Rainmaker," Jimi said, the first time the word passed his lips. But it would be far from the last.

Alone in the Desert, what he'd absorbed from Papa kept Jimi alive. The hardness, the determination, the drive to persist and push back against difficulties. That, and his search for the Rainmaker.

Once the panic lessened, he'd gone back. He'd found Lucy-Anne's body, but nothing else. No sign of the man and his box. He had come at Papa's behest, brought down rain and other things, and then disappeared, as if he too had dissipated with the steam from those fields.

Alone for the first time, Jimi went in search of his mom and sister, but they were long-lost to him. He found no trace, and he came to believe that they'd hidden themselves away from what Papa had become. He did not look for long. Even if he did find them and they took him in, they'd offer only a safe, boring life. That was no longer what he wanted. Jimi believed he was more like his father than even Papa had believed.

Instead, Jimi spent some time searching for the Rainmaker. He'd never even heard the word before that fateful day, but afterwards he researched and found out as much as he could. The Rainmakers came from only one family bloodline, the talent handed down from generation to generation. There were stories from over a century before, when a Rainmaker wandered the Dust Bowl attempting to offer help. Her death was mysterious and violent. Through the following decades there were more reports, most of them disputed and often ridiculed. The family of Rainmakers were usually regarded as fakers, and at worst, as preying on others' misfortune.

Jimi knew it was not fake. But the trail had grown cold, and though he kept looking, there were only rumours about the last Rainmaker family—a man called Jesse and his daughter, Ash. Some said they were both dead and gone. Other whispers claimed they were estranged, and the rainmaking talent had died along with their relationship. The Rainmaker remained on Jimi's mind. As time passed, his Papa—cruel and gruff, strong and powerful—became larger than life, something of a hero in Jimi's eyes. The dream of avenging his father's murder kept him in balance for those first few years on his own in the Desert.

As he grew older, he worked a variety of jobs. Crop picker, ground digger, burger flipper, barman, decorator, driver, store assistant, labourer, woodworker. He was small and slight, like Papa had been, so when he started somewhere new he was always the butt of the joke or, in some cases, the target of bullies.

They only ever targeted him once.

Jimi fought back every single time, and he gained scars as numerous as the jobs that were forced to let him go.

One day, ten years later, when he was in his mid-twenties, a caravan of Soakers stopped by the large roadside diner where he worked. He'd only been there for a few weeks, and he didn't think he had very long left. He was screwing the owner's wife. She was thirty years his senior, but hungry for him every moment they could steal, her appetite voracious. She did things to him he'd never had done before, and allowed him to do things he'd never done, and she told him her sex life had been a decade of drought. Jimi found that funny. She was rescuing herself from her own Desert.

The Soakers parked their wagons on the large lot on the other side of the road, away from the buildings and the other vehicles. Jimi watched from the diner window as the haze settled and the wagons slowly came into view. He'd seen Soakers before, but only in groups of two of three. Now there were a dozen, each wagon different in shape, size, and colour, and the twelve Soakers who crossed the road and approached the diner were equally diverse. They ate and drank, and he served them and talked with them, and became entranced by their stories and their outlook on the world.

By the time they left, an hour later, he knew it was also his time to leave. He did so without looking back, stealing the owner's car and following the Soakers at a cautious distance.

It took a day and a night before one of the wagons peeled off and took a minor road out into the Desert. Jimi followed. In the end it was easy. The Soaker was a woman, old and thin and not at all surprised when he stepped into her firelight. She offered him a drink and a share of her meal, and he shot her in the chest. She fell back, away from the fire, with a deep sigh. She stared at the stars as she died.

Jimi stood there for a long time looking at what he had done. Since picking up Mike's gun he'd kept it oiled and maintained, but it held the same bullets it had been loaded with back then. He hadn't even made sure it still worked.

The first bullet he'd ever shot from the gun had put a hole in this Soaker and taken her from the world.

His heart hammered, so hard that he thought he saw its shockwaves rippling the campfire's flames. *I could have just taken her wagon*, he thought. But she would have come after him. *I could have taken it and driven far away, all across the Desert, and left her out here to survive or die on her own.* But Soakers were a hardy bunch. He had to look ahead without worrying who or what might approach from over his shoulder.

Papa had been right. The first was definitely the hardest.

After the old Soaker woman, killing became so much easier.

Though not quite existing in the shadow of the dam, its influence on the town was strong. Jimi walked in along the main street, and just on the edge of town he crouched by a trickle of a stream and washed blood from himself. The better he looked, the more likely they'd be to help. He smelled the water as he splashed it on himself, tasted it when he washed his face, and he turned aside from the stream just in time to puke. He cried out as he retched, braced on hands and knees as his stomach convulsed, his back arched, and his cracked ribs screamed as he vomited into the dust. There was a little blood in the puke, but he hoped it was only from his mouth. His broken teeth cast shards of pain across his face as the acid bathed open wounds and nerve endings, and he squeezed his eyes shut against the agony. Everything hurt so much more now than when he was being beaten and broken.

Alison had made him swallow the water, and he guessed there was a sick poetry to that. He'd dumped them close to his blazing wagon, hoping the heat would eventually reach them and set their clothing aflame. Even if it didn't, anyone who found the wreck might assume that a couple of Soakers had fought and killed each other. Death was common in the Desert, and those who inhabited its societal fringes—Soakers were closer to the edge than most, save perhaps for the Hotbloods—were rarely mourned. Now, the same water he'd sold to Mosey churned in his guts, infecting his damaged body. Revenge from Alison's ashen grave.

Walking beside the stream on the edge of town he saw the first of the water treatment plants. It was a basic affair, and he'd seen many of its ilk across the Desert. It consisted of several large water containers, each holding several thousand gallons, and a series of pumps, filtering devices, and a final treatment tank. Here at least the system was fairly complex, if a little roughshod, with a long, low timber building which he guessed was used as a community bottling plant. It was from here that two teenagers emerged, a boy and a girl about the age he'd been when he saw Papa die. They saw him and came closer, tentative and cautious. As if his body had been holding itself together until he reached help or safety, a faint took Jimi away. Up and down became fluid, and he slumped to his side, away from the stream and onto the hot, hard ground. He heard the slap of footsteps, then felt the touch of a bottle to his bloodied lips and the tepid flow of blessed fresh water.

During his years in the Desert, Jimi had become good at reading people. He often wore his own face of lies, and seeing deceptive masks on others was useful, and sometimes a matter of survival.

He knew from the first moment the kids' mother saw him that she didn't believe at least half of what he was saying. It was obvious in her clipped tone, her sideways glances at him as she helped him walk, and her silent signals to the teens to keep their distance. He gave her the story he'd come up with about crashing off the highway and rolling into the ditch, and at least she didn't come straight out and say she didn't believe him. She saw he was injured and needed help, and there was no need to lie about that. Her name was Mally and she was a good person. Jimi sensed that in her, and saw it reflected in her two children, whose innocent concern for an injured stranger was heartening. If more people were like them, and fewer like him, the Desert would not be such a dangerous place.

Mally knew that many of his injuries weren't from a crash. She didn't address this until she sat him on a bench outside a store and sent the teens inside to buy bandages and painkillers.

"Russ has a pickup, I'll ask him to go and tow your car." She took out her phone, but her finger hovered over the screen. She was inviting Jimi's real story, giving him time. She was good, yes, but also strong. The safety of her children came before everything, and she sensed that he was dangerous.

"Car's totalled," he said.

"Russ can still fetch your belongings. Bag, whatever." She glanced him up and down. She must have felt the gun in his belt when she helped him walk into town. Plenty of people carried guns, but it would have made her more wary.

"Nothing important," he said. He felt hot and queasy, pain from his broken teeth drilling into his skull, each breath and movement hurting his cracked ribs and wounded shoulder. His stomach gurgled and lurched. Every part of him hurt, and the thought of puking again was terrible.

But he was moving with purpose, an aim in mind for the first time in years. All the pain and discomfort did nothing to change that.

"So where're you headed?" Mally asked.

Jimi sighed and shifted on the bench, trying to find a more comfortable position that didn't exist.

"You seem nice," Jimi said. "Your kids, too. Nice kids."

"They are. It's important to be kind, don't you think? Now more than ever."

Jimi thought of Papa, devoid of affection and dying in the mud. And the Rainmaker who'd brought down the things that had killed Papa, and Mike and Lucy-Anne. Once he'd started running from that old life he had never looked back, and he'd relied on the kindness of strangers many times since. "Sure. Kind is good."

"So what do you need?" Mally asked.

"You're talking as if you want me gone."

"This is a good town. Peaceful. We've had our share of trouble, but we avoid it when we can. And deal with it when we have to."

"I'm no trouble to you," Jimi said, and he meant it. He had the cash he always kept in his pocket, and trouble took time and exerted a price. He was paying some of that price now.

Mally's expression showed that she didn't believe him. He could hardly blame her.

"A car. I can pay for it. That medicine your kids are fetching, I'll pay for that too."

"And then you'll go?"

"Sure. I'll go. No trouble." He smiled at her, and however tough she was, she was also perceptive. Whatever she saw in his eyes made her look away, and she glanced back at the store.

"Nice to have your own water," Jimi said. "I've spent time with Soakers. I know what a pain it is treating enough to supply a town this size."

"We make do, and we all contribute."

"Sure," Jimi said. He was fishing and she knew it, but she didn't know what he was fishing for.

"Guess you won't need to worry now there's a Rainmaker again."

She frowned at him. "What're you on about?"

"I saw it on the news. Before the crash, before I lost my cell phone. Reports of a woman, a Rainmaker, somewhere in the Desert in a little town…" Jimi trailed off, frowning, as if trying to recall the town's name.

"You don't believe that crap?"

"Sure I do."

Mally laughed.

"I'll need a new cell phone, too," Jimi said.

Mally's son and daughter emerged from the store, both carrying paper bags.

"Just leave the bags here," he said. "Thanks." He reached into his pocket and pulled out his wallet. Much of what people surviving in the Desert dealt with was cash only. Papa had taught him that, and it was a lesson well learnt. He handed Mally a handful of folded notes and smiled at the boy and girl.

"Aren't we taking him to Doc Merryweather?" the girl asked.

"We should ask Russ to fetch his car back to town," the boy said.

"He's not staying," Mally said. She took the cash and flicked through it. "This'll cover a car and a cell."

"Thank you."

"And a full charge, too, to get you where you want to go."

Jimi nodded, closed his eyes, and lifted his face to the sun. *She means as far away as possible*, he thought, and he was fine with that. Mally and her kids didn't need the trouble that hung around him like a stink.

As Mally led her son and daughter away from the wounded man she knew was trouble, Jimi reached for the paper bags, eager for whatever chemical relief they might contain.

He still didn't know the name of the town as he watched it dwindle in his rear-view mirror. He drove far enough away that they wouldn't be able to track him when someone found the bullet-ridden car and the bodies by the reservoir, then he paused to start up the phone Mally had given him. Along with the car it had eaten up most of his cash, but she'd handed a few notes back to him with the phone. Jimi had felt a twinge of guilt. It was people like her who helped people like him survive, even though people like him kept her awake at nights.

As the cell phone connected, he popped another handful of painkillers. He'd wound the bandages as tightly as he could around his broken ribs, and used a hardening putty compound pressed into his two broken teeth to cover the exposed nerves. It was meant to be temporary until he could get it fixed. The pain kept him alert.

The cell phone buzzed when it was ready and connected to the net, and it only took him a minute to search for the word

'Rainmaker'. There were thousands of hits, but he filtered for the most recent and a handful of stories came up.

Stories about a young woman bringing rain to a town, causing flash floods, and rumours of creatures tumbling down from previously clear, sun-bleached skies.

Excited, senses aflame, Jimi read the story again and again, thinking, *He had a kid. And now she's doing the same thing.*

The Rainmaker's daughter was in a town called Abbey Springs.

JESSE

He had not opened the box containing his apparatus in almost twenty years, since that time on the poppy farm when Wolf died before his eyes and the hard-faced woman put a bullet in his face. He'd always ensured it was close and safe because it was precious and important to him. It was also the most dangerous thing he'd ever seen, known, and made with his own hands. A few times over the years—most of them soon after he'd shut it away—he'd felt an attraction to the power it afforded him.

But he'd never been tempted to plug those needles into his arms. Not after bloody rain and strange creatures fell from the sky conjured by him, and people died. The Shore haunted his dreams still, but much less frequently over the years. Time faded even the deepest of nightmares.

Now, the clasp on his apparatus case was rusted shut. The hook was fixed tight on the eye, and no matter how much he prised and pushed, he could not shift it.

"Try this," Karina said.

"I thought you were asleep."

"Can't." She held out a knife she'd taken from her jeans pocket where they were dumped next to her bed. She'd ensured they had a twin room, not a double. The more time they spent together, the more Jesse realised they were strangers. He felt that he knew her less now than before they'd even met, which was strange, and sad. He sensed no regret in her, and that was sadder still.

He opened the knife. It was smooth, sharp, well oiled, and he wondered what else it had been used for. After what she'd told him about her time out in the Desert, he really didn't want to know. He glanced at where she lay in bed, on her side and looking at him. In the poor lamplight he couldn't read her expression, if she had any at all.

"I don't want to damage it," he said, holding the knife up. The five-inch blade was thick, serrated on its top edge. It looked vicious.

"You won't. It's strong."

He sat with his legs crossed, box between his knees, and started easing the blade beneath the seized hook. He put pressure on the handle, holding his breath. It grated, ground, and then popped free with a brief, high creak.

In the corner of the room Rocky raised her head, little more than a shadow with ears against the wall.

"Okay, girl, nothing to worry about." But Jesse had to wonder. The hook stood proud of the fixing plate, and for some reason he thought of a rabbit frozen in headlights. Rocky's ears shadowed against the wall, maybe.

Karina said she couldn't sleep, but her breathing was long and deep, and if she was feigning it she was a good actress. He felt a twinge of annoyance that she could nod off to sleep while he was opening his apparatus and facing it for the first time in years. But she wasn't to know this was the first time. She hadn't asked, he hadn't told her, and she'd been gone for so long. He thought he'd caught her looking at his arms while he was driving, searching for fresh scars.

Fingertips on the lid, ready to open the box, he looked at Karina again. There were scars on her body that he didn't remember, and new scars on the inside that he had not been there to soothe. The last time he'd seen her like this was more than nine years ago, and there was no sense of familiarity. She was leaner than he remembered, heavily tanned, and she wore a style of underwear he had never seen on her before. Even in repose she looked different, her expression moulded more by her years in the Desert than the two decades they had spent together before. Their marriage, their love, had barely left its mark on her, on the outside at least. The parts of her he might still know were on the inside, buried deep.

He looked her up and down, almost guiltily, as if caught eyeing a stranger's body. He hadn't been with a woman since Karina had left. For a long while that was because they were still married— he was still her husband and the father of their child, however much she hated him—but lately he thought it had been more down to habit. When they'd been together their sex life had been comfortable, a familiar intimacy. Her sharing a casual tale about fucking a stranger out beneath the stars had cut him deep, even more so because he didn't think she'd told him to hurt him. She was beyond that. It was simply another part of the story of her quest across the Desert. Just another moment, like the man she'd told him she'd killed. Perhaps there were more lovers in her wake, and more bodies.

"Rocky," he whispered. He tapped the bed beside him. "Here." The dog raised her head again, then rose stiffly from sleep, tail wagging as she walked to the bed and jumped on. She circled into a ball, nose to tail, and it felt good to have his dog next to him. Though it was sweltering hot in the motel room and sweat dribbled down his sides and back, he needed the warmth.

He gripped the box's lid and lifted. The hinges creaked, but he pushed harder and it ground open. He laid the box on the bed before him and eased the lid so it was open all the way, and then he took in a long, deep breath. He smelled oil and rust and inanimate decay. He smelled rain. It startled him, but was not unpleasant. The apparatus was as familiar as his own hand, even though he hadn't laid eyes on it in years. He revisited it in his dreams, and the pale light in the motel room suited his dreamlike recollection of the device and its many parts. Shadows hunkered beneath and between components.

Jesse picked up the bedside lamp and moved it next to the box, and the shadows and light playing across and around its constituent parts moved right to left, giving it a shocking sense of movement. He drew in a sharp breath, then rested the lamp against his dog's curled back. It settled, the apparatus grew still again, and Jesse slowly started to breathe more evenly.

In one corner there were a few dried leaves. In another, the water stains of old rain, dark blotches that had marked the bare wood forever. Parts of the apparatus were as rusted as the lock and hinges on the outside, but others were surprisingly clean and untouched by time. A glass dial with a range of numbers had only a scattering of dust marring its surface. He had removed the dial's red indicator because actual readings—temperature, pressure, altitude and time—were unimportant. An electrical circuit board with three hair-thin connectors had a layer of dust across it. He leaned close and blew, breathed the dust in and waved it away, and it played a complex moving constellation in the lamplight.

Two long wires, tipped with fine golden needles, snaked across and around the apparatus where he had ripped them from his arms and dropped them inside all those years ago. He picked up one wire and ran it between his fingers until he came to the needle, expecting to see his own dried blood darkening its surface. But there was only a pale dullness to the gold, as if this most intimate part of the apparatus no longer remembered him.

He heard Karina stir and move, and for a moment he felt annoyed, as if she was disturbing something private and intimate.

Get a fucking grip! Jesse thought, and he turned to look at his wife. She was sitting up on the bed, her back against the wall and knees drawn up to her chest.

"Can that thing help?"

"Help?"

"Find her?"

"I'll never use it again." He looked down at his old apparatus. The lamplight seemed to have drifted, shadows and textures edged slightly into another landscape. Perhaps Rocky had moved. Karina's expression had also changed. She looked stern, distant, her mask back on now that she was awake.

"I always hated it, what it did to you."

"Didn't know you cared." He smiled at her, then berated himself when she glared back.

"Once. It was you who didn't care."

"You always knew about this thing, what I was, what I did. As soon as we met, I made sure you knew."

"Telling me didn't help, didn't mean anything. I was young. It sounded like a fairy tale. It was a long way from seeing for myself."

"Yeah."

"So can you use it to find Ash? See how she is? Maybe even let her know we're looking for her?"

"It's not a phone." He rested his hands on the edges of the wooden box, the entire apparatus within his grasp.

"I remember a lot, Jesse. I might have hated your obsession, but you talked about it often, sometimes in your sleep. You told me all the things your mom said when you were little, and the advice she gave you. She told you there was a link between living Rainmakers, a connection through their apparatus, or whatever. So I don't care if it isn't easy for you. Now Ash has made a new apparatus, so if you can do it, then just fucking do it." Her eyes lingered on the box, and Jesse thought he saw something other than disgust. Fascination, maybe. More likely, hope.

"My mom said a lot of things that didn't necessarily apply to me. Each Rainmaker's experience is as diverse as their style of apparatus."

"But you can try? You can do that, can't you?"

Jesse tapped the edge of the box, wondering, thinking, remembering. He'd sworn he would never, ever use it again, not after last time and what he'd seen and sensed in that place, The Shore.

Just nightmares, he thought. He still suffered them even now, and over the years he'd begun to think they were constructs from that terrible time. The idea that they were actual memories was unbearable. *I changed things in my head. Made things that were never there.*

But Karina was right. His mother had told him a lot.

You might see somewhere when you start building and using your apparatus. A strange place. It's difficult to describe, and it's different for everyone. My father, your grandfather, saw a long beach with an almost motionless sea on one side, and tall chalk cliffs with their heads hidden in heat haze on the other. Sand was nearly white, he said. The skies flitting with clouds. And the creatures he saw, bobbing without making waves and burrowing on the beach, were animals of the sea.

I saw something different. The shore of a giant lake, the waves breaking against an eroded bank. Low rolling hills around me and ahead of me, speckled with occasional empty buildings. A uniformly grey sky, and animals I knew, and also some I didn't. And in the distance a group of... penguins? People? I never knew. Sometimes they seemed to notice me. And when they did... it was like being seen by something other. *As if the whole place paused and looked at me, not just that strange, distant huddle. They were not only the eyes, but the intelligence. They never came closer, although I sensed they wanted to. They saw me.*

But Jesse, it's nothing to be afraid of. And because the places we see are so different, that just shows they're not real at all, son. They're in our minds. So wherever you go, whatever you see, that's just a result of your connection to the apparatus, and something to do with how the rains come. I'm not sure any of us has ever really understood, but I don't want you to be afraid. What we do is wonderful. We mustn't let our fears stop us.

"Some of what she told me was true, some not. I think she was starting to understand how rainmaking was changing, just as our world changed. In her time she sensed some of the danger in what she did, and I encountered that danger face to face in those poppy fields. For Ash, it was even worse. I think the rainmaking mirrors our world and what we've done to the planet. The place she went to, the place she called Skunksville, was more degraded and corrupted than my own."

"But you have to try," Karina said. "You've hidden away for so long while I've been searching the Desert. Do some searching for yourself."

"It needs cleaning. Some of the cables might have petrified, the connections broken, and I'd need to prime it. I'm not the person I was when I last closed this lid."

"Not the man you used to be," Karina said.

"Charming," he said.

"Charm never was my thing."

Jesse picked up both rubber-sheathed wires, each more than two metres long, connecting the apparatus to the needles that were meant to connect to him. He had the lumpy scar tissue on his forearms and the hollows of his elbows, and he'd sworn he never would again slip these needles through his skin. *Maybe I don't need to*, he thought. As a young boy first using his apparatus, he'd sometimes experienced flashes of vision, like the dregs of dreams, just from touching individual components. These times he had felt even closer to his mom than usual, as if he was sheltering in her warmth even though she was dead.

He pulled the wires, lifting his arms so that some of the tangles fell away. He should clean the components like he'd said, service and prime them, make it ready to be part of him again.

But just a touch wouldn't harm.

He let the wires fall through his hands, then closed his thumbs and forefingers around the needles.

They were cold to the touch. He held them up before him for a while, then lowered his hands to rest on his knees.

The apparatus moved, but it was only Rocky shifting position.

The window creaked, perhaps beneath the breath of a growing breeze. But it was probably only the frame shrinking in the cooling night air.

"Anything?" Karina asked, eager for any response that might take them from this grotty motel room and closer to Ash.

"Nothing." Jesse was surprised to find that he felt a cutting disappointment. It was no surprise that he'd lost something of himself after so many years of falling fallow, but a small part of him had wanted to feel something.

"Maybe you'll have to—" Karina began, but Jesse heard no more.

It happened in the space of a single blink. As his eyes closed the world went away, and he saw into the place he had not visited or sensed for so long. His own secret world of The Shore had not been as calm as his grandfather's, nor as benign as his mother's. He recognised the landscape instantly, and it was like reliving an old nightmare from many years before, as rich and dreadful as ever. The debris-strewn ground. The ruins of buildings in the near distance, dilapidated and tumbled. The angry skies, boiling black with twisting skeins of deep red, red as agony, bright as baking lava or exposed flesh.

Creatures fluttered and flew, crawled and stalked, some that looked vaguely familiar like the animals of Earth and many, many more that did not. There were feathers and scales, bare skin and fur, and in almost every instance, teeth and claws. In all his years he had never seen The Shore so alive, and so laden with threat.

In the distance stood that huddle of humanoid shapes, tall and broad. Though featureless, he knew that their pale faces were looking right at him.

One blink, an instant too short to measure, and yet The Shore was alive and active. However differently Ash viewed that strange place—for her it was Skunksville, and it had *always* been more alive and tactile to her than it had to him—she had been there recently to set it alight.

He sensed her, a nearness that both shocked and saddened him. He wondered if she sensed him.

And then those humanoid shapes were moving. They skittered and sprinted across the desolate landscape on sharp chitinous limbs, throwing up sparks that looked so much like the stars of light and power that would extrude from those golden needles, were they buried in his flesh.

He let go of the needles and snapped back to the hotel room. Rocky was barking. His legs had kicked out, knocking the apparatus to one side. One needle still touched his foot and he kicked it away, and then Karina was there, hands on his shoulders shaking him, concerned face close to his.

He wrapped his arms around his wife and pulled her close. He buried his face in her neck and smelled her hair and skin and sweat. Despite how much she had changed, so much about holding her felt the same.

After a couple of hesitant moments, the tension left her and she hugged him back. They were both damp and musty with sweat, but Jesse relished the contact. He needed it. For a few precious seconds he believed Karina needed it as well.

Then she disengaged and pulled back. Keeping her hands on his shoulders, she looked down into his eyes.

"Tell me," she said.

"It's alive. It's *aflame*. We have to stop her. We have to find her, and this time we have to stop her forever."

KARINA

Karina was eager to get started. It was almost dawn, and though neither of them had really slept, she felt time moving past and leaving her in place. It was another eight hours to Collier, and days had passed since the photo of Ash had been taken. The urgency Karina felt was rich and sharp, the need to move and keep moving more powerful than ever before during her years in the Desert.

Jesse showered while she went for something to eat and drink. She had Rocky on her leash. She sniffed and trotted, happy to be out, though she kept glancing back as if to make sure Karina was still there. It felt good to be walking her, but also strange. The dog was Jesse's. She'd spent years hating and resenting him for running to the literal hills. But as time moved on he had faded into her history, like the echo of a voice she no longer knew. Being back with him now had brought that echo in close once more, and she realised it had never really gone at all. She had simply shut Jesse away, boxed him up and put him aside in her mind. Now, he was close again in so many ways. The way he smiled with one corner of his mouth when he was sad but trying to make peace. The small snort he sometimes let out when he laughed. How he looked at her when he thought she wasn't looking and glanced away when she was. He was renewing his memories of her, and she had changed so much. She had experienced a more varied and challenging life than Jesse since Ash had gone—he had grown still, fleeing to Hillside and into the bottle, and yet stuck in the moment by what he had done. She had ridden the terrible waves of the repercussions.

Rocky tugged at her leash, pulling her towards a rough gravelled area beside a small restaurant. As the dog took a leak she tensed as she heard the snick of a door being unlocked. She was attuned to threats, always with one eye open for danger. The Desert was a dangerous place. Jesse pretended he understood that, but really he had no idea. She had been here for a long time, knew the hard-baked ground beneath her feet, the dusting winds, the cries of pain and ghosts of foul deeds carried on the breeze.

The diner's front door opened and a woman appeared in the doorway. She nodded at Karina and smiled at Rocky.

"Cute dog," she said.

"She is."

"You'll pick up if she takes a shit in my front yard?"

Karina hadn't even considered that. "Of course," she said, and she thought, *Please Rocky, don't take a dump.*

"New in town?" the woman asked.

"Just passing through. You're open?"

"Not until eight. Just airing the place while I start cooking."

"I smell coffee," Karina said, so relaxed by the smell. It was always a lure for her. She'd lost count of the number of people she'd shared a cup of joe with around a campfire, or sitting in an RV, or on the front porch of a hotel or guest house.

The woman eyed her and Rocky again, leaning on the door jamb. "Pour you a cup if you like, it's fresh. Happy to make a first sale before opening, to be honest."

"That'd be great," Karina said. "Oh, and…?"

"Sure. I'll cook you something."

She looked down at Rocky.

"She's welcome. Long as she's done her business outside."

Inside, the woman poured a mug of coffee and placed it on the counter. The diner reminded Karina of a dozen places she'd worked across the Desert. Small, maybe fifteen tables, and a colourful selection of lush landscape art covering the walls, a paean to better times. The landscapes portrayed green valleys and forested hillsides, clear rivers and clearer skies, blue oceans and golden beaches. She thought briefly of something Jesse had told her long ago about glimpses of a strange landscape when he was plugged into his apparatus. His imagination had sounded darker and less ordered.

"Getcha?" the woman asked. She reminded Karina of her mother. A little gruff, with laughter lines around her eyes. A face that betrayed a life well lived, and a manner that spoke of cautious optimism. She wished she could see herself reflected in that face.

"Got any eggs?"

"Fresh from my own chickens."

"How about some French toast for two?"

"Sure thing. To go?"

"Great." Karina sipped her coffee and groaned in delight. "I'll take two more coffees, too."

"Sure, honey. I'll be right back." She went through a beaded curtain into the kitchen, and once out of sight she called back, "TV remote's on the counter."

Karina flicked on the TV and searched for a local news station. PBTV flickered up, with a tall, thin woman presenting a weather forecast. Dry, dusty, hot as fuck. She followed it with a high pollen count, elevated pollution levels, and the familiar advice to stay out of the sun between the hours of ten and two.

There was a time when the warnings were heeded, but people get used to things, and weary, and adapt to the times however trying the times are. Karina used sunscreen whenever she could, but she rarely followed the advice. Four hours hidden away each day was four hours not looking for Ash.

She drank more coffee and scratched Rocky behind the ears, as the sounds of food preparation came from the kitchen. The owner softly sang an old tune whose name Karina had forgotten. She smiled. Her mother used to sing to herself while she was cooking or painting, or sometimes when she was just out for a walk.

The TV played background noise, jingles segueing into an hourly news item. Karina kept one ear open as ever, and one eye on the screen. News of more drone strikes in Rio, more terrible bush fires in California with over eight hundred confirmed dead, the assassination of the South African president, the worsening famine in India; death and chaos and the horror that had always contributed to the news, only now it was closer to home for everyone. Though she kept abreast of events, her view had become more focussed and particular to her quest. Famines and hurricanes, droughts and rising oceans—all these things were terrible, but she couldn't do anything about them. Her headspace was no longer expansive enough to contain them, so she absorbed only news from the Desert. She filtered and went deeper, investigating anything that might lead her closer to Ash.

That was how she'd heard rumours of a Rainmaker several days ago.

And that was the word she heard now.

"...the small Idaho town of Abbey Springs. Late yesterday the town was hit by a freak rainstorm that caused a flash flood, resulting in damage to property and an unknown number of casualties. Rumours abound of a Rainmaker having brought down

the rain, along with some allegedly dangerous creatures. Several people were attacked, and local sources claim that at least two have died from venomous bites. This footage claims to show the Rainmaker at work. Be warned, there is some nudity."

Karina took a sharp breath as grainy cell phone footage filled the screen. It was hazy, filmed by someone walking across a ruined landscape of burnt buildings pummelled by a deluge. The camera panned back and forth, and for an instant it settled on someone kneeling in the rain.

Karina leaned close to the TV on the counter, wishing she could freeze or pause the image. The camera shifted from the kneeling figure to a naked woman standing in the rain. The women covered herself, though the broadcaster had already pixelated her image. As she turned away, so did the camera, moving back to the kneeling figure and closing in.

"I can do you some—" the woman said, leaning through the curtain from the kitchen. Karina held up her hand, palm out, and the diner owner fell silent.

"That's Ash," Karina said. The image was jumpy and blurred— but yes, it was Ash, connected to an apparatus Karina couldn't focus on, arms held out and face turned to the sky to revel in the rain she was bringing down.

The woman from earlier, dressed now, slipped into view. The image paused and Karina snorted in frustration.

"Ya know her?"

"My daughter." As Karina leaned in even closer, looking at the paused image, the newscaster appeared on the screen once more.

"These stills from later footage appear to show the young woman connected to some sort of device."

Ash's arms, needles inserted, wires trailing. Blood flowing. The apparatus, blurred, contained in an open guitar case.

"*The family of Rainmakers were once alleged to be—*"

Karina shut off the TV and sat with her hands flat on the counter, staring at the wall but seeing something and somewhere further away.

"I'll pack your food," the woman said.

"Abbey Springs," Karina said.

"Maybe a hundred miles south-west. Never been there myself, but I know a couple who spent some time there last year, helping rebuild a school. They lost part of the town to a fire and—"

"I need to go." Karina stood and moved for the door, dragging Rocky with her, then paused and drew some cash from her pocket. She dropped it on the counter.

"Wait." The woman disappeared back into the kitchen, and returned a moment later with a cardboard takeout box. "You need food. You look… honey, forgive me, but you look like shit." She turned to her coffee machine and grabbed two takeout cups, poured, clipped on the lids. "Food for the soul."

"Thank you," Karina said, reaching into her pocket.

The woman held her palm out. "Please. Go find your girl."

Eight in the morning, clear sky, already ninety degrees in the shade, the world was nothing like it had been yesterday. The rest of Karina's life started today.

JIMI

Jimi drove fast. Pedal to the metal through the night. Headlights beaming ahead, the left light flickering, fading, blooming again with a bad connection. Winking at the darkness, teasing. The dust of lost ages and broken things heavy in the air. Blown by evening breezes, the land exhaling again as it drifted towards another night of pained sleep. Vehicles coming from the other direction appeared as ghostly smudges in the dust, then a growing glare, then separating into twin eyes beaming at him as they whispered or roared by, heading into his past. If they kept going perhaps they would come across Jimi as a Soaker, Jimi wandering the Desert as a lost man, Jimi as a teen kneeling beside the wet, swollen body of his dead Papa.

Jimi drove into the future. It was a future he had hardly let himself imagine, where he might meet the Rainmaker responsible for his father's death.

He popped pills. They sat heavy in his stomach, seeming to swell and burn. Fists of discomfort in a body filled with pain. Teeth burning in his mouth, bleeding into his jaw, face, skull. Blurring his vision. Throwing dust into his eyes to smudge the night even more, making fleeting, dancing shapes in the car headlamps. Ribs stabbing him whenever he took in anything but a shallow breath.

Another fist of pills. Too many. He washed them down with water, wishing for something stronger.

Bumps and bruises, cuts and scrapes and breaks, all had time to make themselves known. Cell propped on the dashboard, GPS guiding him with a point of light in the spiderwebbed dark. Numbers counting down in one corner, time in the other. Digits ticking him into the future, closer to the end of this part of his life. Closer to the true end, as well. He drove towards death. So long as the Rainmaker's came before his own, he would be content.

His point of light moved across the Desert. He might have rolled along these roads before. He didn't know. Didn't care. These were new roads now, lines on a small screen like cracks in reality, the point of light his drifting soul, through and along them to a destination not visible.

Not visible, but only one hundred and ninety-two miles away... ninety-one... ninety...

More pills. Anti-inflammatories, painkillers, others he didn't know.

One hundred and sixty-five miles...

Jimi drove fast. Pedal to the metal through the night. Leaving his old life behind and heading towards whatever was to come. Driving along the lines and cracks of that interstitial moment between the past and a future full of promise. Full of dreams of murder.

ASH

"I saw you naked in the rain."

We've taken shelter in one of the burned buildings at the edge of Abbey Springs. Most of the wooden walls and roof have gone, but the substantial brick chimneybreast remains, and it offers some shelter from the night. The rain stopped hours ago, but I still feel the storm inside, pressing on me with its negative pressure. And I still feel the thrill of being plugged in.

After everything that happened, I'm surprised to find myself still in the eye. I'll make the most of every calm moment I can hold in my grasp.

"Yeah," Ccc says. "Sorry about that." She doesn't sound sorry.

"No need to be."

"The rain felt good," Cee says. "Like… no rain I've ever felt before."

"Fresh," I say. "Pure."

"Right. Until it started raining blood."

I stare into the far corner of the ruined room, where walls and ceilings have come down to form a muddled pile of debris. This building was only singed by the fire, a glancing blow that brought it down but didn't incinerate it totally. It sits on the boundary between the Burn and other areas of town, balanced between life and death.

When we arrived, there was a small yellow frog sat on a charred pile of wall studs. I stomped on it, catching it unawares. Maybe it was drowsy from its fall from that place—

—*Skunksville*—

—but it didn't move as it disappeared beneath my boot. I hated the sensation of it popping. I felt it shift from alive to dead in the blink of an eye.

"That was a mistake," I say. "I never meant for the blood to come down. Nor anything else."

I can see Skunksville, smell it, feel it, as if I'm still there or some of it has come here. I'm still in the eye, but perhaps this is the eye of a different storm.

"I never thought you did mean to do that," Cee says. "It was a mistake. You started bleeding, then the sky bled too. Is that how it works? Is it all you and that machine?"

I have no idea how to tell Cee about Skunksville. My father never really explained it fully because he said he couldn't. Trying to describe it was like trying to describe a dream, he said, and all our dreams are different. "It'll be different next time," I say. "I'm rusty. I need to get the feel for it again, to know my new apparatus more fully." The guitar case is beside me in the shadows. It needs cleaning and drying, but I can't face opening it right now. We should leave, but the idea of walking is exhausting. I've never felt so tired.

"These rains, though," Cee says, and she grins.

"Imagine being like that all the time," I say. "Naked in the rain, washing away all the bad stuff. And now the rain is me."

"No one saw us come in here, but we still have to leave," Cee says. "Are you...?"

"I'm okay. Thanks, Cee. Most people would have run a hundred miles."

"I'm not most people."

"Yeah, I'm starting to get that." I lean across and kiss her on the cheek, and even in the shadows I feel the heat of her blush. "You're the friend I need right now."

"So, what's the plan?"

"What you said. We need to go, but I want to do it again soon. I *need* to. Next time I'll have a better hold on things, but I can't do it again here. I didn't mean to hurt anyone."

"You didn't hurt anyone," Cee lies, and I love her for it. "Okay, you stay here with our stuff and rest. Stay out of sight. I'll get us a ride."

Cee leaves, out into the shadows where anything could be watching.

The wounds in my forearms ache and burn as I think of Skunksville. I'll do better next time. I'll be more in control. I'll talk to those things and tell them who I am.

"I'm the Rainmaker," I whisper to the shadows. "Your world is my world."

Water and blood drip from the ruins as I wait for my friend to return.

JIMI

As he drove through the night, Jimi flipped through news reports from Abbey Springs. The main channels carried only vague mentions, if anything at all, because they were mostly obsessed with the Rio situation and the California fires. The Desert was often an embarrassment. Ten dead in a train wreck in New York was news. A thousand dead from a rash of tornados in the Desert was not. Death was part of Desert life, and many of those living outside preferred to turn their attention away. They couldn't help, so they didn't see. He dug deeper, then found what he sought as a throwaway report at the end of a local news broadcast.

He drove as he watched, one eye on the screen, one on the road. He was risking an accident, driving on the edge, but he'd been living there for years. He saw no reason to take more care now that he might be moving closer to the Rainmaker, and revenge. If anything, he should be closer to the edge, not further away.

He saw the new Rainmaker kneeling with that weird box wired into her arms. He remembered the man doing the same in fields of dying poppies, Papa pacing around him, heat blurring the air between them, insects buzzing, rain coming.

Rain fell.

A woman span and danced.

A foot splashed in a puddle, footage shaking as the person holding the cell phone stumbled.

He drove, foot heavy on the gas, and more of his attention was on the screen now than on the road ahead of him, viewing the past and yet looking to the future.

More rain. The dancing woman covering herself.

And then the Rainmaker, blood running down her arms, and though her eyes were closed she turned as the camera was aimed at her.

Jimi's heartbeat increased. His left hand gripped the steering wheel tighter as the face turned his way. She wasn't him, but part of her was. The chin. The nose. The same face turned up into the spatters of blood that started to fall.

A horn blared and Jimi snapped his attention back to the road, swerving right into his lane moments before the head-on crash that would have killed him. The horn faded behind him and he whooped and shouted, swore at the dusty darkness. He glanced at the screen again but the footage had ended.

She *must* be that bastard's daughter! Her appearance was a surprise, to the world and to him. But though the Rainmaker's trail had gone cold years ago, he had never really stopped looking. He had been waiting for something like this.

He tried to push his foot harder on the gas, to reach Abbey Springs as quickly as possible, but he was already driving as fast as he could go.

The dot on the GPS moved across cracks and lines and the forgotten memory of a dried-up riverbed.

Thirty-two miles...

He swallowed another couple of pills, swilling them down with tepid water.

Twenty-eight...

His cell phone chimed with notifications of the word 'Rainmaker'.

Seventeen...

Jimi started breathing deeper to shut out his pain, readying himself, trying to build a story for when he arrived.

What he wanted to do most in this world was to find the daughter of the Rainmaker and hack her head from her neck, slowly, and hold it up for the world, and her father, to see.

Ten miles.

CEE

C ee hated leaving Ash on her own, but it was dark, the streets were quiet, and the ruined house seemed as good a place as any in which to hide for a couple more hours.

They needed to get the hell away from Abbey Springs, but there was no way they could walk. The Desert would swallow them up, and it was likely they were now known throughout the town, and probably beyond. Known, and maybe wanted. Cee knew that the creatures that had fallen with the rain *had* hurt people, and possibly worse than hurt. She was pretty sure Ash knew that too.

The ground was still damp from the downpour, but it was surprising how quickly a land starved for so long could absorb so much rain. The surface dust was muddy and clung to her boots, but the torrents of water that had washed between buildings had already drained away, seeping into the thirsty ground, changing the landscape in a short period of time. Much of the Burn had been swept clear of a lot of debris. Maybe it was a trick of the poor light, but the ruined part of town seemed somehow smoother. If only such a downpour could sweep heartache and pain from the land.

Cee had seen weird things in the Desert, but nothing as odd as the creatures that had fallen in the rain. *Swept up from the*

Desert in tornados, perhaps? Gathered up in distant storms and tossed down in Ash's rain? She thought that highly unlikely, but to think about it too much was a distraction. Ash was amazing. That's all Cee had to focus on. She'd seen many weird things in the Desert, and now she had witnessed one more.

It was early morning. The sun sat below the eastern horizon, setting fire to dust in the air and casting a flaming rainbow of deep autumn colours across the Desert. The town was just starting to stir, though Cee suspected that much of it had not rested easy. If she was to find a car it had to be quick, and she'd have to take it from a quiet part of town. She'd lost her hat somewhere, and though she'd dressed in different clothes from her damp backpack, she knew that she and Ash were marked people. The last thing she wanted now was to be apprehended.

She had Ash to look out for. The strangest person she had ever known, and after what had happened, she was also the most vulnerable. The only blessing was that she had somehow remained in the eye of the storm that plagued her mind, but there was no saying how long that might last. Cee had only known her for a few short days, but Ash had quickly become the most important thing in her life.

Moving away from the Burn, past fallen and abandoned buildings and into the surviving part of town, the world around her began to wake up. She walked along a quiet street of houses, an affluent neighbourhood where buildings were set back from the road, surrounded by pale, sun-hardened ground where lawns and planting beds had once been maintained. Patches of devil grass grew here and there, and hardy trees bloomed with wan green leaves reaching for the sky. Lawn sprinklers lay dead and rusted. One home in four was boarded up and abandoned, falling into disrepair. A few doors opened and closed as people went about their day. Cars started to purr, and a couple of vehicles rolled along the dusty road towards the centre of town. In one front yard, three young kids were playing ball, and they paused to shield their eyes from the rising sun and watch her walk by. She smiled and waved, and two of the kids waved back. The third turned around and ran back into the house, screen door slamming shut behind him. Cee walked faster in case he'd recognised her. It didn't feel nice being so paranoid.

She could have hot-wired eight out of ten of the cars she saw parked in driveways or on the street, but this wasn't the right kind of neighbourhood. The car would be missed too soon. She needed an older vehicle, even a gas-driven truck, that would attract no attention and might not be missed for a while.

The sun was rising. The town was waking. The clock ticked.

At the junction of two streets she passed a house with a hat on a table on the front porch. The doors and windows were closed and the building seemed quiet. It was a risk, but one she had to take to stop herself being recognised. That would happen soon, if it hadn't already.

She took a casual stroll across the house's front yard, up three steps to the porch, across to the table. There were two chairs there, a couple of books and empty beer bottles, and she paused for just a moment as she viewed the domestic scene from outside. Such peace and contentedness was something she had never known. These people still struggled, she was sure—everyone did, with the famine hitting home in waves, and the Desert growing more parched and desolate year by year—but they still had a chance to sit and read, to drink, to share each other's space and time.

She would find time to do that with Ash. It wouldn't always be running and hiding. Ash would find her level, Cee trusted her in that. Next time it would be better, she'd find the rainmaking easier, and as success grew so her mind would settle, and a version of peace would come. Maybe one day she and Ash would sit on a porch with a beer and reminisce about the old days when they were on the road.

Cee picked up the wide-brimmed sunhat and left the porch. She pulled the hat down tight so that her face was hidden in shadow, and walked along the sidewalk as if she had a right to be there.

The sun was up. The town was awake. The clock kept ticking.

JIMI

"I'm looking for the Burn."

"Why'd you want to go there?"

"I'm looking for the woman who brought rain." He didn't use the word 'Rainmaker'. These people might not know who or what she was.

"You're not from Abbey Springs."

"No."

"Jesus, kid. Didn't take you people long to arrive." The old man hefted another cardboard box into the back of his truck. He was thin and weathered, skin wrinkled as an old leather jacket from decades in the sun and heat. But he was strong, with the look of someone who'd done manual labour his whole life.

"So do you know where she is?"

The man wiped his brow with a dirty handkerchief from his pocket. He looked Jimi up and down. "So what happened to you?"

"I had a car accident a couple of days ago."

"Sure you did. Or maybe someone got tired of you asking dumb questions."

"No, sir. Car accident. I ran off the road into the ditch, blowout, banged my face on the wheel."

"No woman brought rain. It was a storm, a real squaller, been and gone and done fuck all good for the town, other than wash away a load of shit and a couple of people. Friends of mine."

"But the woman at the centre of it—"

"Woman dancing around naked, so I heard. Wish I'd got there quick enough to see. Long time since I've seen pussy that wasn't on a fucking screen."

"Do you know where they are now?"

"The naked woman?" A smile twitched the corner of the man's mouth.

Jimi changed tack. "Is there somewhere good for breakfast, sir?"

"Nope."

Jimi frowned. It wasn't a big town, and from what he'd seen online a good portion of it had been taken in the recent fire, melted back into the Desert. But it must have a cafe or restaurant or bar, or even a coffee stall in a grocery store. He needed food, and a bathroom. He needed a place where people might be more willing to talk about what had happened without busting his balls.

"Really?" he asked.

"You can eat at Caz's, if you like." He nodded along the street. "That way, first right, coffee stop on the corner. But it's not good. Caz'd burn water. Take your life in your hands eating there, son."

"I'll risk it." Jimi offered a smile which he hoped didn't display what he was really thinking about doing to the sarcastic old fuck. *Push him down, knife to his throat, get him to tell me the fucking truth while he's pissing his pants.*

But that might not get him what he wanted, and word would soon travel around town.

"No magic," the old guy said as Jimi walked away along the hot pavement.

"Sorry?"

"The rain yesterday. Bullshit you might've read about. You're just the first, but I'm sure we'll get more coming to town, chasing magic and looking for hope. But it was just a flash flood."

"And women dancing naked in the rain," Jimi said.

The old man laughed. "You come all this way to see some naked woman, you got a problem, son."

"Best just whack off to them on the net, eh?" Jimi waved over his shoulder as he headed for Caz's, and felt the old man's eyes on his back every step of the way.

CEE

Cee arrived at a busier part of town, leaving residential streets behind. There were more pedestrians here, and while more people meant a greater chance of being recognised, it was also easier to lose herself among them. The best place to steal a car was from a full parking lot.

Abbey Springs's main commercial centre consisted of two streets and the wide crossroads where they met. There were as many stores boarded up as there were open, and those still doing business were now opening to a new day. She kept her head down, walking with purpose but trying not to catch anyone's eye. She heard snatches of a few conversations about the day before.

…washed away…

…sat there with those things in her arms…

…just a fucking storm, people making a fairy tale outta things…

…Rainmaker, just like years ago in…

…died from a poison bite, rattler disturbed by the flood probably…

…a spider, but didn't know that species, even young Davey Holt who collects the damn things, he didn't recognise it, said maybe it came from…

When Cee reached the large crossroads she paused in the shadow of a boarded-up bar on one corner. The roads were growing busier and the sky was already ablaze, heat skimming from the roads and blurring the air already tinged with fumes, even though eighty per cent of the cars were pre-charged or solar powered. Just another day in the Desert.

Diagonally across from where she stood was a splash of colour. Caz's Coffee Shop had a pink and yellow awning, and the tables and chairs being set out on the sidewalk in front of the cafe were the same colour. Cee would have killed for a coffee, but what caught her attention was a car turning into a narrow alleyway between Caz's and an adjacent building. On the wall of the alley, painted in yellow and pink, were the words 'Customer Parking Lot'. Hidden away, yet not too much. And if she had a coffee in hand, she'd be just another customer picking up a coffee on her way somewhere.

Cee stood on the corner, waiting for the pedestrian lights to change, then crossed to the sidewalk in front of Caz's. She saw her reflection in the window, and even she'd have found it hard to identify herself. That was good. But if she went inside she'd be inviting someone to look at her face, and that was a risk that wasn't worth taking. Maybe when she'd stolen a car and made it back to Ash, they'd have time to pick up a coffee before leaving Abbey Springs forever.

She bypassed Caz's, breathing in deeply as if mere fumes might give her a caffeine hit, and headed down the wide alley to Caz's parking lot. It was an undeveloped lot surrounded by other buildings, with some yellow and pink bunting strung between posts to give it a splash of the cafe's colour.

The owner of the car she'd just seen pulling in to park walked past her on his way out to the street. When he smiled, she glared at him from beneath her hat until he looked away.

Fucking stupid! she thought. *Should have kept your head down, looked away!* But he'd passed her now, and as she approached the half dozen vehicles in the parking lot she looked over her shoulder. The man reached the end of the alley and disappeared towards Caz's entrance without looking back.

Good. Coffee on his mind.

Even better, the three-year-old silver Ford Tyne he'd been driving was probably the most stealable car here.

Without pausing to look around and raise suspicions from anyone who might have been watching from surrounding windows or hidden doorways, Cee went to the driver's door and slipped out her knife. She flicked it open, and with her other hand she unclipped the belt on her shorts and pulled it loose of the hoops.

If the guy was here for a takeout, she might have five minutes before he returned. The fastest she'd ever broken into a car was forty seconds, but that had been three or four years ago. She was out of practice.

She worked the tip of the knife into the gap between the doors, then aimed the belt's clasp pin at the keyhole. It looked clean and shiny and probably never used, but this was one of the models that still included a manual lock in case the battery failed on keyless entry. She moved the knife back and forth until she felt the point slip into the locking mechanism, gently pushed the belt pin into the keyhole as the magnetic lock twitched it in her hand, then she held the knife true and gave its handle a hard thump with her hip. She heard a crunch and wiggled the belt, but the door remained locked. Sometimes it needed a couple of good impacts, occasionally three, but she still had time. She leaned to the left, ready to hit the knife again.

Someone kicked the back of her knees hard and she went down. She dropped the belt but tried to keep hold of the knife.

A heavy boot kicked her hand away from the knife handle and snapped it from the blade. She rolled forward, reaching to snatch up the belt as she did so, missing. Her roll was clumsy, and though her right shoulder took most of the impact, she still crunched her right cheek into the ground as her weight shifted. She planted her feet on the ground and reached for the pistol at the small of her back as she came to her knees. Her hand just brushed the grip when a weight fell on her and crushed her down. Her head smacked against the concrete.

"Knew you were up to no good," the man said. His whole weight bore down on her, crushing her hand and arm beneath her. She couldn't even move her fingers, let alone reach for the gun. He pressed her free hand to the ground, elbow pushed into her chest. His whole body rested on her, and the more she struggled, the more he pushed her down. His sweating, grinning face was above hers, blotting out the sun.

She head-butted him in the face.

He grunted and kneed her in the thigh. He was still grinning, even as the first drips of blood fell from his upper lip and onto her neck.

"Fighter, eh? Okay, let's fight. See who comes out on top."

"Killed bigger than you," Cee said. She butted him again.

"Ha!" he said. He shook his head. Blood and spit sprayed and made her squint and close her eyes. She tried to snap her leg up into his crotch, but he kneed her again, deadening her thigh. "Thought I recognised you. You were at the Burn. So how about—"

She heard the thud and saw blurred movement above and behind the man. His whole weight slumped down on her, but he was mostly still now, the weight passive instead of aggressive. As she tensed and prepared to roll him off, he was shoved from her and into the side of his car. He groaned. A shape stepped over Cee and stomped on the man, centre-mass. She heard the meaty impact of leather against flesh and the gush of air escaping his lungs.

"Okay!" she said. She rolled away and came up to her knees, drew the gun with bloodied fingers. "That's enough." She stood, gun by her side but finger curled through the trigger. Since the Hotbloods, she only had maybe six bullets left in the magazine. More ammunition was on her list, but it was a pretty fucking long list.

"Sure?" the man asked. "Just one more for luck?"

Cee wiped her eyes, bent to pick up the crushed summer hat, and slipped it back on without taking her eye from this new man. He was small, carried his own scars, and he stood awkwardly from some obvious new injuries. His eyes were wide, and she saw something frightening in them. A reflection of her own. The violence fed him, even though his smile was open and infectious. He was happy about something, and Cee wasn't convinced it was all to do with the bastard he'd just kicked into a shivering ball.

The man stepped aside. "My name's Jimi," he said, "and I'd totally get it if you wanted to put a bullet in this fucker's eye."

The floored man froze and looked up at her. His face was smeared with blood, and she hoped she'd broken his nose. His eyes were white and wide in their bloody mask.

"No need," she said, but she stepped past Jimi and kicked the man hard in the face. He curled in on himself again.

"Pity," Jimi said. "Still, at least he can give you this." He tapped the man's pockets until he found the car's keyless fob. He handed it to Cee.

"Thanks," she said. "But—"

"You were trying to steal his car," he said. He shrugged. "Understandable. It's a nice car, the Tyne. Thousand miles on a full charge, hundred and twenty top speed. I had one once."

"Really."

"Yeah. Notoriously easy to steal, but for future reference, always better to use a snub blade in the mechanism, you've got more chance of disengaging the lock with one hit. You were on, what, hit number three when this creep jumped you?"

Cee smiled. She stretched her limbs, examined her skinned knuckles, felt the bump on her head, touched her cheek. A few spots of blood, but nothing that needed immediate attention.

"So you were watching to see if I could break in quicker than you."

Jimi shrugged, smiling.

She nodded at the squirming man at their feet. "And you decided to help a fellow car thief."

Jimi's smile fell. "I don't like guys like him."

"I was stealing his car."

"He wasn't just trying to stop you."

"I'd have ended up killing him."

Jimi checked out her bloodied cheek and the grazed knuckles holding the gun by her side. Then he knelt by the man and grabbed his hair, pulling until he unfurled himself. There was more blood now, and a broken tooth or two. Cee didn't feel an ounce of guilt.

"Hear that?" Jimi asked him. "I just saved your life. I'm feeling pretty righteous, right now."

The man tried to speak but could only dribble blood.

Jimi stood again and leaned on the car. "Sounds like you're a long way from home."

Cee shrugged. She didn't want small talk.

"So where are you off to in such a rush?"

"Away from this dump," Cee said.

"Sure. Don't blame you. I just arrived and I wanna leave already."

"Yeah. Hey, thanks for your help."

"No problem…?"

"Cee."

"No problem, Cee. Guess we'd better go before this prick decides to get feisty again. He's town, we're not."

"How'd you know I'm not from here?" Cee asked.

"You just said you wanted to leave." Jimi glanced away, then back again, grinning. "Hell, sorry, I saw you on the net last night."

Damn, Cee thought. *Is that how I'm going to be remembered?* She looked at the car Jimi was leaning against and for an instant everything froze. *He'll ask if he can come along. He came to town to meet the Rainmaker and now he knows I was there, with her, and he'll ask if he can come.*

Jimi bent to drag the moaning man away from the car.

Cee stepped around them both and opened the door. "Thanks again."

"She's amazing," Jimi said. "Tell her I said so, and I'm not the only one who thinks that."

"I'll tell her," Cee said. She kept the gun in one hand as she strapped in and shut the door, locking it from the inside. She glanced at Jimi and the broken man at his feet, nodded once, then drove the car along the alley and onto the main street. She turned right. As she drove she started to shake, shock and anger cooling her blood.

If Jimi hadn't helped, she really would have done her best to put a bullet into that fucker's chest.

———

Cee drove fast, but not so fast that she attracted attention. She was desperate to get away from Abbey Springs and back into the empty Desert, partly because the man was a resident of the town and she was probably already being sought. But more because of Jimi, and the reason he'd arrived in Abbey Springs. He'd come for Ash, to fete and worship her, and where there was one there would be more.

Ash didn't need that. She wasn't doing her thing for attention or adulation, she was doing it because it was her gift and she wanted to help.

Cee slowed at pedestrian crossings, flipping down the sun visor and pulling the crushed hat low on her head again. Every second that passed brought discovery closer. He was probably in Caz's already, bleeding over the floor and calling the cops or whoever passed for the law here.

Jimi had helped her, but she was more afraid of him than the man he'd hit and kicked away from her. He'd had a look in his eyes that she recognised, one that worried her the more she thought about it. It had been a hunger of sorts. A craving.

She parked close to the edge of the Burn, trying to tuck the car as far out of sight as she could. It ground over debris in a back lane between houses, and by the time she opened the door Ash was already there, peering from behind a wall.

"You found a hat," Ash said.

"And a car."

"What happened to your face?"

"I'll tell you when we're moving. Grab our bags and jump in."

"I'm not feeling so great."

"So get in the back and lie down. I need to drive us away from here."

"West," Ash said.

Cee blinked. She'd not even had a direction or destination in mind, but Ash spoke with such conviction.

"Why west?"

"The fires," Ash said. "I've been thinking about what I did, and what happened, and I know I could have just kept on going... spoken to them, maybe, made contact..." Her eyes went vague and distant, looking somewhere Cee could never see.

"Ash, in the car. Someone might be following us."

Ash nodded and got into the back of the car, guitar case clasped close to her, backpacks dropped on the other rear seat. Cee reversed and started driving again, skirting the ruin of the Burn and meeting the highway at the western edge of town.

"So why towards the fires?" she asked.

"Because maybe I can help put them out."

Cee looked in the mirror and Ash was falling asleep sitting up, mumbling a few more words as her head tipped back and rested against the back of the seat.

"I'll tell them... don't mean any harm."

Cee felt a chill at her words, wondering who 'they' were, why Ash should talk to them. But they were probably the mutterings of someone skimming the edge of madness, just as they now edged around the expanse of the Burn. The eye was passing Ash by, and Cee had to be there for her when the tumult took her again.

JIMI

"What's that way?" Jimi asked the bleeding man.

"Huh?'

"The way she drove her new car. What's that way? The edge of town?"

"The Burn," the man said. "Where the rains came down yesterday."

"Yeah, the rains," Jimi said. He snatched up the woman's belt and the blade broken from her knife, chose a car, and was inside within thirty seconds.

As he drove from the parking lot he resisted the temptation to drive over the bloodied man. Then, as he approached the alley entrance, he reconsidered. The man could identify both of them, and both cars, and he knew where they were going. This was a small town, but probably big enough to have a local police force in operation. A couple of cruisers, maybe. Cops looking for glory and the excuse for a bit of excitement.

He looked in the rear-view mirror at where the man was just pushing himself to his knees. He was staring at the ground, at the dark patch of blood and broken teeth pooled beneath him. Probably counting his blessings.

Jimi put the car in reverse. God bless the silence of electric cars. The man only looked up when he heard the crunch of tyres on gravel.

Jimi hadn't driven a car as nice as this one in a while. He was used to driving his big Soaker wagon, and that had been fifteen years old and the rougher side of run down when he'd acquired it. Mechanically the wagon had run okay, but there'd been springs sticking up through the seats, parts of the inner door linings were missing, and the sleeping mattress behind the seats had always retained the tang of old piss no matter how many times he washed or aired it. The BMW he'd taken from Alison and Josh had been bullet-holed and stained with blood and brains. And the car he'd left in Abbey Springs was already fading from memory, so bland was its ordinariness.

This car felt nice. It ran smoothly, it was almost fully charged with a three-quarter-full standby gas tank, and he'd found a bag of candy and a bottle of soda in the glove box. Not his favourite candy, but it would do. Beggars can't be choosers, as his Papa would have said.

Best of all, it didn't smell of piss.

Jimi took a couple more painkillers from the bottle he kept in his pocket. Only a handful left, and he knew he was popping them too often, but his broken teeth hurt like fuck. Other wounds and injuries and cuts bothered him, but it was his smashed teeth that really screamed.

Reaching the edge of town, the sudden appearance of the Burn came as a shock. One moment he was driving along an abandoned street, structures on either side boarded up or simply empty and dilapidated. The next moment the land opened up before him, buildings eaten by fire, piles of wreckage stacked here and there like burial mounds as far as he could see.

The shock quickly gave way to concern. Shit, had he lost Cee already? His was the only car here, and he peered around, trying to glimpse the silver Tyne.

He stopped the car and climbed onto the hood, then the roof, wincing as his cracked ribs protested. At least that stab of pain distracted from his spiky teeth.

Shadows cast ahead by the early morning sun rising above him over Abbey Springs, he scanned the Burn, the rough trails where the routes of old roads were still apparent, and he wondered what it must have been like.

Water falling from the sky. Rain clouds forming from the clear blue. The first pink patterns of something other than rain as blood spotted the ground, the ruins, the upturned faces of those revelling in the downpour. Life-giving. Life-taking.

He saw a glimmer in the distance to the south-west, and for a moment he thought the sun was reflecting from a puddle left over from yesterday's downpour. But there were no puddles. The ground had sucked in the water, coveting the precious moisture, and the glint was sunlight shining from a single moving vehicle.

Jimi climbed down from the roof and started following at a distance. Once they hit a highway there was no need to stay too close, and hopefully soon the route might become busier, and he'd be able to tuck in behind other cars or even a Soaker convoy. If needs be, he could change vehicles every time he stopped. He still had the knack for jacking cars.

Driving with one hand, he started laying a trail of crumbs on the net that would lead to the Rainmaker. If her bastard father was still alive, and had seen the footage, and was coming to find her—and Jimi hoped for that, prayed for it—then hopefully he would find and follow Jimi's trail.

And if the father wasn't coming, or was dead, Jimi could still avenge his dead Papa.

He'd hack off her head, and she would rain her own blood.

ASH

My dream is of the storm my life has always weathered. "You have to be careful," my father says, and he's older than I've ever seen him. We're sitting in a woodland. There's an apparatus I don't recognise between us, and we each have a wire pinned into our left arm. "It takes you somewhere, and you've got to be so, so careful that you don't allow anything back with you." His haunted eyes. That ragged, healed scar on his face. He looks so old.

"I'll be careful. You'll show me how."

He tries to smile. Only one corner of his mouth raises, and I wonder how careful he had been.

Wind blows, lightning thrashes, sparks creep up the wires into my father's arm and my own. His eyes go wide.

"Storm's coming," I say. "Storm's close."

"I'm here to look after you," a voice says.

Cee, I think, and I'm not sure whether the storm in my dreams and the rains I brought down the night before are one and the same. I open my eyes and I'm dozing in the back seat of a car.

"Where are we?"

"Heading west."

"To the fires."

"Yeah."

I sit up. The guitar case is in the footwell and I press my leg against it, comforted by the contact. It still feels damp.

"Maybe the fires will burn the storm away," I say. Cee glances at me in the rear-view mirror. She looks worried.

"You okay?" she asks.

"Not sure. Not sure I've ever been okay."

She doesn't reply to that, and I take it as answer enough. I feel distant from almost everything as the eye moves further from me, but the tumult takes me elsewhere.

It takes me back *there.*

Be so, so careful that you don't allow anything back with you, Dad's voice echoes in my memories like the rumble of forgotten thunder.

In my mind's eye I see Skunksville. The rust-red sand beneath my feet. The angry skies, pulsing and boiling like a spreading bruise. Those shapes noticing me, turning and coming for me in an excited huddle as if they had been waiting for this moment, waiting for me, for so long.

I didn't bring them back, I think, unsure whether I spoke it as well. But I think about those other creatures that have fallen with my rains, and wonder whether they could have come from the blood-coloured sands of Skunksville.

And I wonder how close those other, larger shapes will be next time I plug myself in. I feel the need to do so. But also, fear.

"I can't bring them back with me," I say, and in Cee's eyes in the mirror I see a glut of storm-red clouds, as if reflected from my own. My forearms itch with a terrible need.

Like a living thing, the guitar case against my leg issues a comforting, tempting warmth.

JESSE

As Karina drove through the night and towards dawn, Jesse began to wish he hadn't sat in the back seat with Rocky. He'd done so to keep an eye on online activity without the glare of the screen distracting Karina from the road ahead, and he'd already found a few strands to follow. One was a series of reports on a small Abbey Springs news site. He had to scroll past mentions of reduced harvest, sinkholes opening across swathes of land to the east of the town, and the community's ongoing efforts to dig wells where the water table was lower and lower each year, until he found mention of the Rainmaker.

It was a series of eyewitness accounts written with no small measure of journalistic scepticism, the last of which was posted the previous day. The photograph and grainy footage were of poorer quality than those he'd seen elsewhere. *Ash kneeling in her rain*, he thought. Some accounts claimed that blood fell from the sky. If he closed his eyes he could almost feel the warm caress of red droplets across his own arms. Another page he kept refreshing was an old-style message board that seemed to have been set up to refute any claims that the storm had been anything other than a natural occurrence. Someone always tries to take the credit, the page claimed, with a photo of Ash, head down, arms bleeding where they were plugged into her apparatus. Jesse examined this picture carefully, ignoring the text and focusing on the apparatus. It was too blurred to make anything out in detail, but he could still tell it was more refined and streamlined than her first effort from years ago. This new apparatus reminded him of his own, more than her childhood construct.

Part of him was excited about that, even proud. The same part of him that regretted taking the back seat, because he was closer to his apparatus back here. It was in the trunk, and it called.

He kept one hand on the back of his sleeping dog's neck, scratching and squeezing as Rocky snored and twitched. In his other hand, his cell phone. He tapped and scrolled, and he kept returning to the mention that interested him most. At first, he'd glanced at it and moved past, because something about the posts made them sound like they were confused, maybe even made up.

Rainmaker, still wet, but moving.

No clouds here.

Not the Rainmaker right now.

Her blood still falls.

The Rainmaker and her friend, travelling west.

This last was accompanied by a photo, taken through a dusty windshield and zoomed in, of the rear end of a vehicle. The light was poor—it had been uploaded only a few minutes earlier, and the wide skies were the same early morning shades of fire and autumn that Jesse could see outside now—but he filtered the photo through some software to sharpen and refine the image, and when he'd zoomed in some more he uploaded the image to a vehicle recognition app.

"I think she's in a silver Ford Tyne," he said.

"Where?"

"West of Abbey Springs. Where are we now?"

"A few miles east of the town," Karina said. She sounded tired. She'd been driving for a couple of hours and she'd turned down his offers to take over. His nervousness over the speed she was driving had lessened a little, but he knew why she wanted to maintain control. She still didn't trust him. She'd come to him for help in finding their daughter, but Karina still believed she was the one most determined.

That was not the case. Not now. Not after what he'd seen and sensed after touching his apparatus for the first time in so many years.

"Straight through?" he asked.

"Where have you found her?"

"On a weird message board, linked to a general social media hub. Keyword search brings it up."

"And?"

"Dunno. Something about it feels odd."

"Have you found any other sightings?"

"Not since the footage you saw. That's all over the net now, too."

"If she's stayed in the town, she'll still be there if we follow that car and it's a false lead," Karina said.

"She won't have stayed."

"What makes you so sure?"

"I wouldn't."

"And she's like you?"

He heard the bitterness in her voice, or maybe it was an attempt at humour.

"When it comes to this, yeah," he said.

Karina didn't reply, maybe because she had nothing good to say. They locked eyes in the rear-view and Jesse smiled, but he could only see her eyes, and if she smiled back it didn't reach them. One hand still on Rocky's neck, cell in the other, it was his forearms that itched. He hadn't felt the itch that strongly for a long, long time, and though it made him sick and afraid, and conjured memories that he had successfully consigned to nightmares for so long, there was a strange hunger there as well. It could only damage and hurt him and others, but the apparatus called to him, singing sweet songs of yearning. This was his subconscious, the part of him that could never deny what he was and what he had done. The part of him as natural as breathing.

He did not turn and reach for the old, battered box. But he could not shake the terrifying idea of just plugging in and letting go.

The power, the sense of control, the flicker of sparks along the needles and into his arms, the tickle of rain...

...and that place he had promised never to visit ever, ever again. The Shore.

"We're not far from her," Karina said.

"If she does it again it might be worse."

"Part of this is about stopping her," Karina said. "That's why I came to you. But my main aim is to save her, bring her back home to me."

Jesse didn't reply. *What if she can't be saved?* he thought. *What if she can't be stopped?* He understood that was why Karina insisted on driving now. She needed to maintain control because she was still afraid of what he might do.

"Abbey Springs ahead," Karina said. "I'm driving straight through."

Jesse refreshed the screen on his cell. Another message popped up.

I hope the Rainmaker makes rain again soon. The whole world's waiting.

I'm not, Jesse thought, but he felt the springs and dials, capacitors and coils of his apparatus as if every element of it was fresh in his memory and hands and veins, and he wondered whether he'd been lying to himself all along.

CEE

An hour after leaving Abbey Springs, Cee wasn't looking in the rear-view quite so much. A couple of times she saw cars behind them, and one followed along the highway for a few miles before turning off. If Jimi was following them, he was keeping his distance.

Also in the rear-view, she saw Ash asleep. She looked troubled even with her eyes closed and head lolling on her left shoulder, and Cee wished she could ease her suffering.

That's what I'm doing, she thought. *I'm looking after her.* But she wasn't sure. She didn't know whether driving towards the fires so that Ash could bring down rain was looking after her at all.

Her scraped cheek had stopped bleeding and dried into crisp scabs. She'd picked out a couple of slivers of gravel, but she'd need to give it closer attention when they stopped. The car's charge was holding well, but they'd need a bathroom break, and food and coffee, and she was still on edge about the stolen car. At any moment she expected the flashing light of the law in her mirror, and several times she considered ditching the car.

Yeah, right. Because stealing this one was so easy.

As shadows grew shorter and the skies burned with the familiar scorched shades of day, Cee at last began to settle. They were making good time and Ash was resting, and two hours after leaving town they were over a hundred miles away. Sometimes the road behind them didn't display even a glimmer of sun on glass or metal. Abbey Springs was behind them, and Cee began to consider what might lie ahead.

The raging bush fires that Ash wanted to go towards were a familiar aspect of Desert life. With countless miles of farmland abandoned to the drought, and relentless sun and elevated temperatures becoming the norm, so too were the conflagrations that regularly scorched thousands of square miles of Desert landscape. Private fire brigades had sprung up, and with frequent lack of water, new and imaginative methods had been developed to protect against fires. Often preventative more than reactive, this sometimes involved huge swathes of the landscape's surrounding communities being stripped of any plant life, living or dead, and scarified down to the hard-packed subsoil. These places were intended to act as fire breaks, but they couldn't halt the violent winds that accompanied the bush fires from carrying blazing brands to seed fires elsewhere. Many areas of the landscape were scarred by these fire breaks, barren places even by Desert standards. Elsewhere, the scars of old fires showed where such desperate measures had been ineffective. The Burn in Abbey Springs was a familiar sight. Cee had seen a dozen communities that had been burned to the ground, and several times she had been forced to escape the flames.

Moving away from the fires was more usual than heading towards them.

There's nothing usual about this, she thought, looking at Ash in the mirror once more. She looked like a corpse, but Cee could see her eyes moving beneath closed eyelids as she weathered whatever nightmares haunted her. Her father trying to kill her, perhaps. Her time on the road in the Desert, searching for something she had yet to find.

Maybe she was dreaming of whoever or whatever it was that she was determined not to let in.

The road took them into a landscape of low sweeping hills, hillsides spiked with the matchstick corpses of dead trees and brittle copses of those still clinging on to life. They followed a river for a while, winding along a shallow valley, road skipping back and forth over the dried waterway on characterless rusted metal bridges. Sometimes she saw the glimmer of a stream in the wide riverbed, like an exposed vein on the parched cracked hide of the world. More often there was no water at all. In the distance, above the hills, the sky looked different. Still clear and deep blue, but there was a heaviness to it that drew out some of the colour, made it calmer, more washed out. She wiped the inside of the windshield, then set the washers sweeping back and forth. Dust smeared in even arcs. The strange tenseness to the western skies remained.

Smoke, Cee thought. She'd heard that the bush fires and the massive smoke clouds they pushed out could be seen from space. It could be that she was seeing the leading edge of one such vast cloud now.

The road rose towards a low ridge where two shoulders of hills met, and as she climbed she glanced in the rear-view mirror again. The twisting road behind her was hidden behind folds in the land, but where it snaked between hills in the distance she saw sunlight reflected from glass. There was no reason at all to suspect this was Jimi following them after a hundred and thirty miles, and no reason to fear it might be the law. Still, she pushed down on the accelerator.

Cresting the hill and heading down the other side, a strange, unexpected sight greeted her. The river along the valley floor was dammed by fallen trees, tumbled rocks, and packed mud, a structure that had probably degraded and been added to year after year. There was evidence that a good portion of the valley had once been flooded to form an artificial lake, but now the river's flow had slowed and the reservoir was little more than a pond. Gathered around this pond, like large mammals at a watering hole, were six Soaker wagons. None of them were the same, and they made for a startling spectacle in the pale landscape. The sun had scorched colour and life from this place, and the Soaker crew were gathering what water they could to bring life to somewhere else.

The road curved down the hillside and passed close to the parked vehicles, and Cee slowed the car to a crawl. Two Soakers, a man and a woman, offered a wave by way of greeting, and Cee came to a stop. She wound down the window, glancing back at Ash.

She was awake, leaning back in the seat and staring from the side window.

"I smell smoke," Ash said. Cee breathed in but could smell nothing.

"You okay?"

"Thirsty. Hungry."

"We won't be here long. You stay in the car." Cee stood from her seat and stretched, allowing her T-shirt to ride up and expose the pistol tucked in her belt.

The Soakers seemed friendly enough, and Cee smiled as she approached. "Buy some water from you?" she asked. "And if you have some food to spare, that'd be a bonus."

"You're heading the wrong way," the woman said. Closer, Cee could see that she looked tired and drawn, her face ashen. Usually they were tanned and weathered from long years in the sun.

"Fire's drawing in," the man said, pointing vaguely over his shoulder. He was scrawny but strong, dark skin cracked and hard from so long in the Desert. "They've got it under control in the south for now, and thirty miles north from here it's hit a fire break that might hold it back for a day or so. But it's moving quickly from west to east, and Rockfield is right in the way."

"Is that what you're doing?" Cee asked.

"Town needs water now more than ever," the woman said. "Some have evacuated, most are staying to try and save what little they have. So there's money to be made."

The man looked uncomfortable. The woman glanced aside. Cee wondered if they were making money at all, or if they were helping out simply because they could.

"So why're you going that way?" the man asked.

"Same reason," Cee said. "To help."

The woman turned and walked back towards the Soaker wagons pumping water out from the shrinking reservoir.

"How can you help?" the man asked.

"We'll do what we can," Cee said. "It's good to help out, right?"

The woman reached her wagon and climbed into the cab. A few second later she jumped down again, a plastic water bottle in each hand.

"Sure, if the pay's good," the man said. He smiled, and Cee thought she saw the truth behind that smile that she had already suspected—that for these two Soakers at least, it wasn't always about the pay.

"Ten bucks per bottle," the woman said. "For you, I'll call it twenty for two. I'll throw in a couple bags of chips."

Cee laughed and dug a twenty from her pocket. "Thanks. Are there others?"

"Helping?" the man asked. "Sure. The townsfolk. And some fire department choppers from Cali trying to protect the wealthier parts of town."

"Thanks for the water and chips," Cee said.

"Maybe see you soon," the woman said.

Cee nodded and walked back to the car, and for a moment she considered asking them to delay Jimi if they saw him pass by. She didn't know why she felt threatened by him—he'd helped her, after all—but the idea of Ash drawing fans, gathering a tribe or a cult around her, didn't sit well. *She needs peace*, she thought. *She needs calm so that she gets better, not worse.*

And here they were, driving into the fires of hell.

She handed Ash one plastic bottle and a bag of chips and kept the rest for herself, lifting her bottle in a toast to the Soakers as she drove on. She sipped tentatively, expecting the dank grittiness of untreated wild water. But it was pure, with only a residual tang of the chemicals used to make it potable. Offering the Soakers a silent thanks, she drove past the dried-up valley and towards the darkening bank of smoke manifesting on the horizon.

"Clouds," Ash said.

"Clouds of smoke."

"Time to make my own clouds." Cee heard her rummaging, and when she glanced back she saw the guitar case open on the seat and Ash grasping one of the needles in both hands.

"Don't worry," Ash said. "I've been thinking about this, and what happened, and the storms that have taken me and made me their own. I think it was always because I've been afraid. It's *me* who should be making the storms *my* own. I'll be unafraid, and make them all… my… own."

"What if—?"

"Don't worry," Ash said again. "Just drive for the fires. I'll only plug in fully when I know I have control. When I know I can talk to them, and keep them away. I have to be so, so careful that I don't allow anything to come back with me."

Cee drove down out of the hills and towards the smudge of a distant town and the darkening wall of smoke that formed a cliff in the skies beyond. Soon she saw a scatter of pale white clouds forming in the sky, low above the car.

And these were not clouds of smoke.

KARINA

"She's heading for one of the big bush fires," Jesse said from the back seat.

"You're sure?"

"I'm seeing footage from fires maybe only forty miles from us."

They'd been driving for over four hours. Karina had refused Jesse's offer to swap, not because she thought she could drive faster, but because she needed to maintain some level of control. She'd brought Jesse into this because she hadn't been sure she could confront Ash on her own and save her from whatever she was going through. Even after years searching for her girl, she knew that the strongest link existed between her and her father. Their insecurities, talents, and curses were inextricably bound. She hated it, but as soon as she'd heard the first whisper about the new Rainmaker she'd accepted it as well. It was the part of Jesse's life she had grown to despise, but it was also the most solid, incontestable aspect of their history together. Now, she needed to drive so that it meant she was pushing them forward, not him.

And she wasn't sure what Jesse might do when they found her. *We have to stop her*, he'd said, and he'd tried stopping her once before. Karina had spent too long looking for her daughter to watch Jesse hurt her all over again. She was resigned to the fact that she needed him to find Ash, but then it would be down to Karina to save her.

"A fire makes sense," Jesse said.

"So she can help?"

"She'll be feeling… vulnerable. But maybe powerful, too."

"And scared," Karina said. "Maybe she won't want to do it again. After what happened in Abbey Springs, maybe she's running."

"Why do you think that?"

"Because you did."

Jesse's silence did not sound wounded or hurt. Maybe he realised she was speaking the truth.

"I'm not sure she's quite all there," he said.

"Hardly surprising, after what you did to her."

"But there's something else," Jesse said. Karina glanced in the mirror and saw him looking down at his cell phone. Unguarded, she saw what she hoped was his honest, open expression. He looked sad and haunted, but he was also worried. "She's got help. And that could mean she's being steered or coerced."

"No one can make you do that shit, can they?"

"Not me, no."

"But?"

"But we don't know how damaged she is."

"By what you did to her."

He nodded.

"So who's helping her?"

"The report I'm following is intermittent and fragmented. As if whoever's posting is driving as well, and following them, maybe. But it seems to be a young woman."

"What else?" Karina asked.

"They can see smoke in the distance and clouds in the sky."

"Smoke clouds?"

Jesse didn't answer.

"Jesse?"

"Rain clouds," he said. "They look like rain clouds, just starting to form. She's getting ready to do it again."

Karina, in control, drove faster.

JIMI

"Soakers," Jimi said. He smiled and waved, and a couple of them waved back as he drove by. The sight of wagons parked around the shrunken reservoir, sucking up scant supplies, gave him an unexpected pang. He'd been a Soaker for years, and the solo lifestyle he'd chosen had suited him well, wandering and making money and feeling a level of respect directed at him from some communities.

The Soakers watched him drive past, and he wondered how recently the two women had passed by.

He'd seen the deepening haze of the distant fires in the west, and he knew where they were going, and why. Jimi had seen bush fires before, and once he'd been drafted in to help fight a small blaze threatening a collection of farmsteads on the Idaho plains. He'd made a few thousand dollars out of that, and one of the local irrigation engineers had fallen for him. *My hero*, she'd called him. He'd even considered hanging around for a while—because she was nice, and he'd sort of fallen for her, too—but others hadn't trusted him. It would have ended badly. Most things did for Jimi.

The idea of following Ash and her friend into the flames ignited a nervous excitement that tickled his guts.

I see smoke clouds in the distance, he wrote on the message board he was using. His previous posts were attracting comments and plenty of shares, and he took a couple of photos through the windshield showing the sweeping landscape and vast skies. The photos didn't yet pick up the haze of distant smoke, but he made sure to include a road sign, casually but carefully in focus. He considered what to write next, cell phone held to his mouth ready to dictate another post.

The idea of what might lie ahead was a balm for his injuries, and as he spoke he imagined he was talking directly to the man who had killed his Papa.

"She's going to put out the fires," he said, and his words translated to text that was sent into the aether.

Driving down from the hills, he saw the glint of sunlight from a car in the distance. More distant, the textured spread of a town across the horizon, and the looming shadow of smoke hanging above it.

Closer, higher, the clear blue sky was scattered with forming clouds.

"She's making rain clouds," he said. He took more pictures as he drove. *Come on, Daddy*, he thought. *Come and find your daughter.*

ASH

I t wasn't loss of control that had been her undoing, it was never having control in the first place. Her father hadn't taught her well—he had never quelled the fear, only built on it with warnings and cautions—and when her attempts had started going wrong, he had blamed her rather than himself.

Now she has found Cee. Ash has never had a friend like Cee before. She makes her feel confident and assured. Not safe—feeling safe is a mistake, in these times and with these gifts—but unafraid.

I don't fear you, Ash thinks, and the storms within do not change, but they do not threaten. They are part of her, not apart from her. They might well be the greatest part of her. She will not be afraid of herself.

The eye has passed her by, but she wonders whether the eye was ever real at all. It gave her the illusion of control, but perhaps it was simply her way of looking in from the outside. More remote, more detached, the eye observed her passive self. The real her is here and now, with boiling storms inside. She has always been a child of the storm. That's the mistake her father made: making her believe she had any choice.

This time it will be different, she thinks, because she is approaching the storm with control, luring it closer, ensuring she has a grip. She won't allow herself to lose it again. Cee is here with her, protecting her and being her friend, and she's the rock that Ash holds onto as the storm begins to grow. She can feel it ready to rage, and she holds it down. She senses the drop in pressure on the outside as it builds within, and she smiles and grips the needles. They are warm in her fists, warmer than blood. They're possessed of their own power, and the apparatus in the open case is filled with potential. She is eager to plug in and become one with it. She can feel its eagerness to make that so.

"Not yet," she says.

"There are more clouds now," Cee says, and Ash hears the delight in her voice. "Is that you?"

"What do you think?" Ash asks, and she laughs. The skies above them are hers. Clouds form. Moisture condenses. She feels its potential, even without being fully connected.

"I think it's beautiful," Cee says.

"It really is." The calm of the eye has passed by, but Ash has found a new calm as queen of the storm. The power is beguiling but not damaging—she knows its limits and her own, and understands that it is power to be used with wisdom and kindness.

Closing her eyes, she peers into Skunksville. It's like looking through a mist or a veil: the view is foggy and uncertain, the colours muted. She opens herself to the place, allowing in hints of its scent, a damp breeze on her skin, and the sound of straining, crackling, grinding movement, even though the sea is almost completely motionless and the blood-red sands of the beach appear almost solid. It's as if there is something beneath the sand, beneath this strange land, that is slowly and perpetually turning over. She feels a subtle vibration but it could be the car's movement, not something transmitted or sensed from Skunksville.

I'm both here and there, she thinks, and it's a strange feeling. She can sense the movement of the car in her stomach and Cee's proximity is calming, like a cool hand on a fevered brow. She can also feel the damp grittiness of sand beneath her feet and hear a distant lowing that comes from a creature she does not know. There's something about the sound that suggests intelligence, even language, and it is chilling and beautiful.

She sees movement, but unlike the last time she was here, she is merely an observer. The moving creatures are not aware of her. Something with a bright yellow shell skitters from behind a rock on the shore and enters the sea, causing hardly a ripple. The water is thick like oil, or perhaps it's heavy with salt, resistant to rippling. This place is not only stranger than she knows, but stranger than she can understand. Several more of the creatures follow the first, and then something swoops down out of shadows and snatches up the last one in the line. It vanishes again almost instantly, merging into the gloom, or changing colour and hue so effectively that it becomes unseen. Other unrecognisable creatures crawl and fly, slink and slide, and the more she watches, the more Ash becomes aware of them.

But the creatures of Skunksville still do not see her.

Not even when she sees *them*.

They're much further away, gathered in a small group in the shade of the tall cliff that disappears way above. From this distance they might be fungi speckled along the cliff's lower slopes, many of them gathered close, heads bowed like people in prayer or old folk considering the feet that have brought them so far.

I'm here, Ash thinks, and she almost projects it vocally because they fascinate her. The other creatures—birds and spiders, snakes and insects, other things that are similar or combinations of many—appear wild and almost mindless, animals of instinct rather than intellect. These humanoid shapes she sees across the sand and along this strange beach are something else.

Waiting things, she thinks. *Watching things.* Last time she was here they had noticed and started coming towards her. The idea of them reaching her both terrified and delighted, and perhaps that time would come. But it would be a meeting within her control, not theirs.

I am Skunksville. It's my domain as much as theirs. She looks up to the dark, heavy sky, laden with rain that she seeks to control, heavy with blood that she does not. She doesn't quite understand how this can be, but it's here and she accepts it, just as much as the rainmaking is a part of her. Perhaps her father or grandmother tried to understand, but she doesn't think they ever did.

It's not about understanding. It's about accepting.

I'm not afraid, she thinks as a scorpion the size of her hand crawls across her foot. *I don't fear.* A spider drifts by on long trails of silk, caught on the breeze and clasped in like a fist waiting to land. *I'm the master here.*

She clamps her hand tighter around the needles, and veins of lightning arc behind blood-red clouds. The scorpion pauses in its movement, and along the beach one of the humanoid shapes looks up to the sky.

Nothing looks at her. She feels ready. Maintaining control, remaining there, she scrapes one needle across her left forearm and pushes. A sharp prick, and then she feels a gentle pop as it pierces her skin.

The colours become more vibrant, the rich scents of Skunksville even more powerful, and the breeze from calm sea to impossible land carries more spiders and scatters grains of red dust against her cheek.

The place becomes agitated, excited, alive, and still she isn't noticed as the rain begins to fall.

Pure, fresh, bloodless rain.

CEE

As they approached the edge of Rockfield it began to rain, and in the rear-view mirror Cee saw the flare of brake lights as a car slowed and then stopped. A dozen vehicles had passed them heading for the hills, some of them towing trailers or with roof racks packed high with as many belongings as they could fit. These were the inhabitants of the town who had already given up against the approaching conflagration. The smoke here wasn't too bad, but it formed a wall in the western sky beyond town, a dark grey mass blotting out the blue and spreading high up where it was caught by the wind stream.

Cee couldn't blame them for leaving, but she was also unsurprised when some of them slowed and stopped. It was raining. A gentle mist for now, but still enough for her to turn on the wipers. Rain might bring relief in the normal times of drought and hunger and thirst. With a raging fire threatening the town, it brought hope.

"You okay?" Cee asked.

"I'm good," Ash said, and she sounded good. She was calm and at peace, a distracted smile on her face.

"Nothing…?" Cee asked, not wanting to verbalise her fears, knowing Ash would understand.

"It's all good," Ash said.

Cee checked the road ahead then glanced back, down at Ash's arms. Both needles were inserted and the apparatus was open on the seat beside her. There was no blood on her arms, no sparks leaping around the needles, wires, and apparatus, but rather a gentle, bright glow.

"So, where shall we go?" Cee asked.

"Let's head through the town," Ash said. "Stay in the car. Don't draw attention."

"You're still in the eye?" Ash had spoken these words to her as she tried to explain, but they felt strange coming from Cee's own mouth. Almost a different tongue, but one that she was beginning to understand.

"In my own eye," Ash said. "Observing, not observed."

"Okay," Cee said, laughing. A nervous laugh.

"I mean I'm more in control," Ash said. "I'm here and there. Don't worry about me. Just drive."

"Yes, ma'am."

"It's because of you," Ash said, her voice lower and almost lost in the more frequent swish of the wipers. "You make me unafraid." As she spoke, the misty rain turned into a more consistent downpour. They passed another car that had stopped on the road heading out of town, parents and two kids standing on the dusty verge and looking up at the sky. Clouds they might have believed were drifting smoke had opened up, and as rain fell and the morning light dimmed, the clouds grew heavier with greater promise.

Cee drove into the outskirts of the small town, and it was a place preparing for disaster. It was a similar size and layout to Abbey Springs, just another Desert town, with residential areas surrounding a central business district, and a large square at the centre of which lay a park ringed by vibrant trees. Rockfield must

have gone to great efforts to maintain their square. There was even
a bandstand with several racks of folding chairs stacked against
one side, and a dried-up pond that seemed to have been given
over to a skate park for kids. Many of the businesses around the
square were boarded up, but there was an air of bustle to the town
that was not only to do with the sudden unexpected downpour.
People rushed here and there, and though Cee saw some of them
engaged in quick exchanges with friends while glancing up, this
was not a chaos brought on by the rain. It was organisation as the
town prepared for fire.

Loaded cars and trucks were parked away from the buildings
on what had once been the lawned area of the large central
square. Buckets of sand were placed along the sidewalk. A tangle
of hoses snaked in front of one of the square's larger buildings,
maybe the town hall or council building. There were a couple
of small water wagons with hoses coiled on reels. As Cee drove
slowly around the square a few people looked their way, but the
town was large enough that no one knew everyone, and she didn't
feel they stood out too much.

If anyone looked into the back seat, that might be different.
Maybe some of the people here would have heard about what had
happened in Abbey Springs—Jimi's arrival proved that the story
had already travelled far and wide, to those interested in looking—
but she hoped they wouldn't automatically associate this surprise
downpour with a town a hundred and fifty miles away.

"I think we should keep going," Cee said. "Out to the edge of
town, where the fire's due to hit."

"Keep going, yeah," Ash said.

"The rain'll dampen down the buildings. Soak the ground.
And maybe we should go further, wet the ground, try and stop
the fire in its tracks."

"Yeah, stop it."

Ash looked dreamy. Her eyes were still open and she wore a distant smile, but Cee wasn't sure what she was seeing, or how far away it might be.

The closer they came to the western edge of town, the more frantic the activity all around them. Cars headed past them, going east, buildings were being hosed down here and there with precious water, and folk stood in small groups as they looked with worried eyes to the west.

The wall of smoke dwarfed the landscape. It was beyond a gentle rise outside town, past farmsteads where farmers were busy opening gates to allow cattle an open route to freedom. That more than anything brought home the terrible fate soon to befall this place—the animals being set free, rather than the families loading up their lives and fleeing.

The rains became heavier.

"Keep going," Ash said, and Cee couldn't tell whether she was talking to herself.

The road was a shimmering mirror speckled with a million ripples. The pale ground darkened with water. Cee saw no blood in the rain, and neither could she smell it when she opened her window.

No blood. But as they slowed at the summit of the gentle rise and the full scale of the approaching fires became apparent, blood found them.

JIMI

After passing through the town and seeing the silver car stop up the slope ahead of him, Jimi thought of pulling off the road and waiting for the father to come. He'd been putting down a trail of clues for anyone who might be seeking the Rainmaker, and sitting in peace for a while—an hour, a day—might give his injuries time to calm. He'd been popping too many painkillers and caffeine pills, and sometimes his vision blurred, sometimes his bones ached and his organs throbbed, stars of pain settling throughout his exhausted body.

But the rain washed away so many pains and plans with its purity. He opened the car window as he drove and it splashed across his arms and face. It smelled like renewal. This storm would be the edge upon which his present walked, the pivot point between his troubled past and a new, brighter future.

A future where he would make Papa proud.

"I'm more like you than you ever thought," he said into the rain. The car wipers made his future clear, rain blurred it, clear again, and with every sweep the car parked on the crest of the hill came closer.

He was done with waiting. He'd spent his whole life waiting, since seeing Papa die in the mud. He blinked and his vision blurred again, inside the car as well as through the water-smeared windshield.

Jimi did not stop. If Papa's murderer *was* on his way—and it was a big *if*, a stretch of fate—he'd still come, whatever happened in the next few minutes. Jimi could sit and wait by the side of the road, or he could get out in the rain and confront this new Rainmaker. Let her know what her daddy had done. And if he came, Jimi would meet him with his daughter's hacked-off head in one hand, his gun in the other.

Making sure the gun was tucked into the belt at the small of his back, he rolled to a stop close behind the stolen car. As he stood from the vehicle he bit his bottom lip when a wave of dizziness swept over him. He smelled blood, but there was none in the rain. This was all his own.

The Rainmaker's car had pulled off the road, into a gravelled gateway leading to a distant farmstead. For a few moments, as he looked beyond the car and down the gentle slope, and at the monster approaching from the west, Jimi forgot about everything: the pain in his body from the beating he'd taken; the pain in his heart from recent memories of his dead Papa; the car just ahead, and the potential for closure, and revenge, that might wait inside.

The fire ate the world.

It stretched along an uneven line from north to south, a blazing snake slowly twisting and sidewinding its way eastward. Far to the north it halted at a wide dark scar on the landscape, a place where the ground itself had been torn aside in an attempt to smother the flames. To the south the fire line extended up and over a small hill, above which more smoke billowed and boiled. Between these two points the blaze marked the end of the world. Jimi could see nothing beyond, because smoke hung thick, heavy, and high above the fire, a grey cliff that pulsed and moved with violent thermals. Even up on this hill, two or more miles distant, he could feel a breeze brushing past him. Air was drawn in, rushing towards the fire as if eager to meet its end.

"Everything changes from here," Jimi said, and he imagined his words carried on the breeze, flitting past the ears of the familiar woman stepping from the Ford, passing her by, then being drawn across the dry landscape and swallowed by the flames. They would echo into the clouds of smoke, submitted to the fire gods and given heat and import even as they faded away to nothing.

Everything changes from here.

Cee turned and saw him and he started walking, slow and casual. He held his cell phone in his left hand, video function recording. She'd think he was still the Rainmaker fan who'd helped her back in Abbey Springs. She wouldn't suspect anything else. Why would she?

"Hi, Cee," Jimi said. "It's beautiful."

"The fire?" she asked.

"The rain."

And it was. Cool but not cold, and though it had only been falling for a few minutes the rain calmed the terrible Desert heat, already making a statement against the distant blaze. He left boot prints in the damp dust that covered everything. It refreshed his skin, washed dirt down from his hair into his eyes.

"Is she in the car?" He knew the answer, of course. Even if he wasn't sure, Cee's eyes would have given her away.

"I was worried the law might come after us," she said.

"No need to worry about that."

"Why? Where did he go after I left?"

"I had a word with him," Jimi said. "Told him you were important and to leave you alone. You and the Rainmaker."

"Who is it?"

The voice was muffled and sounded weak, distant, but it still sent a thrill up Jimi's spine.

"The guy who helped me back in Abbey Springs." Cee spoke without taking her eyes off Jimi. He liked that. It made him feel important. He noticed her hand close to her hip, thumb hooked into her pocket, and he guessed she had a gun tucked into her waistband. She might be a problem when the time came, but the time wasn't now. For now, he had to be her friend.

He raised the cell phone and aimed it at Cee and her car.

"Hey, no way!" she said, holding her other hand palm out.

"My friends won't believe—"

"No!" Cee took a few steps towards him and the Rainmaker said something he couldn't hear from inside the car.

Jimi lowered the cell phone and tapped off the camera function. He smiled at her. Making friends.

"This isn't a show," Cee said. "Understand?"

"It's amazing."

"Yeah, it is. But let it be amazing just for you, okay?"

"You're saying I can stay?" Jimi was pleased with his performance so far. If she said something he didn't like—no you can't stay, get the fuck away from here you freak—he'd take his chances at being a quicker draw than her. His gun was still in his waistband at his back, but he felt sure he could pull it and shoot in one movement. It wasn't something he'd practised, and it gave him a delicious chill. *Like a gunslinger*, he thought, remembering the old westerns his Papa used to watch, about dusty men in hot places wearing hats and knocking back shots of whiskey and shooting each other. It was another memory of Papa he'd not recalled in years, but which came to him rich and fresh now. Probably because Papa was close to the forefront of his mind. Soon, if things worked as he hoped, he might get to meet the man who had murdered him.

His whole body tingled, pleasure through the pain.

Cee's head tilted as she listened to something else from inside the car. The rain meant that Jimi couldn't hear what its maker was saying, but he liked the sound. It reminded him of the time Papa had died, and that was an important place to be right now.

If I'd been more like him, I might have been able to save him. It was a thought that had haunted him over the years, and he'd spent most of his life between then and now trying to be more like Papa. Stronger. Braver. Harder. He thought he was doing well.

The gun was cold against his back from the rain, and what he had to do was best served that way.

Cee gestured at him to approach. "Just put that away."

Jimi tucked the cell phone into his back pocket, touching the gun with his fingertips as he did. "Amazing, just for me," he said, and he walked a few steps along the verge towards Cee and the car. As he walked, he took in the surroundings: the road heading down from the hill crest and towards the approaching conflagration; the farmstead to their left, a couple of vehicles in the yard but with no signs of activity. Maybe they'd already fled. Several trucks passed them by, grim-faced townsfolk sitting in the back. They were holding an array of hoes, shovels, and rakes, and Jimi realised they were going to try to cut a fire break in the hillside. He couldn't help but be impressed by their hope. He raised a hand, but none of them responded. *They probably think we should be helping.* He almost laughed. If only they knew who was in the back of that car.

"Close enough," Cee said. She took a step back and stood at the car's front wing, allowing Jimi to stand a couple of metres from the car and take a look inside through the open window.

There she was.

"Just like him," he muttered, and he was both here and back there in the poppy fields. He was bathed in fresh rain, and also smelling blood in the downpour and hearing the splashes of creatures hitting the ground. Standing still, tensing up, his wounds screamed in again, making him queasy, making him sway where he stood in the unnatural downpour. When he blinked water from his eyes, he saw Papa lying dead, soaked with water and blood from the skies, swollen from the stings and bites that had taken him. Between blinks, he saw the woman. There was a machine on the seat beside her with wires leading from it and inserted into her forearms, and it was just like the Rainmaker back then. He didn't think it was the same device—the box containing it looked different, and there was something about the way fluid sparks and lights danced across this apparatus and flowed up and down the wires that seemed new—but the act was the same.

"Just like who?" the woman in the car asked.

"Just like the Rainmaker I used to know."

The woman's eyes went wide, then her face relaxed again and she smiled. Jimi wasn't sure, but it didn't look like a smile that touched her eyes or came from her heart.

"You followed my dad. Or maybe your family did, you don't look old enough."

Jimi didn't reply. He'd said the wrong thing, perhaps. Or maybe he'd said exactly the right thing.

"What's your name?" he asked.

"Ash."

"Like the world. Gone to ash."

She nodded slowly, then rested her head back against the seat. Neck exposed. Hands palm-up on her knees.

"Ash?" Cee asked, coming closer.

"I'm good. He's good."

"Why isn't he with you here?" Jimi asked, and Ash glanced up at him again through the open window. She seemed sleepy, almost dopey. It must have been taking a lot out of her.

I'll take more out of her, he thought. *I'll drain her of every ounce of blood and rain it down on her father.*

"He's gone," Cee said.

Jimi froze. Everything around him grew still, and for an instant the world was clear, and he perceived that instant with startling clarity. Even the raindrops stopped falling, and he saw himself reflected in every one of them.

He's gone.

Nothing in Ash's expression conveyed anything to make him doubt Cee's statement.

He's gone.

He remembered him running into the storm, box tucked under his arm, leaving Papa dying in the wet, bloody mud he had created.

"I missed him," Jimi said.

Ash blinked softly, gaze elsewhere. He wondered what she might be seeing but didn't care. He had missed her father, but he would not miss her. Killing her would have to be revenge enough for this life, and after she was dead, he might be able to become something or someone else.

Killing this Rainmaker was all the world could offer him, and Jimi would grasp that chance with both hands.

"I just want to take a photo," he said, and as he reached behind his back he experienced another moment frozen in time. His life slowed to an imperceptible pace, all his focus here and now. His agonies faded, and his head was clear of pain and drugs for the first time in days, as if the thought of what he was doing could block the nerve messages from the damaged parts of his body, and flush the drugs from his mind.

He blinked and took a mental image of the Rainmaker's daughter that he would remember forever. These were her last few seconds of life, and he would look into her eyes as she died, just as his Papa had looked into her father's.

His fingertips brushed the cell phone projecting from his pocket, and he wished he'd kept it in his hand so that he could record what was to come.

He closed his hand around the gun handle, tucked his finger through the trigger guard, and pulled the weapon free, turning as he did.

Cee carried a gun and would have to go first.

CEE

Cee fell to her left against the car's front wing, and as it struck her left hip and she pivoted onto the hood, something punched her high in the right leg. *Shot!* she thought, and her weight and momentum carried her onto the hood, and she twisted and writhed her way across the smooth wet surface, feeling nothing but shock.

The second gunshot planted a cold kiss across her right calf. A third creased the hood close to her face as she slid from the car and onto the wet ground in front of the bumper. She landed hard, tensing herself so the wind wasn't knocked from her, scrabbling onto her hands and knees and crawling around the passenger side of the car. Her right hip felt hot and heavy and not part of her at all, but the pain hadn't yet kicked in. Shock had her in its cool grasp.

Her crawl ended when her leg gave out and she fell onto her side in the mud. She was already tugging the gun from her belt, and as her head struck wet ground with a hard thud she saw beneath the vehicle.

Jimi was walking around the front of the car to finish her off.

From somewhere far away she heard a long, low scream, and a crack of lightning thrashed across the sky, sheeting a thousand ragged lines and imprinting the moment in time.

She aimed beneath the car, steadied her hand, and as Jimi walked past the front wheel she fired twice.

His ankle exploded, changing shape and colour. She waited only to make sure he was down, then reached up for the door handle and hauled it open. She feared that she wouldn't be able to move, lift herself up, find strength, but she managed all three.

Gonna hurt like a motherfucker, she thought, but it wasn't hurting yet, so she took advantage of the white-hot shock and dragged herself across the passenger seat, over the central console and behind the wheel.

"Cee!" Ash screamed, and another sheet of lightning crackled within the clouds of boiling smoke smothering the horizon. The sight was so epic, so Biblical, that Cee caught her breath and could only stare for what seemed like forever.

Jimi hauled himself upright in front of the car, the flames and smoke and arcing lightning his backdrop. He steadied himself on the car's front grille and pointed his gun at the windshield.

The shot skittered from the glass, leaving a long, ploughed furrow from in front of Cee's face to the upper frame.

She started the ignition and slammed her foot down on the gas, and that was when the pain roared in. Her whole hip and stomach and groin exploded into agony as if her blood had been replaced by lava, her bones ground into dust and then poured back in. She managed to grip the wheel so hard that her nails bit through leather to the plastic beneath, mouth open in a scream so pain-filled it came out silent. She was only half aware of the shape slamming onto the hood and rolling against the windshield, and instinct told her to spin the wheel to the left. Jimi struck his hands onto the car chassis in an effort to hold on, and his gun barrel caused another crack in the glass. As the car wheels span and skidded and the vehicle slewed in a half-circle, he slid off.

The passenger door window exploded inwards in a shower of glass and rain. The rain punched Cee in the side of her head so hard that it flipped to the side and impacted her own window, and she thought, *Rain doesn't hit that hard*.

"Cee!" Ash called again. More lightning flashed, thunder cracked, and Cee wasn't sure whether the lightning became a living, forever thing, because her vision was suddenly bright white and pale grey and nothing in between.

I'm fine, she tried to say, but she wasn't sure she spoke the words. She wasn't even sure she thought them as she meant them. *Maxwell has me, he's got me, I'm fine*.

Lightning struck the car three times, rapid metallic *thunks*, and then she was driving along the road back the way they'd come.

We can rest there, she thought. *Maxwell is there, and we can rest, and he'll make me better again. He can put me back together. He always said I should be better*.

From somewhere far away she thought she heard Ash calling her again and again and saying something else, but she couldn't hear anymore because the thunder was too loud, the lightning too bright, and something with too many legs bounced from the cracked windshield and squealed as it fell past the smashed side window. She smelled and tasted blood. Some of it might have been her own. Trying to focus, trying not to fade too fast, Cee steered them back towards Rockfield.

ASH

"Cee!"

She isn't answering. She's driving, steering, but if she can hear me she doesn't know what to say, or can't speak, and there's blood in her hair and on her face, and her head is moving strangely on her neck as the car weaves back and forth across the road. The windshield is scarred from bullet strikes like exclamation marks. Rain blows through the smashed passenger window, and not just rain, because I can smell the blood as well. It's not only Cee's blood. It's from elsewhere. It's from—

—*Skunksville, where it's raining thick and heavy now, and the ground and sky are crawling with creatures that seem to be moving in patterns, there's order to their flight or crawl or scamper. I am the centre of that pattern. They're all coming to me, but that shouldn't be the case. I had no fear for the first time ever—*

—she's been shot at least once—

—*I was at peace, my ability as easy and unconscious as breathing for the first time—*

—she won't talk to me, she can't hear me, and her head's swaying and bobbing as if it's going to fall off—

—*and that peace and contentment, that fearlessness, has all been blown away.*

I can feel Skunkville's angry winds shoving me into the tumult, blasting into me and out of me at the same time. I'm the centre of the storm.

Rain stings my face, like spikes of sharp sand carried on a furious breeze.

Lightning flashes again and again, illuminating the landscape I believed I had come to master at last. Every flash shows those distant humanoid shapes moving closer, because they have noticed me. Of course they have. They've been waiting, and now that control has been violently ripped from me again, they see me, and they're coming.

Stop, I say. *Stay away.* But I don't really speak, and even if I could, they wouldn't listen.

The storm has me out of control. I was crazy to believe it could be any different.

I try to reach for my forearms to draw out the needles, but in the real world I cannot move.

This place which I'd dared to believe I could master and control, Skunksville, now focuses entirely on me, and I can sense unknown creatures falling through me, into the tumult and out via the eye on the other side.

And those figures I have always feared the most are coming closer, running on long legs, spidery arms swinging as if they're grabbing at the air to haul themselves forward. I don't want to see their awful faces when they finally lift their bowed heads to look at me. I don't want to hear their voices, because they will mutter terrible things in an unknown language.

I don't want to let them through.

Cee! I try to shout, unsure whether I'm even making a sound.

But Cee has been shot. Cee can't help me. My anger and rage, my grief and mistakes, are all my own.

JIMI

Writhing in rain and blood, Jimi wasn't sure how much blood was his, and how much was falling from the sky. He had seen and felt the change. From pure fresh rain to something thicker, not every drop was red, but even the water now felt greasy and unclean. He could drown in it if he pressed his nose and mouth close enough to the ground, but he had never considered such a cowardly way out. Not even with the pain from his shattered ankle, like nothing he had ever experienced before. It smothered his other agonies, a white fire that started in his foot and ankle and lower leg and expanded and travelled to consume the rest of him.

He screamed into the storm. The wind had increased, drawn by distant fires but also exhaled by the Rainmaker. There had been a storm years ago when Papa died, but nothing like this.

Crawling towards his car, he was careful to keep his right leg elevated so his broken foot did not touch the ground. He hadn't dared look at it yet, but he felt a sickening swing as he crawled, and every movement was like a dozen blunt blades being driven through his flesh and ground into his bones.

He'd hit Cee, but he didn't know how badly. Once at least, and possibly again when he'd fired at the car as she drove back towards town. Getting shot by her hadn't been part of his plan.

She was faster than he'd expected, more attuned to the danger he presented. But this wasn't over. The Rainmaker had changed in front of his eyes the moment he'd heard her bastard father was gone—from a vague figure in the back of the car, to the main focus of his life.

His arms shook from supporting his weight and his cracked ribs boiled spikes of pain. His splayed fingers disappeared beneath thick mud as he crawled, emerging each time dripping with coppery water. More blood fell. Jimi couldn't help thinking that he'd done that. Before he shot Cee, the Rainmaker brought down only rain.

Blood splashed and pattered around him, and he felt its warm caress across his back, like fingers tapping out a random rhythm. Other things fell, too. Long, thin worms snaked across the top of the mud like sidewinders, seeming to dodge the splashes and ripples of rain. A lone bird lay on the edge of the road, with plumage he had never seen before. Its wing was broken and it flapped itself in frantic circles. Further away something larger landed, and he scanned the road surface, searching for what might have made such an impact. A figure scuttled from view into the ditch on the other side of the road, and he caught a brief impression of scaled legs and a long, heavy tail.

He didn't worry about something stinging or biting or poisoning him, leaving him to die squirming in the mud. His story was not yet done. He saw his future mapped with such clarity that he didn't even raise the gun when a long, thick snake bounced from the hood of his car and slithered to the ground just three metres from where he crouched.

I'm not done yet.

His vision of his future was only minutes long, not hours or days. It was a mile long, not tens or hundreds of miles. It was here, back to the town, the Rainmaker in front of his gun, her blood adding to the blood she was already bringing down.

That's why Jimi was not afraid. His future was set and assured, and any other outcome was not part of his world. Not even with the flames of hell bearing down on him. He saw the bush fires closing from behind, reflected in the car's windows and the infinity-black eyes of the snake that had reared up before him, its head a metre above the ground as it tasted him on the air. He felt the heat of the fire on the back of his neck. Dizziness from blood loss tilted his world.

But Jimi was not afraid. Everything led to that one moment close in his future. Nothing would stop him. He wouldn't let it, and each time he blinked water from his eyes he saw Papa's disfigured corpse.

Jimi had grown up thinking he was nothing like his Papa, but from the moment his Papa had died, all that had changed.

"I'm just like you," he said, staring at the snake. His dead Papa opened his eyes and grinned, his lips deformed from the toxic strings that had killed him.

The snake lowered its head and slithered away from the approaching flames.

Jimi grinned back.

"I'm just like you."

The first time he tried to get into the car he almost passed out and had to lean against the door to catch his breath. His vision swam, stomach clenched, and when his injured foot impacted the door sill he almost puked from the pain. The deluge continued, and looking in the direction of the town he saw that the rains were also falling there. The Rainmaker was still bringing down the storm. He guessed that meant she was still alive, not mangled in a car wreck. That was good enough for him.

He eased himself around and down into the seat, keeping his foot lifted. He'd have to work the accelerator and brake with his left foot, but that wasn't his main concern. If he passed out and drove off the road, there was no way he could crawl all the way back to Rockfield.

Everything became pain. He screamed, he roared, he raged and cried, lifting his leg into the car and trying to prop his knee so that his foot didn't touch the floor or base of the dashboard. He nursed the gun between his legs. Things splashed and thudded down around him, and once or twice something hit the car. He wound up the windows just as a black shape scuttled down the wet windshield and disappeared off the side. A crab crawled down the rear window, segmented legs so long that they braced against the bottom of the window while the thing's body still hung over the top.

The only time he took up the gun was when a canine creature limped into view and stood staring at him from astride the white line. It had powerful jaws, pricked ears, fur seared from its left shoulder and flank.

Did you really fall from out of nowhere? he thought. He'd seen coyotes and wild dogs, had even heard rumours of wolves in the Desert's northern territories, but this was none of these. It was too small for a wolf. It had speckled colourings he did not recognise. Its eyes were loaded with intelligence. It sniffed the air as if sensing his injuries, looked at the gun in his hand, then trotted out of sight behind the car.

Jimi reached for the handle and swung the door closed.

He started driving because he had no choice. He crunched painkillers from his pocket, their bitter, gritty taste filling his mouth and nose.

The fires were closing, a glimpse of hell in the rear-view mirror. The wipers smeared blood, and for the first time he wondered where it all came from, and the pain that must be suffered there to make so much.

CEE

Cee tried to look at Ash but saw only darkness in the mirror, as if she could no longer see that far.

That doesn't make sense. I can see the road ahead.

But could she? Or was she driving blind?

She saw rain and darkness, lit by frequent flashes of lightning that might have been inside her, not without. She couldn't remember her own name, only Ash's, and perhaps that was the only reality. She saw her hands on the wheel and they were both speckled with blood.

That blood on my forearm isn't mine. It's from somewhere else. The blood across my fingers is mine.

It was all the same colour. The windshield was gouged and starred, or maybe it wasn't there at all.

It is. The rain hits it, and some of the rain is too dark, too thick. And those animals I know and others I don't hit it, too.

Creatures bounced from the windshield now and then, and some of them might only have been confused or injured by the storm. A small bird with a broken neck, swept aside by the wipers and stuck in the grille beneath the window. An insect the size of her hand and with sharp-tipped legs that scored lines across the glass. A butterfly with torn wings.

More lightning flashed from inside the car. *From the places I've been shot*, she thought. *I'm leaking lightning with every heartbeat.* The crack of thunder came immediately after, so loud that she saw water droplets jump across glass. She felt it in her bones. In her hip, and face.

Her right leg wasn't working and she drove with her left foot. She sat in a warm puddle. Her left foot still worked, so it wasn't her spine. Probably not.

I've had worse than this, she thought. Her forearms were scarred with such memories. *Maxwell said it was worse than death, so it was worse than this, wasn't it?* She couldn't think straight. She wasn't sure she could drive straight, but they hadn't crashed yet and she was pretty sure they were still moving.

Ash, she tried to say, but her voice was an unformed croak. She was thinking the words, and trying to speak them, but her face wasn't working. Her head was strange.

I should look in the mirror.

She'd have to move to do that. It would mean letting go of the wheel with one hand. She didn't think it was a good idea, in case she saw someone she didn't recognise looking back.

I'll look after you, she tried to say. She thought she was aiming the idea at Ash, but maybe it was to herself as well.

She still didn't know her name, but she could remember her dark times in the past when Maxwell had told her it was worse than death.

Well, that's okay, then, she thought. *I survived that.*

She kept driving through the impossible storm of rain and blood and strange creatures falling from the sky, because she knew they had to reach Rockfield. She drove away from the man who'd come to kill Ash, but who had killed her instead.

Worse than death, and I survived that. He hasn't killed me yet. I'm not dead yet.

She tried to remember her name.

JESSE

"Oh my God."

"Ash," Jesse said.

"It's got to be, hasn't it? Got to be our girl causing that."

"I haven't seen a storm like that before."

"Ever?" Karina asked.

He climbed through from the back and dropped into the passenger seat. Rocky whined a little and Jesse reached back until he felt fur, ruffling and scratching her to peace. He wished someone would ease him down to peace so easily.

"Never," he said. He knew what Karina meant. "It was never that big for me. That violent."

"What does that mean?" Karina asked.

"Exactly what I've been saying. She's stronger than I ever was, much more powerful."

"She needs me more than you ever did."

It was a strange thing to say, and Jesse thought, *No, not at all, I needed you all the time.* But he didn't say it, and he never would. He'd lost that right years ago.

And he was terrified. The power he could see before him, the sheer violence, came from his daughter, his blood.

"I did that," he said. "I made her like that." Perhaps he was appealing to Karina to take some of the blame from him. She wasn't that easy.

"A lot of this is going to be up to you," she said. "We're here to save her, Jesse. Right?"

"Yes, of course."

"Not to kill her."

The words sliced through him like a keen knife. He'd never intended to kill his girl, and believing he had was the worst thing that had ever happened to him. The opportunity he had now was something he'd never dared hope for.

"Not to kill her," he said. "Never that."

"What are we going to find in there?" Karina asked.

"Put your foot down." Jesse's stomach churned, his reconstructed jaw ached. Every part of him wanted to go in the opposite direction.

The boiling storm looked like a living thing. It was vast, the clouds stacked miles high, dark, heavy, and forbidding. They were given life by the constant thrashes of lightning that arced through and around them, like slashes of pure light cut into bruised flesh. At the huge storm's base, lightning cracked down to the land, several strikes every second, dancing back and forth beneath the cloud banks and giving the impression of a huge living thing balancing on delicate legs of fire.

As they approached Rockfield and the violent storm that squatted over it, the first spots of rain hit the car. The wipers activated and smeared damp dust across the windshield. More rain fell, and Jesse felt a dizzying anxiety.

He was waiting for blood.

If none came, maybe that would mean Ash had mastered this ability at last.

Ever since Karina had arrived in his front yard and told him that Ash was still alive and rainmaking again, he had been torn in two, split by the terrible thing he had done and the effect it had had upon her. Perhaps the whole experience had driven Ash to madness, and any new attempt at rainmaking would be even worse than it had been before, for him or her. The people he had killed had been bad people, but still their deaths continued to haunt his dreams.

Or maybe on returning, she had refined her new apparatus and herself. Found a balance. Managed to bring down rain and nothing else from Skunksville.

The wipers smeared only rainwater and dust. *Maybe it's okay*, he thought. *Maybe Abbey Springs was just a blip, an accident on her way to mastering this.*

"What's that?" Karina asked.

"Car come off the road," Jesse said. "We should stop and..." He trailed off.

Karina slowed the Land Rover as they neared the car with its nose down in the ditch, and Jesse could already make out the shape in the driver's seat. He could see the streaks of pink watery blood running down the vehicle's pale blue paintwork. A strange creature the size of a cat clung to the driver's torso, head dipping back and forth into the meaty mess of his or her face.

"Oh fucking hell," Karina said, and she accelerated past the wreck. "Jesse, we've got to find her and stop her."

He could not answer. The next time the wipers swept back and forth they smeared blood, and this time they remained fully on. The downpour went from a shower to a deluge as they closed on Rockfield, and the headlamps flickered on even though it was early afternoon. A shape darted across the road ahead of them and disappeared beneath the vehicle. He listened for a bump or crunch but heard nothing.

"Jesse!"

"Yes."

"We've got to find Ash and help her!"

"Yes," he said again. *But you said stop her*, he thought.

Karina drove them into the impossible storm his girl was bringing down.

KARINA

They saw two more dead people just before they passed the first buildings at the edge of town. An adult and a child, huddled against a fence separating the road from a field of dead trees. The trees might once have borne fruit but their branches were stark and lifeless now. Someone had weaved hundreds of metres of bunting through and around their branches, and it hung heavy with water and blood.

The woman had long auburn hair knotted by the storm, and both arms were clutched protectively around the child. Karina knew they were dead because crows were perched on their heads and shoulders, pecking at their eyes.

She imagined hugging her own daughter back into her arms, helping her, protecting her against this fucking curse that had haunted her family forever.

"I approach her first," Karina said.

"But what if—"

"It's me!" she shouted.

"Yeah. Okay."

She glanced sidelong at Jesse and saw his terror. She was afraid too, but she'd not let it get in the way of finding and caring for Ash. She never had before. He'd locked down with his fear and never learned to live with it. She'd confronted her own every day.

Never like this, though. The idea that her own daughter was doing this drove in a terror so rich and powerful that Karina felt sick. It made her feel more removed from the world than she ever had before, but having Jesse with her helped her to cling on.

They drove into Rockfield, the pulsing, breathing mass of the storm above and around them. Blood was diluted by rain. The fall was heavy but steady, and so different from the storm she'd driven through to get to Jesse's place. That had been violent but chaotic, battering her left and right with wind and rain. This storm had been conjured from nothing, and its sick magic clawed at her, trying to find its way inside her mind. She might be haunted by this moment forever.

On their left was a fire station, with several firefighters gathered around their truck. They were in full uniform. One of them danced a grotesque jig, reaching around to grab at something that must have been inside her jacket and pressed close to her back. The others paused to watch, shocked and surprised, and Karina drove past. She did not glance in her mirror to see how the situation played out. She wasn't here to help anyone else.

"Karina!" Jesse shouted, and she slammed on the brakes. The car slid and skidded to a halt as something loped down a street to their left. She couldn't make out what it was. A dog, perhaps.

"What the hell?" Jesse asked.

"Where will she be?"

"I don't know."

"Jesse! Where will our daughter be?"

"At the centre of things," he said, but he looked as lost as she felt. "Just drive." He glanced at the back seat and at first she thought he was looking at Rocky. Then she realised.

"You think you can find her with that?"

"I don't know. I could try."

"You connected with her before, didn't you?"

"In a way." He said no more but remained turned around in his seat.

"What, you're scared?" she asked.

"Petrified," he said. He climbed into the back seat. "More room back here. Keep driving. Find the centre of town."

Karina drove on. She saw a couple of shapes dropping from the sky, one in the distance, one much closer. Both were small. Neither moved once they hit the ground. The streets were quiet, the townsfolk already fled ahead of the incoming fires or sheltering indoors. She wondered how long it had taken them to realise this was no normal storm.

Something struck the roof and she heard claws scrabbling for purchase. Her gun was between her legs, tucked under her left thigh so that it wouldn't slip down to the floor. She started to reach for it, but the scraping sound stopped and she glimpsed something drop past the passenger window from the corner of her eye. She pressed on the gas, but there was no sign of anything in the road behind them.

Ash could be anywhere. In one of the buildings, or the vehicles, crouched in a yard or in a field beyond the edge of town. So close to Ash, Karina felt a sudden flash of hopelessness.

"Jesse, hurry," she said. "It's getting worse."

That was when she saw the car that had crashed into a parked vehicle in the town square, and the woman who stood leaning against the open door, and what was wrong with her head. It was the same woman she'd seen in the clip of Ash from Abbey Springs, the naked dancer. Now she held a gun and tracked it back and forth, aiming at nothing and everything. The right side of her face was a bloody mess, her jaw hung down, and Karina was sure she could see the bright flash of teeth or bone through her cheek.

When she saw and heard their car, the woman started shooting.

ASH

'm jolted back into the world. My apparatus ends up on the floor behind Cee's seat and one of the needles tugs at my arm. The pain is like an electric shock. I'm startled back to reality and I'm grateful to be pulled away from that place, but Cee is keening a high-pitched whine, and shivering even though the rain is warm. I call her name but she doesn't answer. The car has crunched into another, and the storm within me is still released, still raging. Lightning flashes without and within, and cracks of thunder match my beating heart.

Cee pushes the door open and goes to stand outside the car. She is instantly soaked, but the side of her face, neck, and shoulder is already wet with blood. Her head still shifts and twitches as if her neck isn't quite strong enough to hold it upright. Her keening rises in tone, and she holds onto the door with one hand, aiming her gun with the other.

"Cee, he might be out there!" I shout. I can see the street distorted through the window. It seems quiet, apart from the storm. I reach for the door handle but the wires aren't long enough. I grip the needle in my left arm, but when I touch it a painful kick goes through me and throws me back across the seat, as if I have completed a circuit in myself. *The storm wants to remain*, I think. The apparatus holds me tight. Skunksville doesn't want its newfound route from there to here closed off again.

I try to ease the storm, but it's driven by my anger and grief. I can see how badly Cee is hurt, and I wonder that she isn't already dead.

I should stop this. I should end it.

There's movement outside. A small group of people, perhaps a family, runs along the sidewalk. Cee tracks them with the gun, and for a terrible moment I think she's going to shoot. I take in a breath to shout, but then a car stops across the street from us. It's a Land Rover.

Cee shifts her aim and shoots. I don't see where the bullet hits, and Cee lowers the gun a little, head tilted or slumped onto her right shoulder.

The car door opens. A woman steps out, hands up, careful to remain mostly behind the door, and... I lean closer to the window, holding my breath so that it does not mist the glass... I squint, and realise...

It's my mother.

It's my mother!

"No, Cee..." I say, but my voice is so weak that it sounds like someone talking from some unknown distance. Or a voice from a dream. Maybe the me of Skunksville is saying those words into that distant storm, and all I hear are echoes.

Cee aims across the street, but her arm is shaking, the gun wavering. Something runs along the middle of the road, between us and my mother. It's a crab-like creature, and I have seen its like in Skunksville.

They're falling through, I think, and I wonder how close those humanoid shapes are to me right now. The me over there, not the me over here. *I have to stop this now, before—*

I look at the needles in my arms. The wounds are bleeding because it's all gone wrong again, and I reach out to tug at the wires and—

The car's other door opens and my father steps out.

"We're her parents, and we're here to help," I hear my mother shout. The words are almost lost to the storm, but I have never forgotten that voice.

"Kilt her," Cee says through the ruins of her face. "Ya *kilt* her!"

And then she starts shooting again.

JIMI

Through the rain of blood, through the searing pain, Jimi took in the chaotic scene in Rockfield's main street and felt his life change again.

Cee had collided with a parked car and was leaning against the open driver's door. She fired three shots across the street at two people who had emerged from a Land Rover parked in front of a closed bar. The woman might have been Cee's mother. Jimi guessed that because he recognised the man instantly.

The Rainmaker.

She lied to me, he's not gone, but now it's only me who gets to kill him. He pressed his foot on the accelerator. He couldn't hear the gunshots over the storm and another roll of thunder, but he saw the rain misted and blasted away from the gun barrel one more time before Cee sensed his car and turned to look.

He hoped that none of those three shots hit the son of a bitch who had killed his Papa.

His car's front wing clipped the back of the crashed car, and in that instant he saw the damage he'd already done to Cee. Her entire right hip and leg was soaked with blood, and the right side of her face was deformed and broken, eye flooded red and swirling in its socket.

His car struck her and crushed her against the inside of the open driver's door. The gun flew from her hand as she bent in half and flipped forward, her face impacting Jimi's car's hood with a heavy wet thud. The crunching sound was bone and metal hinges as the door was torn away, breaking apart just as Cee was broken, their damaged elements cracking and parting and merging. His car continued past the crashed vehicle and he jigged the steering wheel to the left, hoping to avoid crunching into any more parked cars. The momentum kept Cee splayed across the hood, her right hand opening and closing as if feeling for the gun she'd dropped.

Jimi went to slam on the brakes, instinctively using his right foot to do so. Agony exploded as his broken foot struck the pedal and his shattered ankle gave way, bending his foot sideways, blinding him with spine-crushing pain. He screamed as the car mounted the sidewalk and slammed into a brick wall between the bar and a boarded-up fast food joint. He was flung forward into the steering column, cracked ribs taking the full impact. Winded, his scream was silent, and through narrow, watering eyes he saw what little was left of Cee. She'd been cut in half by the impact, her lower part disappeared somewhere beneath the car, her torso with splayed arms sliding down to rest on the front of the hood where it was crumpled against the brick wall. The rain washed her blood away, but plenty more flowed. Her blood-flooded eye looked into him, through him, and perhaps it was the impact of a heavy raindrop on lashes that made it seem to blink.

Jimi pushed back in his seat, trying to catch a breath. He reached for the gun between his legs but it had fallen down by his feet, and at that moment it was too far away.

He's alive, he thought. *He's not dead. He's alive, for me!*

He would tell the Rainmaker who he was before killing the mother of his child, and then his child, in front of him. And maybe after all that he would even leave the wretched man alive to live the rest of his life without them.

Or maybe he'd just kill the Rainmaker first.

He had waited so long, and now his was a life rich with possibilities. He laughed at the agonies coursing through him. The pain fed him. It was the only way to move on.

As he took a deep breath and leaned down to grab his gun, the world around him exploded.

JESSE

The horribly injured woman said something into the storm but her words were slurred, her face disfigured. As Jesse took one step from the Land Rover, she started shooting. He crouched, saw Karina do the same, heard the hard *thunk* of a bullet striking the vehicle close to him, the sound of a shattering window, and then a car struck the shooting woman and crushed her and swept her up. As it slewed to the left and crossed the street, he ran for Karina, but she was already standing and heading for the doorless car.

Has she already killed Ash? Jesse wondered, because something awful had happened here. The car struck a building ten metres along the street and he saw and heard the sickening impact as the woman, hopefully already dead, slumped down across the car's hood.

"Karina!" he shouted, and he ran after his wife.

He caught sight of Ash in the car's rear seat. His daughter, his girl no more. Her eyes were wide open, her mouth agape. She wasn't looking at him, but at the ruin of the car crushed against the wall beyond the bar.

"Ash," Karina said into the storm. "Ash! We've come to—"

Everything changed in an instant.

The world came apart, and at the moment it happened Jesse

saw something happen to Ash. Her eyes narrowed, and her mouth closed into a fierce, bitter line.

Lightning thrashed and cracked and arced across the sky all around them. It struck a four-storey building further along the street, glass blasting outward, wood splitting and shattering and catching fire. It lit up the low clouds and glimmered in a billion raindrops, turning them to falling fire. The thunderous explosion was instantaneous, and windows along the street exploded from the shock waves. Water on the road jumped, and Jesse pressed his hands across his ears. He went to his knees and saw Karina do the same, and she twisted around to look at him.

Jesse looked at the car, his daughter in the back seat, her eyes closed now, face pressed against the side window where she'd slumped.

She can't help it, he thought. *Which means she can't stop it.*

Blood and rain splashed down around them. Creatures fell, some remaining motionless where they landed, others fleeing and hiding beneath cars, or taking flight into the deluge. Jesse stomped on a small scorpion struggling on its back in the water, and dreadful memories came to blur present and past. A snake fell across his shoulders and he waved his arms, spinning in a circle until it fell and slithered away towards the Land Rover.

Karina stood by the car where the door had been torn away and Jesse joined her. He looked across at the crashed car and saw movement inside. He had no idea what the hell was happening, but here was Ash, and they had come all this way to find her.

"Jesse!" Karina shouted. "We need to stop this!"

Jesse leaned into the car and looked at Ash. She was slumped against the back door, both arms connected into her new apparatus. Sparks flowed back and forth along the wires like luminous ants, and gathered around where the needles entered her arms. She was bleeding. She was breathing heavily and quickly, eyes rolling beneath their closed lids.

Jesse reached for one of the needles.

"Hey!" a voice shouted.

Karina grabbed his arm. Jesse glanced back over his shoulder. A man stood beside the crashed car, leaning against it, balanced on one foot. He was aiming a gun at them.

"Where's your—" Jesse began.

"In the car," Karina said.

"Hey, you know me? You know me, Rainmaker?"

Jesse didn't know him. He stood beside Karina, and from the corner of his mouth said, "Get in the car."

"If I move he might shoot."

Jesse gauged the distance. The man was maybe twenty metres away, far enough to have to shout into the wind and rain to be heard, but his aim was steady. He was wide-eyed and frenzied. Jesse noted his damaged ankle and foot. If only they could start moving he'd never keep up with them, but he'd also never miss if he started shooting now.

"No, I don't know you," Jesse said.

"You knew my Papa."

"I doubt that."

Something heavy landed in the street. It struggled to its feet, then limped off between buildings.

"This remind you of anything?" the man asked.

"No," Jesse replied. *Yes*, he thought. *Of course it reminds me.* But he still didn't know this man.

"My name's Jimi," the man said.

Jesse shrugged. "In the car," he said, shifting to the side to give Karina room.

"My father called himself Wolf."

The scorpion in his beard. The fury in his eyes.

"Oh, fuck," Jesse muttered.

Something larger landed nearby, its vicious claws scrabbling for purchase on unfamiliar ground.

Lightning. Thunder. A gust of wind driving a horizontal rain of blood, and the blood became bullets.

Jimi's first three gunshots were aimed elsewhere.

ASH

I saw her come apart.

The grief is rich and raw. I've never felt anything like it, even after what my father did, when I fled and found myself alone. Cee made me realise how precious companionship and friendship is, and how wretched it feels when that is stolen away.

I'm trapped in this place. I can't move. I'm not my own, myself. I am the storm, violent and unhinged. I am the chaotic eye. Skunksville is stinking and dead, and our world must seem so rich and lustrous in comparison. Even the world of the Desert. I am the escape, and I see and sense so many creatures taking it. I can hardly blame them.

And those other things are coming. Humanoids, always in the distance and unknown. Now they are closer, moving swiftly on their long limbs with heads still lowered. Closer, closer, and as they approach I can make them out more clearly. Sixteen, eighteen, twenty-three of them, they are similar in appearance yet with distinguishing features. One has a silver streak across the top of its lowered head like a scratch on painted metal. One has three limbs instead of four, one arm truncated and waving around like a leaf in a storm. Another has a shifting fringe around its midriff like a skirt of fleshy petals. Arms drive as they run, legs push, wide feet pound at the ground.

And these people of Skunksville have scales instead of skin, claws instead of fingers, and as they close on me I realise they are not people at all. What I have always assumed to be heads lowered in contemplation raise and unfurl into a splay of long, probing limbs, tasting at the air. And then reaching for me.

They've always been waiting for this moment, I think, and they are further from human than anything I have ever seen. I see their eyes, set in a thick stem of a face beneath the head of waving, sensing proboscis.

In those eyes lies a dreadful, ecstatic intelligence.

The storm falls through me, and so do they.

KARINA

Karina barely heard the gunshot as it was swallowed in the storm, but she felt a flick at her left ear and then the sharp sting of pain. Jesse shoved her into the car's bloodied driver's seat and crouched down behind the open door, and past him she saw the man whose name was Jimi hop alongside his crashed car, leaning against it as he strived for a better angle. *He could just shoot Jesse in the back*, she thought, but something told her he didn't want to. He wanted to cause Jesse pain. He was aiming at her.

She pressed a hand to her ear and it came away bloodied. She cursed herself for leaving the gun in the Land Rover, but she'd been so keen to find Ash, so eager to see her girl again, and here she was—unconscious, hooked up to another fucking apparatus, her face clouded with the dreadful storm she was bringing down upon them all.

She heard a shout outside, and Jimi turned and started shooting in a different direction, along the street and away from them. She couldn't quite make out what he was firing at. She saw a shape through the water and blood flowing down the windshield, which itself was cracked and starred, and it might have been anything. She hoped it wasn't another person. It looked about the right size, but something about the way it moved was wrong.

"What now?"

"His foot's injured," Jesse said. "We run, he won't be able to follow."

"I'm not leaving her! We've just found her!"

"I wasn't thinking that. Scoot over."

Karina climbed across into the passenger seat as Jesse knelt into the car, reaching into the back for his girl. Karina sobbed once, hard, and Jesse glanced at her. She loved him then. She always had, somewhere deep beneath the hate.

"We'll help her," he said.

Another gunshot.

"What *is* that?"

"Keeping him from us, that's what." He spoke as if he knew what it might be, but now wasn't the time for her to ask. "You okay?" He was looking at her bloody ear.

She waved him away and turned to Ash. "Can't you just pull those things out?"

"I don't know what that'll do to her."

"You don't *know*?"

"She's in much deeper than I ever was."

Karina looked into the storm, searching for Jimi. He was no longer beside his crashed car. *Good*, she thought, *maybe whatever he was shooting at—*

Something crawled into view along the middle of the street. It was moving slowly, obviously injured, and it was like nothing she had ever seen before.

"Holy fuck," she said.

Lightning flashed, and in the poor light the flash imprinted the thing on her mind. It was the size of a tall, broad human, clothed in scales, limbs long and tipped with vicious claws, and its head consisted of a waving mass of feelers or tentacles. A couple of them trailed through puddles as it dragged itself along. The others waved as if tasting the air or plucking raindrops before they struck the ground.

"Jesse…" she said.

"We need to move," he said. "We'll get her out the back door. I'll carry her, you stay close with the apparatus."

"What about him?" She couldn't see Jimi. He'd stopped shooting. Neither of these facts made her feel any safer.

"Maybe it got him," Jesse said, standing beside her open door. "Come on!"

The thing in the street was only a few metres away, hauling itself along with no apparent purpose. She didn't think it knew they were there. *If only I'd brought the—*

Three more shots rang out and the thing flipped over onto its back, limbs kicking at the ground as if to propel it away. It stiffened, relaxed, tensed again, and then grew still.

"How about that, Rainmaker!" Jimi shouted from beside his car. "Huh? You see that? Bullseye!"

"Jesse, get in the car, don't give him a clear shot."

"He wants to kill me last."

"Who is he?"

"Doesn't matter."

Jimi aimed the gun and half hopped, half hobbled forward, crying out as he moved.

She didn't hear what must have been an empty click from the gun. But she saw his look of surprise, then frustration.

He froze, then looked back at his wrecked car.

"Jesse, now, go and tackle him *now*!"

Jimi was hobbling slowly back towards his car, maybe for a reload. Jesse shook his head. "We've got to get Ash to safety."

"But he can hardly walk and he's out of bullets!"

"He's not the most dangerous thing out there."

Something impacted heavily on a rooftop nearby, smashing glass and broken shingles onto the road. From further away she heard a scream diluted by rain. The idea that her daughter was causing this chaos was devastating, and Karina reached towards the apparatus to tear it apart, bring her back from wherever she was.

Jesse grabbed her hand and held tight. "It'll kill you!"

"Then you do it!"

"It might kill me, too."

I don't care, she thought. But she realised that right then, neither did Jesse.

As he stood out in the rain and opened the rear door that Ash was leaning against, Karina saw Jimi reach his own crashed car and lean inside.

"Jesse."

"I know. Grab the guitar case, lift it, climb through as I lift her out. Try not to touch its workings or let the wires pull too tight."

She did as he suggested, placing one hand on Ash's cheek first. She felt so hot that she must have been burning up, like she had lightning inside.

"Out and to the Land Rover," Jesse said.

Jimi was leaning against his car again, face turned up to the sky. Trying not to pass out.

Jesse eased Ash into his arms and grabbed her beneath the armpits. He pulled and she slid off the back seat, and Karina climbed through and picked up the apparatus. He was going to drag her across the street, not lift her, and she realised that made sense. It meant her arms would trail by her side, so that the needles and wires would hang free.

Karina stood from the car, the apparatus carried in both arms, held out before her. Rain stung her injured ear.

Back along the street, past the Land Rover, someone dashed from behind a building and across the road. They were silent, fast, and something about their sprint spoke of panic.

A shape darted after them, and for a moment she thought it was another person. Then it leapt and brought them down. The victim let out a terrible scream, slamming down onto the road and sliding into the flooded gutter. They struggled, but not for long. The thrashing figure slammed its limbs up and down, striking its prey with sickeningly wet impacts, and Karina looked away when she saw blood and shreds of clothing and flesh adding to the rain.

"Jesse!"

"Into the car."

Behind the scent of fresh rain and blood she caught a whiff of smoke. She'd almost forgotten about the fires.

As they crossed the road she glanced back at the fallen victim and the creature settled on their back. Waving tentacles sprouting from its upper parts were probing the opened flesh of its prey, intimate touches landing here, there, and then each tentacle stiffened and drove in. She heard a crunch as the skull cracked in two.

Just as they arrived at the Land Rover and Jesse reached for the door, holding Ash against him with one arm, Jimi let out a loud laugh. He was hobbling towards them again, left arm holding a makeshift crutch, right arm waving as he attempted to aim the gun.

"Look at you, all together!" he shouted. "I got my fuckin' ducks in a row!"

Jesse pulled the rear door open.

Rocky leapt out, barking, and ran straight at Jimi.

Karina stepped behind the open door as Jesse heaved Ash up into the back seat. She grunted and groaned, and Karina placed the guitar case carefully onto her daughter's legs and stomach.

Jimi got off two wild shots before the dog bounded into him, leaping to clamp her teeth around his arm, and he fell back without a sound and struck the road hard. Rocky shook her head, and Jimi tried to bring the gun around to press it to the dog's side.

"Rocky, away!" Jesse shouted.

The dog leapt from the fallen man and darted onto the sidewalk, disappearing around the far side of the Land Rover.

"In!" Jesse said.

Karina climbed in over Ash and her apparatus, lifting her daughter's head and placing it in her lap.

Jimi fired again just as Jesse climbed into the back seat. One bullet took out the open door's window, another *thunked* into the door's core.

Jesse grunted, climbed into the front and dropped into the driver's seat, opening the door and whistling. Rocky jumped into his lap and scrambled across into the passenger seat.

Karina risked a quick glance through the window as Jimi aimed and grinned, then a shape leapt on his legs and dragged him away between two buildings.

Jesse started the engine. The windshield darkened, then shattered. Karina ducked down again, leaning over Ash to protect her daughter's body with her own.

"Gun's in the footwell!" she shouted, and when she looked between the seats she saw that Jesse was already leaning down to retrieve the weapon, and that the smashed windshield was full of something other than wind and rain and blood.

The creature scrabbled at the smooth, water-slicked hood, striving for purchase so that it could force its way in through the ragged opening. The thick tendrils of its head felt around the opening and grabbed onto the dashboard, steering wheel, and the upper window surround, then its body tilted up and it looked inside.

Karina met its stare.

It looked down at Jesse, then back at Karina, its expression and attitude filled with a dreadful intelligence. For a crazy moment, she thought it had Ash's eyes.

Jesse slipped the vehicle into reverse and pressed on the gas. They jarred and jerked backwards, wheels grinding against the kerb before bumping over something soft. *The dead person*, she thought. Jesse pushed down harder on the gas and they accelerated backwards, causing the creature to slip back down the hood.

Jesse sat up and fired twice. The thing fell from the hood and out of sight.

Karina sat up. "Jimi?"

"Don't know." Jesse's voice was strained and she knew he'd taken a bullet. She didn't know where. Now was not the time to ask.

He moved into drive and hit the gas again. Jimi's car was splayed across the sidewalk thirty metres ahead of them, but there was no sign of him; for now at least no one was shooting at them.

They moved forward but did not bump over the fallen creature. *It's gone*, she thought, but before she could warn Jesse a shape leapt at them from the night, slamming into the car, limbs piercing the bodywork to clasp itself up and towards the smashed windshield again.

Jesse acted instinctively, spinning the wheel to the left, mounting the kerb and sidewalk and crashing into the bar's front wall just a few paces from Jimi's wrecked car. The impact threw

Karina forward into the back of the front seats and she fell into the footwell, Ash landing on top of her.

Ash's eyes flickered opened. "Mom," she said.

Two more gunshots sounded, then Jesse tumbled from the car and pulled open the back door, staring down at them, grabbing Ash again beneath the arms and starting to drag her out, gun still clasped in his right hand.

Karina saw blood staining Jesse's right side.

Rocky barked and jumped over Karina, her claws raking her arm and shoulder as she squeezed past Ash and Jesse and trotted out of sight.

"Rocky, here!" Jesse said, but he was looking back and forth between Karina and the apparatus that Ash was still attached to. Ash stared at her too, eyes wide, eyes Karina had seen only moments ago in the unnatural face of the thing trying to kill them. She didn't know what that meant. She was probably imagining things.

"Karina!" Jesse snapped.

She struggled upright and carried the apparatus from the car as Jesse backed across the sidewalk. The Land Rover had cracked a wall and smashed through the bar's front window, and after a quick glance over his shoulder he backed up to the opening, stepped over the low sill and pushed inside past the vehicle's hood. Ash helped, half-walking as he half-dragged her.

"He killed Cee," Ash said.

"Yes." Karina couldn't find any more words, but now wasn't the time for talking. Ash's eyes closed again, and it looked like she was crying tears of blood.

Inside the bar it was darker, quieter, and Karina took a deep breath to try to level herself. Jesse kept carrying Ash backwards, shoving chairs aside with one foot, and Karina followed with the apparatus still fixed into both of Ash's forearms.

"What the fuck are those things, Jesse?"

He shook his head.

"We need to put her down and take these needles out."

Jesse slumped back against the bar, and Ash began to slip from his hands as he slid down to the floor. He let out a long, low groan as he placed her gently down beside him. Then Rocky was at his side, and his eyes closed, and Karina heard someone or something scrambling into the bar behind them.

JIMI

Whatever it was, it fucking stank worse than a skunk.

Jimi kicked himself away from the creature hunched against the wall. It was shaking as it bled out, the blood darker than it should have been. He'd put two bullets into its head just as its grotesque mouth snapped down on his shattered foot. He might have lost his toes, but he couldn't bear to look.

It didn't matter.

And the dead thing, whatever the hell it was and wherever the hell it had come from, fucking *stank*!

"This way, mister!" Someone emerged from the shadows. A short boy, maybe sixteen years old, eyes wide with a mixture of excitement and fear. "Shit, that thing bite you?" The boy grabbed one arm and dragged Jimi, screaming, into the alley and away from the dead thing. It was darker in there, but the scene was still revealed in flashes of lightning near and far. A couple of parked delivery trucks. A pile of refuse in bags chewed open by rats or dogs, or other things. A kid's plastic playhouse, multicoloured and happy and incongruous in such a place.

The boy dropped his arm and backed away. "You okay, mister?"

"No," Jimi said. He bit his lip, trying to drive back the dizziness that threatened. He didn't think he was losing too much blood, but he was a wreck. Every stab of pain made him more determined. *I don't have time for this!* He hated the idea of those things getting the Rainmaker and his family before him. *And just what the fuck were they?* he thought, and then the kid answered and Jimi realised he'd been speaking aloud.

"Right? What the fuck, eh? Like blood raining down, probably dust or something taken up in thermals from the fire. Desert dust getting wet and making it look all red like blood, but those other things falling down, eh? What the fuck? I heard about a rain of fish once, in South America or somewhere, and they think a tornado took them up from a lake and dropped them down again, but I seen things here too big for that, and things I think don't belong here, weird fucking things. A snake with two heads, mister, what do you think of that? My daddy said his pa's pa saw one of them once in the Pacific during the war, but here and now? I dunno, something weird." He nodded at the corpse close to the mouth of the alley. "And those big things with, like, an octopus on their heads? I saw one land on Mrs Doubleday's car and all the windows smashed out, and it tried walking but one of its legs was broke and it's still going round in circles now, and is that hair on its head? Or fungus?"

"I need your help to stand," Jimi said.

"Oh, right, yeah." The kid picked up Jimi like he was hardly anything, propping him against the wall. "And all this thunder and lightning and stuff, you think the Rainmaker's here? I saw her online, my pal Casey told me about it, said there was some girl dancing naked on the news—that's why I watched, gotta be honest, but maybe she's come here now? She brought snakes down with the rain in Abbey Springs, that's what I heard."

"I heard that too. Yeah, she's here."

"Cool. Maybe she'll put out all the fire."

"You seen the fires?" Jimi asked.

"No, mister, we're getting ready to leave, me and my family. I was just picking up food from McMurty's, then the rain started and I heard stuff in the street, a crash then shooting." He stood back from Jimi, pausing in his gushing talk to look him up and down. "You get shot?"

"Got bit," Jimi said, showing the boy his holed arm.

"Shit. You'll need to clean that."

"I need a crutch, I'll get back to my car then. Your family must be worried."

The kid frowned. Red rain flowed from his huge mop of soaked hair and down his face. Jimi had been naive and open like him once. Despite what Papa did for a living, Jimi'd had a positive outlook on the world. The Rainmaker had taken all that away.

"Kid!" Jimi said. "A crutch. Something to lean on." He held up his gun. "And ammo, or another gun."

"Wait here, mister." He ran back along the alley.

"Hey!" Jimi called. The kid held up one hand and disappeared around a corner.

Jimi leaned back against the wall. The kid hadn't abandoned him, he was sure of that, and he'd give him a minute. He needed that time to gather himself, prepare for what was to come. His leg was alight with pain. Every bit of him hurt, but he fed from it, absorbing agonies from his smashed teeth, shot and bitten ankle, mauled arm, crushed ribs. He swallowed the pain and prepared to let it all out again in one single direction. He tasted blood, unsure whether it came from his mouth, or inside from his cracked ribs nicking his lungs, or from somewhere outside.

The kid returned after just a couple of minutes. In his left hand he had a pump-action shotgun, in his right a heavy plastic bag. He was grinning.

"Crutch," he said, handing Jimi the shotgun. He delved into the bag and brought out a pistol, holding that out to Jimi, too. "Got me one as well!" he said as Jimi took the weapon, pulling his own gun from the bag. "Lots of ammo! McMurty's got a sporting goods part out back, he's supposed to keep it locked up. He ain't there but I'll call him and tell him what I took, he'll understand. We can pay him later, he knows my pa."

Jimi checked the pistol's clip was full. "Shotgun loaded?"

"Six shells."

"Good work, kid."

"Come on, then! You can come with us, we're getting the hell out."

"How close is the fire?"

"Can't you smell it?"

Jimi couldn't.

"It's fucking close, mister. Come on, we got room in our truck, we're going east. I can't wait to tell my family about those weird creatures. Or maybe they already know." The kid frowned, and his fear shone through for the first time.

"I'm not coming," Jimi said.

"Huh? Course you are."

"Go to your family. Watch out for those things."

The kid shook his head, frowning. Looked around. "But I thought you were coming with me?"

Jimi shook his head. "Fuck off, kid."

The boy backed away, glancing at the pistol in Jimi's hand, the shotgun he held against his side as a crutch. Then he turned and ran along the alley, only glancing back as he rounded the corner and disappeared from Jimi's life forever. Jimi had run away like that once, afraid and confused, but there had been no one waiting at the end of his run.

Every step he'd taken had led here.

"Save your family," Jimi muttered. Using the shotgun as a walking stick, gun ready in his other hand, he hobbled back into the street, heading in a diagonal towards the crashed Land Rover and smashed bar-front window.

Halfway across the road, he took in a deep breath and smelled smoke and fire. It was raining blood, towering cliffs of smoke and fire were closing on the town, and demons stalked the streets. Jimi gritted his teeth against the pain as he walked through hell.

JESSE

Jesse heard a bark from Rocky, a shout from Karina, and he felt Ash's weight on his outstretched right leg, the warmth of a daughter he had assumed dead and cold more important to him than the furnace of pain in his right side.

Her world, he thought. *This is Skunksville, but I still know some of it.*

Rocky barked non-stop, and he thought Karina might have shouted his name as she lifted his right arm and tugged the weapon from his grasp.

The Shore was mine, but those things… they were there, too, in the distance. Her world, my world. Different, and the same.

He caught a sudden whiff of ozone from the components of Ash's apparatus, and his eyes snapped open as he thought, *Maybe I know how to stop all this.*

He pointed, eyes wide, and Karina turned and fired four times at the thing crawling through the smashed front window. It jerked and rolled, and the fourth shot struck one of its piercing eyes. It shuddered several times, and the dozen long tentacles protruding from its strange head were the last parts of it to grow still. They clasped and waved at the air in an almost beautiful dance, before curling in on themselves like the legs of a dying spider.

Karina crouched by his side, one hand on his shoulder, the other passing gently across his stomach. Jesse gasped and bit down a shout.

"I'm okay!"

"You're not."

"I think... I might know how to stop this. Stop her."

"You mean help her?" Karina was so close she was almost a blur. She was soaked, fierce with blood.

"Sit her against the bar," Jesse said. "Is she still awake?"

"In and out," Karina said. "She recognised me, but I'm not sure she's in control anymore. What are you going to do?"

"I'm going in through her apparatus."

"Is that safe?"

"Safe?" Jesse laughed, then cried out as it hurt his stomach. He had no idea how severe the wound was, and he didn't want to know. He might only need a few minutes. After that, whatever would be would be.

Karina grabbed his shirt and pressed her face close to his. "You mean to help her, Jesse. Right?"

"Right," he said, because he heard the fear in her voice, the mistrust after last time. "Of course." But he wasn't sure about any of this. And he knew that if he couldn't help her, couldn't stop her, then he might only be left with one alternative.

Ash had opened something up, and Jesse had to close it.

"What about that hopping bastard?"

"Son of the drug dealer I killed," Jesse said.

"Holy shit."

"Yeah. So we've got to get somewhere safe, somewhere he won't find us, before I—"

"I can protect you both."

"I don't doubt it," Jesse said. "But it's too much of a risk. If something happened to Ash while she was still connected…"

"It might stay like this?"

Jesse shook his head, because he really didn't know. "We need to move," he said. "A basement, somewhere out back." He glanced at Ash, and her apparatus. It seemed to pulse with a life of its own, and he remembered what that was like. Exciting. Chilling. When he was young and building his own apparatus he'd been fired up with a passion to change the world.

Perhaps he still could.

Something howled outside, a sound not from a human mouth. It rose and rose until it was beyond his range of hearing.

A car sped along the road, and he caught sight of its silver chassis as it flashed by the damaged bar frontage. It was silent but for the shush of wheels splashing through water.

The storm growled again, still directly above the town, and Ash. This was her storm, and the only way he could stop it was to be in her world. Take *possession* of her storm. Because he recognised the creatures in the streets of Rockfield, and maybe The Shore and her Skunksville weren't as different, and as individual, as he had always believed. He had no idea if it would work, but it was the only move he could think to make, and he was the only one who could do it. He believed that Ash had come here to practise her skill and save the town from the encroaching flames, but the cost was too great.

A fire would go out. But those things, and whatever else might fall, could spread and procreate.

"Ash," he said. He nudged her shoulder and her head rolled, then she startled upright and looked at him.

"He killed her," she said.

"You've got to help me," he said. "We have to—"

She screamed.

It was shocking, long and loud, and her eyes rolled before her head tipped back and hit the bar front.

"I'll drag her," Karina said, shaken. "But can you lift this?" She tapped the guitar case.

Jesse wasn't sure he could even lift himself, but he had to try. Everything depended on him now. Karina had searched for and found their daughter, but now only he could save her.

He tried to stand but could hardly move. There was no strength in his legs and the waves of pain from his gut made him almost pass out. Only Karina shouting his name kept him there, and he was sweating, panting.

"No time," he said. "We'll have to do it here."

"And Jimi?"

"Maybe he's dead. Maybe he's gone. Keep watch… Don't hesitate. If you see him, you shoot, understand?"

"Just whatever you're planning, hurry!"

"You think I've got a plan?" He tried to laugh but it hurt too much, so he simply reached for Ash's left arm, plucked out the needle, and plunged it into his own right forearm. The pain was sharp and bright and brief, and then he felt a rush of something he had missed for so long.

Not pleasure. Not joy. It was more like belonging.

Ash stiffened and froze, and he wasn't sure she was still breathing. His world began to blur, and overlaid across it was another. He saw the strange sea and high cliffs and the beach in between, and he understood that the mysterious place she went to was nothing like his own.

His Shore had been worse than his mother's version of this place, and Skunksville was much, much worse than his. The decline echoed the fall of their world and the terrible changes they had wrought over it. It was so obvious and awful that his vision blurred with useless, wretched tears.

He could see her in the distance, standing on the beach with one foot planted in the still, oily sea, one on the blood-red sand. There were no waves, no currents, and he recognised that this land was still and dead, apart from the things even now seeking escape through Ash. Creatures large and small spiralled towards her like water into a hole, rolling and running, slithering and tumbling and flying, and from every one of them he sensed a burst of relief and excitement.

And most of all, hunger.

Ash, he said, and his voice was shatteringly loud. She turned to him, looking back over her right shoulder. He'd expected rage, or hate, or even delight in what she was doing. What he hadn't expected was horror.

Dad, Ash said, her voice loud as if it was spoken directly into his ear, *help me! I'm the storm and it won't let me go.*

Seeing his girl in such distress gave Jesse strength. They were in this together, and as father and daughter they would survive together.

He took his first few steps along the beach of Skunksville.

ASH

I never believed I would lose control.

I stand on the beach and I'm a conduit, not a conductor of things. I try to slow them down but I can't. I try to ease back on the storm flowing through me, but the storm is a living thing that has me in its grasp. It refuses to let go. It has always been waiting for me to return, weaker and more vulnerable than ever before.

Seeing Jimi kill Cee changed everything.

Ash, my father says, and his voice is a shock, his uttering my name more so. He's close behind me and I can feel the warmth of his presence. I can't imagine how difficult it is for him to be here, although I can see how it's possible—I still have an eye onto the real world, and I can see the bright trails of wires into my arm and his like constant streaks of lightning. He's come here for me, and it's all because he couldn't stop me before. I realise now that he never meant to kill me, only save me.

"I never knew how hard it would be," I say. The creatures of Skunksville rush towards me and disappear as they draw close, and I know they are falling with the rain. My father does not disappear. He does not fall.

I never went anywhere like this, he says. He looks around, his eyes terrified and fascinated. At the sea, so calm compared to the upset in my soul. At the cliffs, impossibly high and unattainable.

And at the dreadful beach, with its denizens seeking freedom through me. I wonder if they have been waiting a long time, but I'm not sure time means much here. Another of the tall humanoid shapes approaches, its eyes fixed on us as it fades into the storm.

That one might kill my mother. It might kill me.

Our talent is from a gentler time, my darling girl. There's nothing gentle about it anymore, however much you want it, and are desperate for it to help.

"Then tell me how to stop it," I plead. "You tried before, but I wasn't ready for it to end then. I was younger, selfish, more headstrong. But I'm ready now."

I think maybe we have to do it together, he says. He holds out his hands, and this time they're empty. He's not holding a hypodermic ready to inject me. He's offering togetherness and kindness, not violence and fear.

I take his hands, and they feel warm against the coolness of this place.

"How?" I ask.

How have you ever gone back? he asks. *We close it down. Together, we can let go of the storm.*

For a moment I am already mourning losing this terrible, wonderful power. I could bring rain to dry places, tend harsh thirsts, water the Desert.

But it's become clear that I cannot bring *only* rain. The other things that fall are as much to do with my state of mind as they are the state of this world, and ours. In this world of change and drought, hunger and chaos, I can never find myself completely at peace. The danger outweighs the benefits. I have to let go.

My father understands my conflict. His relief is all the more palpable when I offer him a smile.

I wonder what he would have done if I'd refused. But I suppose I already know. The past tells me that. And he didn't come all this way for nothing.

KARINA

Jesse and Ash leaned against the bar and each other, eyes closed, and Karina had never felt so afraid of the storm.

Because I'm alone, she thought, but then Rocky growled by her side. Her hackles rose and she looked at the smashed portion of the front windows, where the Land Rover's nose protruded into the bar and lightning flashed and pinkish water flowed. Karina crouched in front of her husband and daughter and pointed the gun. A shadow might have passed the gap, but it was difficult to make out because of the changing light.

"What's up, girl?" she asked. The dog growled again, deeper and lower, and she stroked her flank. She didn't flinch.

Someone pushed at the main door. Rocky barked. The door rattled in its frame, locked but loose, and Karina swung her gun that way. Thunder rolled overhead and the windows lit up from the outside, and a hunched shape was imprinted halfway along like an old photo negative.

Rocky ran and leapt as the figure appeared in the smashed window. A shot cracked, the bullet thudding into wood somewhere to Karina's left. She wanted to fire back but Rocky was in the way, head shaking where she was clamped onto the figure, and Karina saw that it was Jimi, bloodied and broken and leaning around the ragged edge of the shattered window to get another shot. He was screaming, and it sounded like fury as much as pain. Rocky had his shooting arm in his mouth, and Jimi was doing his best to tug his hand free. He fired again, this bullet shattering the mirror above the bar.

"Rocky, away!" Karina shouted, trying to remember how Jesse had controlled her out in the street. The dog took no notice.

She grunted, aimed as best she could. She didn't want to hit the dog, but it would only take one lucky shot from Jimi for her life to become more of a ruin than it already was. She had searched too far and too long for her daughter to lose her now. She shuffled to her right, putting herself between Jimi and Ash, then pulled the trigger.

The remains of the window broke apart in a rain of glass. Rocky dropped away from Jimi's arm and scampered across the bar towards the far corner, whining.

Jimi fell, and Karina thought she heard his own cry. She aimed and fired again but she couldn't make him out.

She didn't know how many bullets she had left. She had to conserve them until she could be sure.

She stood, remaining in front of Ash. He must have fallen outside behind the low sill wall, lying flat on the sidewalk perhaps, maybe with a bullet in his chest. The idea of taking his life made her feel sick, but she'd have killed a dozen Jimis to protect her girl. A hundred.

Something moved on the Land Rover's roof, sliding down the windshield and landing on the hood, and Karina muttered, "Fuck!" and squeezed the trigger. The bullet slammed a hole in the windshield, missing the flapping shape of the large rook. The bird found its feet, shook itself, then took flight back into the storm.

Jimi struggled to his feet behind the low brick sill. He was covered in blood, weak, using a long dark shape to support himself, and Karina did not hesitate for a second. She aimed centre-mass and pulled the trigger.

The gun merely clicked. *Empty, jammed, safety—*

Jimi lifted his crutch and swung its end into his other hand.

Shotgun! Karina thought, and she froze in place, stuck between running at him and falling back to protect Ash.

The shotgun fired just as Jimi's weakened leg gave way and he slipped to his right.

Karina felt the blast pluck at her shirt and sting her hip. She saw Jimi hit the sidewalk again, shotgun barrel striking the windowsill and spinning from his hands.

She heard a grunt behind her, and a groan, and the long, slow slither of a body sliding to the floor. She closed her eyes in silent prayer to no one she believed in, and as she turned around she felt her whole world turning on the same axis, changing, and becoming somewhere very different.

Half of Jesse's face was missing, his jaw hanging off, teeth shattered, tongue a raw wet mass. His throat vented blood in a terrible flow.

Now the other side of your face will have a scar, she thought, and then she opened her mouth and vented a sob of shock and grief.

Jesse stared at her, but he was seeing nothing, and the glimmer in his remaining eye was simply the reflection of another, more violent flash of lightning.

The thunder rolled in like an earthquake, shattering more windows and setting car alarms singing.

Beside her dead father, Ash opened her mouth and added her own scream to the mournful chorus.

ASH

I see my father die twice. In Skunksville his eyes go pale, his face grows slack, and everything that makes him *him* vanishes. From a living, thinking being to a shell, the change is almost instantaneous. I still have his hands grasped in mine.

He doesn't fall. He simply becomes another part of my dead world.

Dad, I try to say, but I can't speak. I'm too busy—

—screaming, because he's dead and I can feel the wet warmth of him on my cheek and shoulder, and the pain in my face might have been caused by a pellet from the shotgun or one of my father's shattered teeth.

We are so close, I think. The moment before my father died we had found some strange epiphany, a confidence that we could do what we sought, together. It was a feeling of strength, but also love. Satisfaction. An easing of the pain and anger that drove my tumult, in the knowledge that together, we were stronger than the storm.

Now I'm left alone, and once more I balance on the precipice. On one side, fury and rage and an unbridled desire to bring down as much agony and horror as I am able. Hell awaits, if only I can open the door.

On the other side there is control, and an understanding that my father has always been right.

I hang above both, and holding my decision, freezing my action, is the scene before me, playing out in the real world when so much of me is in Skunksville that I can do little to help.

Physically, at least.

My mom falls to her knees, looking at me and my dead father. In her face I see the reflection of my own pain and confusion.

Behind her Jimi, covered in blood that I hope is all his own, hauls himself up onto the jagged edge of broken glass in the window frame, and in one hand he's lifting the shotgun around to bear on us both.

I come down on the side of rage and horror.

JIMI

Jimi had never believed that so much pain was possible, yet the comforting flush of joy tingling through him was all he could focus on. That, and the shattered face of his Papa's murderer. Now his wife and daughter would join him.

Jimi was in pieces. Bleeding from a dozen wounds, emitting a constant low whine, he did everything he could to pull himself upright. Glass bit into his palm as he held onto the windowsill, but he only gripped harder. His shattered foot and ankle spilled him sideways, but he pushed against the break. Every explosion of pain gave him purpose. Each moment flooded with white-hot agony brought a different measure of peace.

He lifted the shotgun to prop it on the broken sill, pumped it, and readied to fire it one-handed. His finger curled around the trigger. The mother knelt with her back to him. The daughter sat against the bar, screaming, with scattered meat from her father's broken head speckled across her face. The dog whimpered and whelped by his dead master's side.

It was delicious.

Something struck his broken left foot. It was a large red bird, with a long beak and luminous wings. It flapped itself upright and started pecking at the open meat of his ankle. Jimi drew in a shocked gasp and pulled his leg up to kick at it, but it followed, pecking more frantically as its meal was moved away. The pain scorched like acid. A scatter of large beetles drifted down around him on gossamer wings. Several landed on his arm and immediately clamped on with vicious barbed jaws. A small yellow frog bounced from a shard of broken glass and rolled to the puddled sidewalk, spreading webbed legs and leaping for his stomach. He winced back and the frog slithered down his skin, and he felt several jabs as spines along its back raked at him. The pin-prickle wounds pulsed cool before exploding into bright points of pain, and Jimi opened his mouth to scream, tasting the mix of rain and blood. A large, winged creature fell behind him and he heard the scatter of claws before teeth clamped onto his arm. He twisted and thrashed, tugged his arm back, finger squeezing the trigger and sending a shot harmlessly into the bar's ceiling. He rolled onto his back, kicking, waving his arms, thrashing, screaming, and in that position he could look up at the storm clouds low overhead.

Water and blood fell all around, and there were other things, too. They fell onto him and around him, some creatures that looked almost familiar, and many more that did not. The one thing that connected them all was their bites and stings, their claws and sharp spines, and their need to inflict the most terrible agonies upon him. The larger animal shook its head and ripped another chunk of flesh from his arm. The bird tipped its head back and swallowed something it had pecked from his leg.

Jimi screamed again and again, and something long and bristly darted into his mouth and wormed its way down his throat. It stole his air and smothered his scream and started chewing at his gullet, eating him from the inside out.

He managed to roll onto all fours and crawl towards the crashed Land Rover. Creatures hung from his skin, gnawed at his flesh, and for every one that fell or pulled away with a morsel of him in its mouth, two more latched on. Something sank razor teeth through his jeans and into his right testicle. A small lizard crawled over his left eye and probed at it with hooked claws, tugging away his closed eyelid to get at the succulent eyeball beneath.

He reached for the Land Rover's open door just as something large and heavy landed on its roof. The remaining window glass shattered outwards and the shape rolled off and hit the ground close to Jimi.

He forgot about the shotgun, the women, the dog, his father's dead killer, and even the agonies that drowned him. His mind became consumed by the horribly familiar thing before him, the size of a tall human but so inhuman that his mind struggled to comprehend it.

He could not scream. He could no longer breathe. The other creatures biting and eating him all fell away, as if in supplication to the thing now before him. It whistled softly, and Jimi thought he heard humour in its voice, and saw it in the thing's horrible, knowing stare.

Such human eyes, and they looked like—

It leaned forward and the tendrils around its face clasped onto his head and pulled him towards its yawning, beaked mouth.

ASH

Before dying, he gave me back control. He made me understand I had a choice. As I take the needle from my arm and withdraw from that violent, dead world, I take one last look at my father standing beside me on that beach, his lifeless eyes staring towards impossible horizons. I understand that this is as close to him as I have ever been, and ever will be again.

I slump back and bang my head against the bar. I keep my face turned away. Even though I can feel his weight against my shoulder, I have no desire to see what has become of my father here. I grasp hold of that final image I have of him in my other world. It was perhaps the most intimate moment between us since I was a child.

From the corner of my eye, I see what is happening on the sidewalk beyond the shattered window. Despite everything Jimi has taken from me, I'm glad the small wall below the windowsill is there. I don't want to see him being taken apart.

"Mom." She's kneeling just past my feet, also looking outside. She's breathing hard, bleeding from her ear and hip.

"Mom!"

She turns, glances at my dead father, then looks at me. We lock eyes and it feels strong, solid, and she doesn't look away. She doesn't want to see anything but me, and I'm filled with a rush of love, and a deep sadness at everything she must have been through. I see the depth of those experiences in her eyes.

"Here," I say, beckoning her to me. I still hold the needle in my left hand, and with my right I reach along my father's arm to the needle there. I draw it out and feel his blood on my fingers. Still warm. It doesn't seem fair.

"It's stopped raining," my mom says.

"Yeah."

"Is that you?"

I nod.

"Are you okay?"

I can't answer because I'm not sure, but she's not really talking about me. She's talking about the storm.

"Here," I say again, and she crawls to me and sits close to my other side.

"That thing," she says, and it's as if her words draw its attention. It lifts its bloody head from behind the low wall, turns, and stares into the bar. It's still chewing, and I see a scrap of Jimi's clothing caught on its beak-like mouth. Its tendrils wave, smelling or tasting the air. The lightning has ceased, the deluge is now just a misting rain, and in the sudden silence the sound of chewing is repulsive. Beyond that sound I can hear shouts, screaming, a distant gunshot.

That's all on me, I think, but I can't confront the truth of my deeds just yet. It will drive me mad.

The dog huddles against my dead father's legs but looks up at me, as if understanding I am the centre of things here.

The creature places two limbs over the wall and down into the scattered glass inside the bar. It pulls itself in, probing its head forwards and staring at us with those strange, familiar eyes.

The dog growls.

There's another gunshot from somewhere closer, and a large truck powers past along the road outside. In its wake I catch the scent of fire, carried on the air now that the torrents of rain no longer wash it down.

The creature stares at me for a few more seconds, and *into* me. I feel a strange contact there, like a memory of myself that never was. Then it turns and runs away. In seconds it disappears around the back of the crashed Land Rover, and I hear it scampering into the distance. I wish I could draw it back and return it to the place it came from, but I don't think I'm that strong. I fear that if I ever go there again I'll end up staying forever.

Once there, I might become a conduit to worse things.

My mother hugs me to her, and despite the rain and the blood, the shooting and death, hers is a smell that takes me home.

KARINA

Karina tried the Land Rover, but it had two flat tyres and the engine whirred with the grind of something broken. The car Cee and Ash had arrived in was totalled. And Jimi's car still had Cee's broken body spread across the crumpled, ruined hood.

The wall of smoke to the west was vast, and the approaching fire, seemingly untouched by Ash's rains, was so close that it had whipped up a storm of its own. Voracious, the blaze drew air through the town, and people were fleeing into the headwind. A family of four ran along the street, hardly sparing a glance for the two women and their dog. Several cars passed by filled with people and their belongings. A man caught Karina's eyes, his stare haunted, and she wondered what he'd seen.

There were dead animals scattered across the street, and more running wild. She saw two of those larger creatures, too. One of them lay dead across the road in the entrance to an alley, a small dog sniffing at the corpse. It was good that the fire would take it away. She thought she saw another in the distance, darting across a side street. Karina hoped the flames would do away with everything Ash had brought down with her storm.

Jesse will be burned to nothing, she thought. She felt tears threatening, but she could not afford them now. Maybe later.

"Mom, wait," Ash said. She went to the Land Rover's open back door and hauled out the flat box containing Jesse's apparatus.

"Ash, no, we can't…" Karina trailed off as Ash heaved the box through the bar's smashed window. She stared after it for a second or two, then turned to her mother.

"They should burn together. Dad, his apparatus, and mine. That's it. That's the end of the Rainmakers."

Not quite, Karina thought, but it wasn't something she could say right then. The responsibility would always weigh heavy on Ash.

"We need to go," Karina said.

"You're okay to walk?"

"Walk? I'm thinking of running." Karina felt her hip where the shotgun blast had whisked past. She thought there might be a pellet or two stuck in there.

"Then let's run," Ash said. She smiled, but it bore such sadness. Karina was glad that she had turned to run before she saw the first of her mother's tears.

Wind roared through Rockfield, sucked in by the approaching conflagration. The rains had dampened down the dust, at least, but litter and the remains of dead trees danced through the air as they sprinted. The growl of the fire was a living thing, storming out of the desert at the town it would soon consume. Karina felt the intense heat at her back, and when she heard the first series of thuds and *whoomps* as buildings and vehicles at the edge of town exploded into flames, the idea that they weren't going to make it hit home. Rocky ran ahead and waited, again and again, barking back at them to hurry, *hurry*. Her hip hurt, and her ear, and she couldn't help feeling that she was leaving part of herself behind to sizzle away in the brutal flames, back there with her husband. The Karina who had hated him for years, and returned for his help when it most mattered, was not the woman now running along the street behind her tortured, tattered daughter. This was all new terrain, and though finding Ash was all she had lived for, it had also taken so much. The future remained a frightening place that part of her didn't wish to face. She raged at that, shouted and swore at it, and Rocky added her bark, and Ash her voice. Screaming at their fears and demons, they approached the edge of town where a dozen cars and trucks were parked by the roadside, people milling around as if unsure what to do.

As Karina began to wonder who she might ask for help, a truck rolled to a halt beside them. It was a Soaker wagon, its huge water tank trailing a series of hoses still dripping precious water. The cab door opened and a tall old woman jumped out. She was scorched around the edges, and her bare arms and legs were covered with soot. Her eyes, wide and glaring in her dirty face, told everyone what they needed to know even before she spoke.

"Town's finished. Need to go east, all of you. We're gonna set a fire break into the old river valley a couple of miles east of here, so just make sure you get past there before stopping. This bitch is a bad one, and she's getting worse."

"Thanks for trying," someone said.

"Yeah. Well, didn't do no good," the old woman said.

"You gave us some time," someone else said.

"You seen those things?" a man asked. "Monsters falling out of the sky with the rain and blood?"

The old Soaker rolled her eyes. Then she turned and pointed back into the town. "That's the monster." The wall of flame and smoke, maybe a mile away, was changing colour as it started to eat up the furthest edge of the town. The flames were higher and more violent, the smoke billowed a darker black. The sound was tremendous, a steady roar that shook the ground, interspersed with explosions as houses and vehicles succumbed.

"Get going," she said. "Got some room in my truck for anyone's not got wheels."

Karina waited for a few seconds, watching the townsfolk as they turned to each other, sharing hope and friendship before climbing into the parked vehicles and starting out into the Desert.

"Even got room for your mutt," the Soaker woman said.

"She's called Rocky," Karina said.

"Rocky," the woman said. The dog perked up her ears at hearing her name. "Eye of the tiger."

"Thanks," Ash said.

"No worries." She looked Ash and Karina up and down. "Looks like you've been through it. Just the two of you?"

"Just us," Karina said.

Ash sat in the middle seat, and Karina leaned against the door and watched in the mirror as the town went up behind them. It was horrible and beautiful, and so much of her history added to the brightness of those flames, and the oily blackness of the smoke.

Ash held her hand and squeezed. Karina looked away from the flames and down at her daughter's hand in her own. On Ash's forearm, a recent wound leaked a single tear of blood.

ASH

As morning gives way to afternoon, Rocky moves around the yard. This is her familiar place, and between stints of lying in the sun, shade, and sun again, she sniffs around the cabin and yard and sometimes ventures into the woods. She knows the shadows and paths, and the best places to bathe in the sun. She seems at peace and at home. Sometimes, though, I catch her staring at the cabin's front door even though Mom and I are outside, working on the gardens or trying to figure out some of the devices used for drawing water or powering Hillside. Now and then she stares for ten minutes or more, then rests her nose on her paws and whines.

Sometimes I look at the doorway too, and imagine him standing there. I wonder if he ever stood there staring out at the yard and thinking of me. I guess he probably did.

It took us nine days to make our way here. From the moment we left Rockfield in the Soaker wagon, this was the destination Mom had in mind. She hasn't called it home, but I know that's how she's starting to think of it. I'm hoping I can do the same.

I watch Mom working in the garden and I can see how fit she is, lean and strong from years in the Desert. I've asked her about that time, and usually she replies that it doesn't matter anymore, she found me, we're together again, and her past was burnt away in that terrible fire. To begin with I thought she meant Dad and his body, but I think it's a lot more than that. It's his apparatus and mine, burnt to atoms and adding their own energy to the cleansing flames. It's the long, long story of her years in the wild. One day maybe she'll tell me, but I'm happy with her as she is now, and I don't really need to know.

Someday, I'll also tell her about my time in the Desert. She has yet to ask.

"You gonna help me or are you sitting on your butt all day?" she calls.

I raise a hand and smile, and she smiles back. "I'll just grab a drink."

Mom nods and stretches, pressing both hands into the small of her back and looking to the sky. There are a few wispy clouds high up, and sometimes I feel a gentle chill as they pass in front of the sun.

I head across the yard and up the steps into the cabin. It was built by my father, the man who I spent years believing tried to kill me. In reality he'd been trying to save me, and though it took much longer than he'd hoped, I guess he finally succeeded.

There's not much inside that reminds me of him. It's pretty sparse, and in the few weeks we've been here my mother and I have added our own touches to the cabin, inside and out. Making it home. She's even talking about building a new bedroom on the side, and Jenny from the local town says she knows people who'll help. I fill two water bottles with clear, fresh water and glance around again. I like to imagine him sitting here, but it also makes me sad for all those lost years. I've been on my own in the Desert for so long, so I know what he must have been feeling sitting here, stroking his dog, reading his books, or just staring from the window. I know loneliness. Cee helped me survive it and weather it for a short while, and I'll always be grateful to her, and will always miss her. I don't think Dad ever had a Cee.

The top of his bookshelf is empty, and I guess this is where he kept his apparatus. It's a blank space in that room, a black hole, and when I look at it my forearms itch, and between blinks I see flashes of Skunksville. I don't know if they're memories, or brief glimpses of it as it is now. I look away from the empty shelf and the vision vanishes, and as ever, I vow to fill the space with something else.

Soon. I'll do it soon.

I scratch at my arms where the scars have yet to fully heal and go back out into the sun. Lying across the yard in the shadow of a healthy tree, Rocky whines once and lowers her head again, staring at me.

"Hey, Rocky!" She wags her tail. She was looking for someone else, but I hope she can sense my father in me and feel our connection. I hope she can see the good side of both of us.

"Dying of thirst over here!" Mom shouts from around the side of the cabin.

"On my way." And I am. But I stand on the porch for a moment longer, looking across the yard at the woodlands surrounding us, and the uneven road that leads down to Blueton. It's another hot day, and though we've come a long way north, I know the Desert will always be on my mind. It's growing, too, and one day, if things don't change, if *people* don't change, it will catch us up.

Until then we'll stay here and do our part, and I'm coming to terms with the fact that I'm only really meant to do as much as anyone else. No more. I remain in the eye of a storm that has passed on, and I think I might grow comfortable here.

We'll be content at Hillside. It's a good place, a safe place, and we're building new memories upon those already here.

Best of all, sometimes it rains.

ACKNOWLEDGEMENTS

Thanks to my editor Cath Trechman, who always makes my books better. Also big thanks, as ever, to my agent and friend Howard Morhaim.

ABOUT THE AUTHOR

Tim Lebbon is an award-winning author of over forty novels, and hundreds of novellas and short stories. His books have been adapted twice for the big screen (*The Silence* and *Pay The Ghost*), and he has several more projects in development. He lives in South Wales with his wife. In Wales, it rains all the time. For more information visit his website: timlebbon.net. Follow him on Twitter and Instagram @timlebbon

For more fantastic fiction, author events,
exclusive excerpts, competitions, limited editions and more

VISIT OUR WEBSITE
titanbooks.com

LIKE US ON FACEBOOK
facebook.com/titanbooks

FOLLOW US ON TWITTER AND INSTAGRAM
@TitanBooks

EMAIL US
readerfeedback@titanemail.com